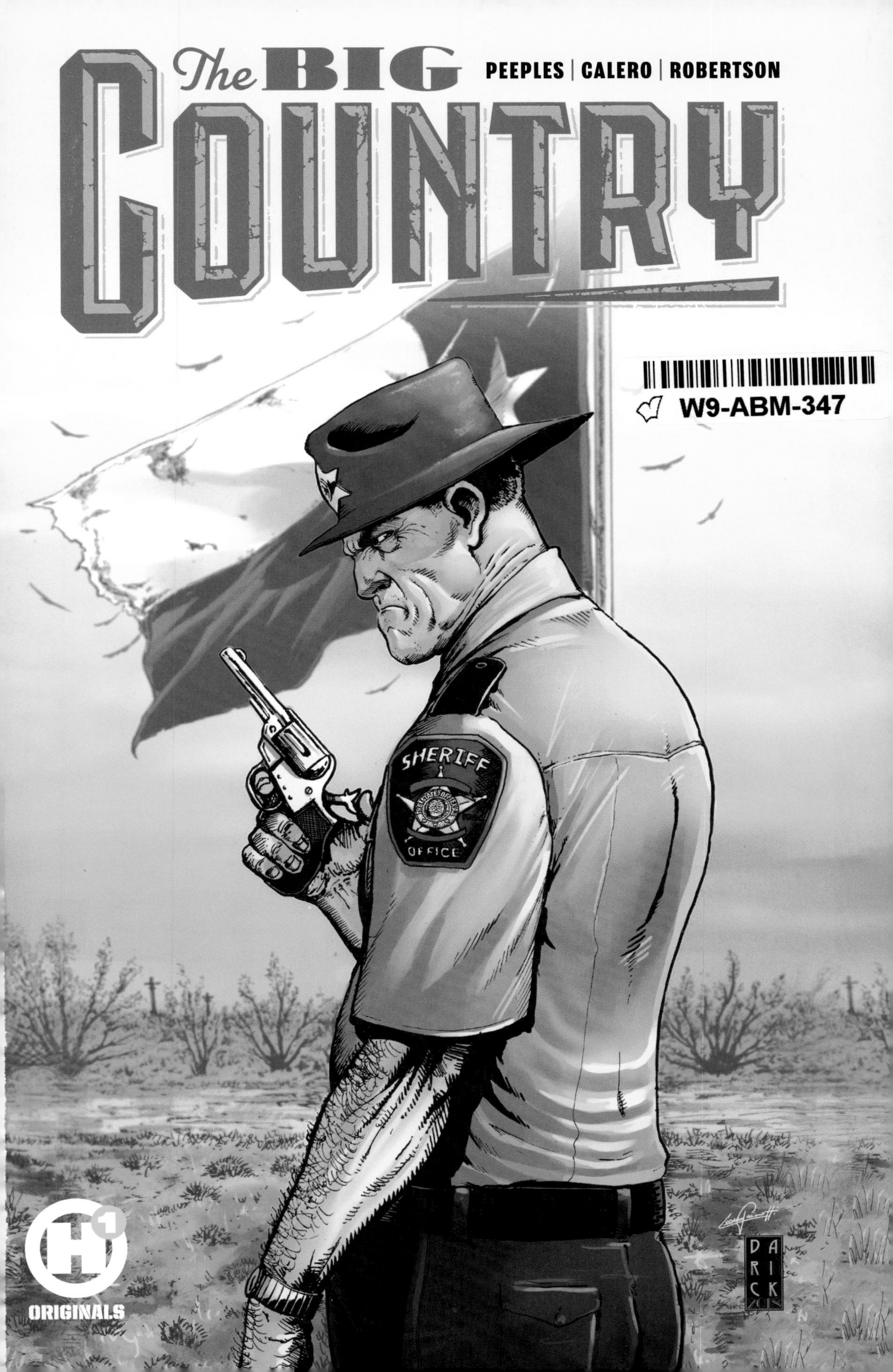
The BIG
COUNTRY
PEEPLES | CALERO | ROBERTSON
SHERIFF
OFFICE
H1
ORIGINALS

WRITER | **QUINTON PEEPLES**
ARTIST AND COLORIST | **DENNIS CALERO**
COLOR ASSIST | **LISA LUBERA**
COVER AND TITLE PAGE ILLUSTRATION | **DARICK ROBERTSON**
COVER COLORS | **BRYAN VALENZA**
TITLE PAGE COLORS | **LEONARDO PACIAROTTI**
LETTERS | **ANDWORLD DESIGN**

DIRECTOR OF CREATIVE DEVELOPMENT | **MARK WAID**
CHIEF CREATIVE OFFICER | **JOHN CASSADAY**
SENIOR EDITOR | **FABRICE SAPOLSKY**
ASSISTANT EDITOR | **AMANDA LUCIDO**
LOGO DESIGN | **RIAN HUGHES**
SENIOR ART DIRECTOR | **JERRY FRISSEN**

CEO AND PUBLISHER | **FABRICE GIGER**
COO | **ALEX DONOGHUE**
CFO | **GUILLAUME NOUGARET**
DIRECTOR OF SALES AND MARKETING | **AILEN LUJO**
SALES AND MARKETING ASSISTANT | **ANDREA TORRES**
SALES REPRESENTATIVE | **HARLEY SALBACKA**
PRODUCTION COORDINATOR | **ALISA TRAGER**
DIRECTOR, LICENSING | **EDMOND LEE**
CTO | **BRUNO BARBERI**
RIGHTS AND LICENSING | **LICENSING@HUMANOIDS.COM**
PRESS AND SOCIAL MEDIA | **PR@HUMANOIDS.COM**

THE BIG COUNTRY. This title is a publication of Humanoids, Inc.
8033 Sunset Blvd. #628, Los Angeles, CA 90046.

Library of Congress Control Number: 2019910137

H1 is an imprint of Humanoids, Inc.

SPECIAL THANKS FROM QUINTON PEEPLES:
To Tricia, Georgia and Mason. Thank you for showing me a better way.

SPECIAL THANKS FROM DENNIS CALERO:
To my daughter, Paloma Calero, who can read this book someday.

HUMANOIDS

SAN ANGELO, TEXAS, 1978

Childhood memories are supposed to be nice. Right?

Playing in the backyard. Riding bikes. Summer nights and June bugs.

I have those. And a couple others.

They say you can't trust memories from when you were a kid.

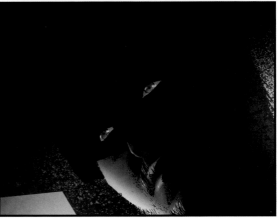

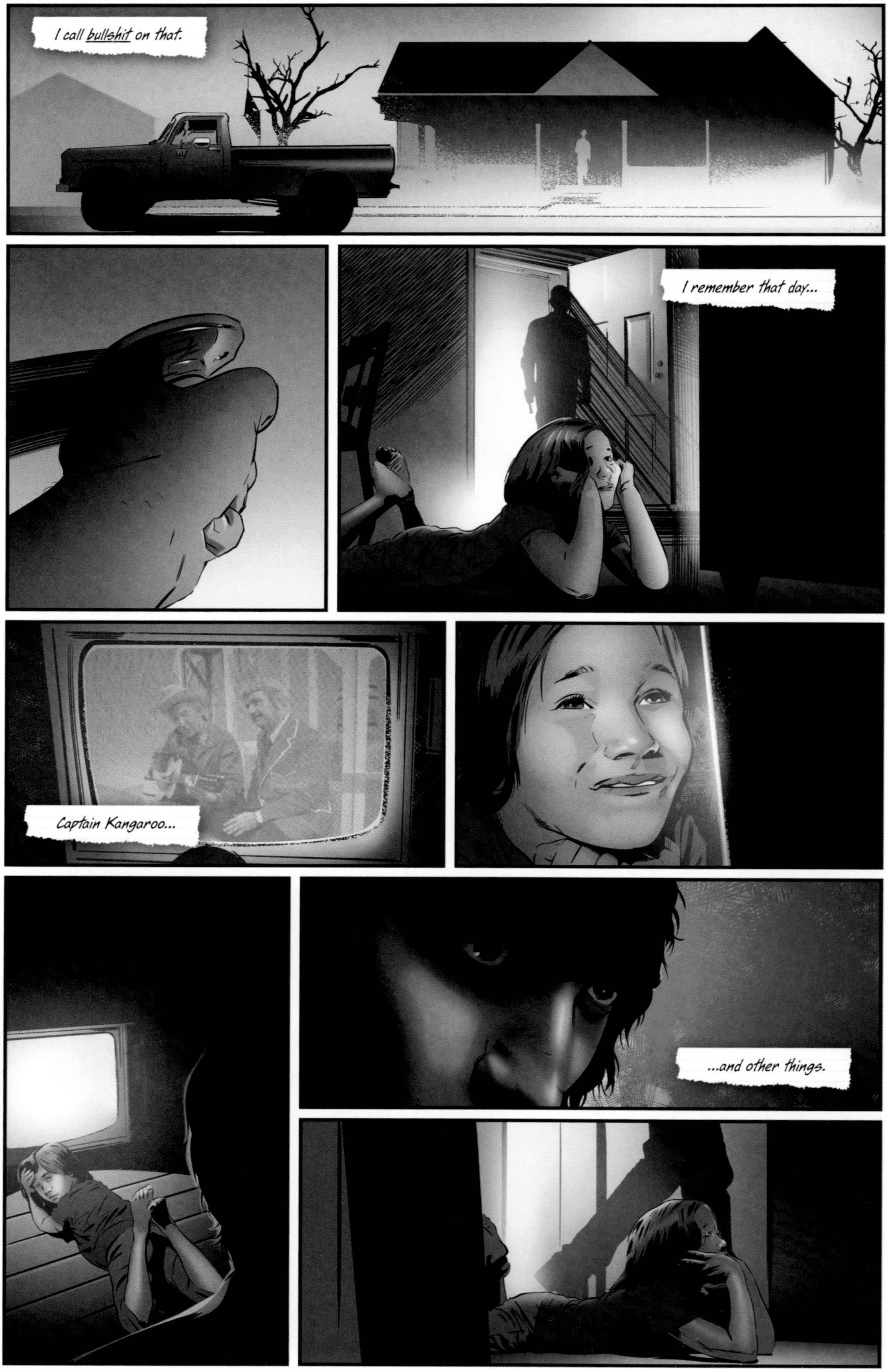
I call bullshit on that.
I remember that day...
Captain Kangaroo...
...and other things.

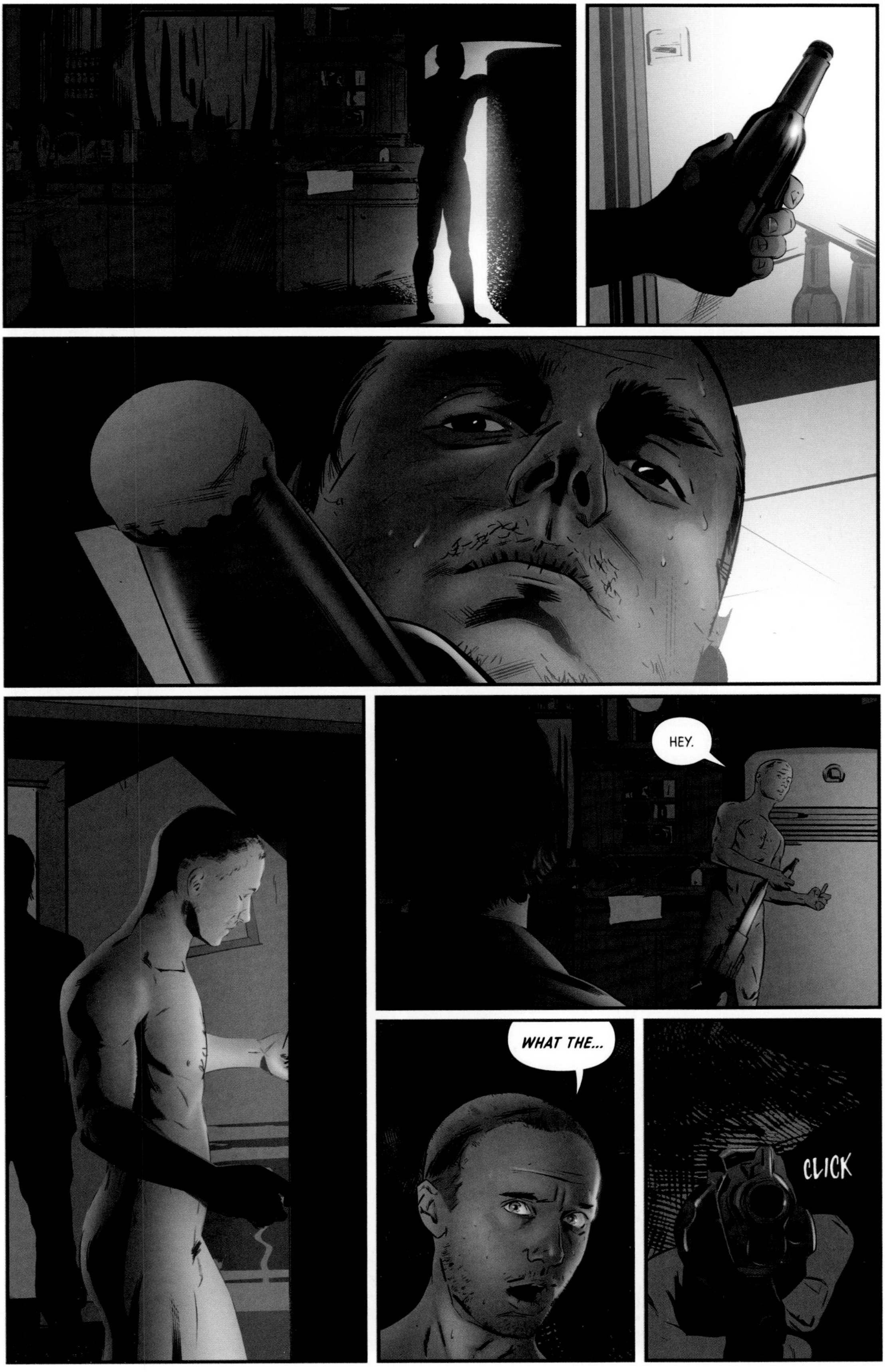
HEY.
WHAT THE...
CLICK

BLAM

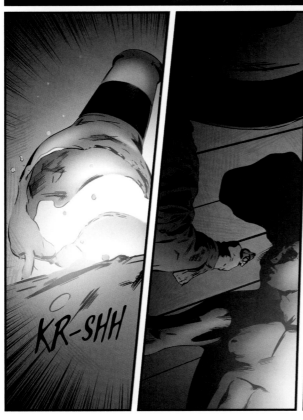

KR-SHH

BLAM
BLAM
BLAM

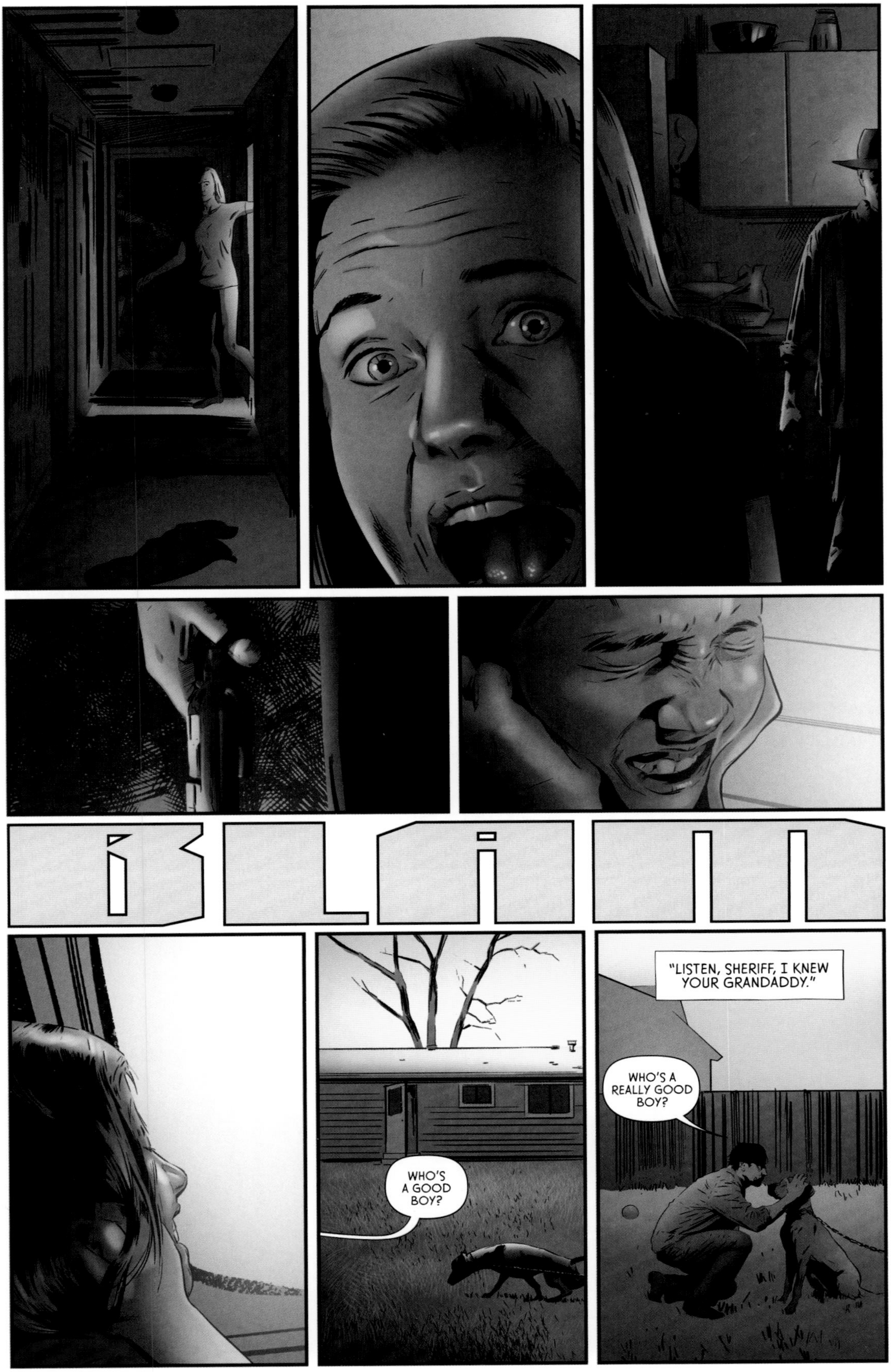
BLAM
"LISTEN, SHERIFF, I KNEW YOUR GRANDADDY."
WHO'S A GOOD BOY?
WHO'S A REALLY GOOD BOY?

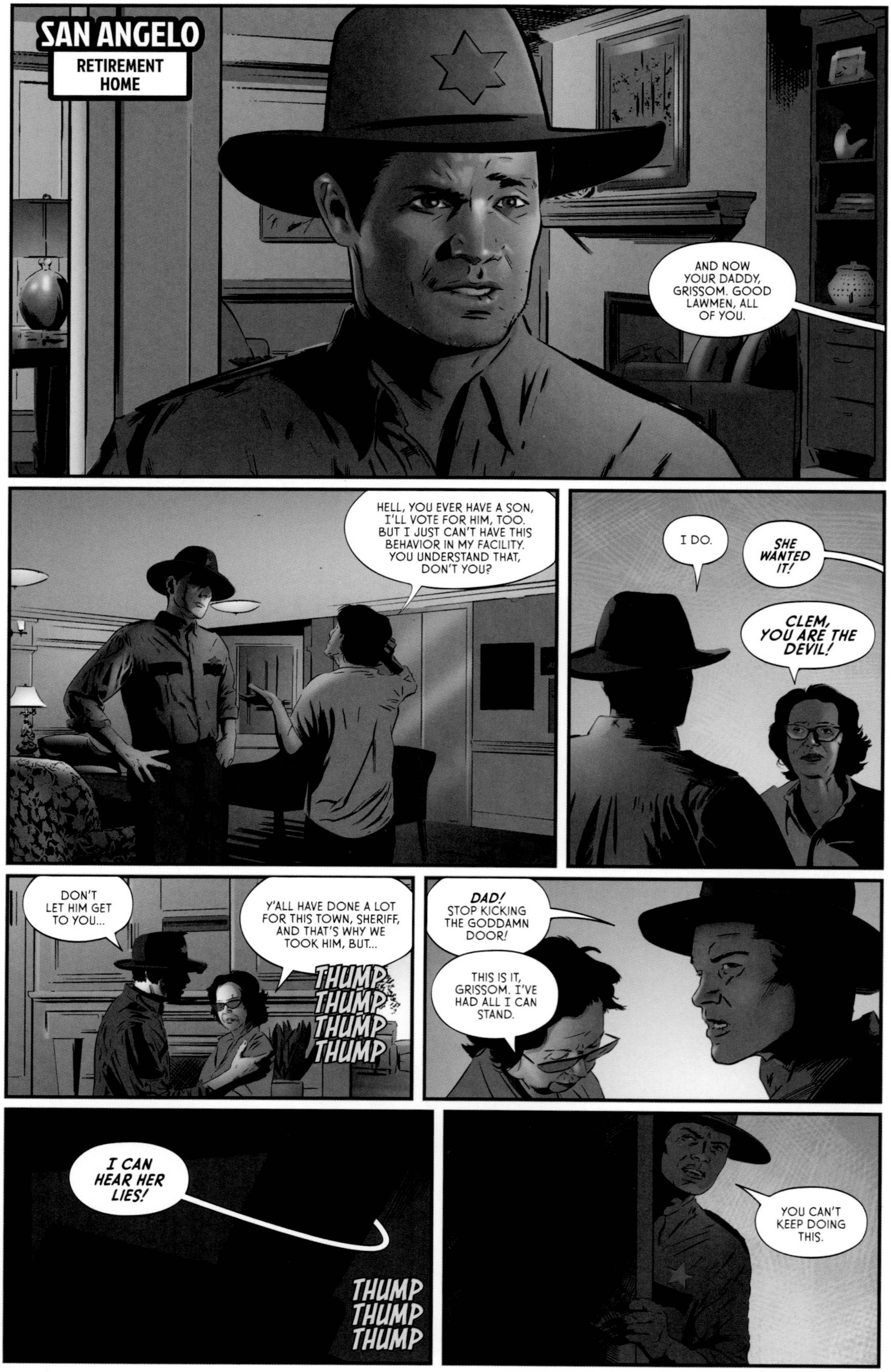
SAN ANGELO
RETIREMENT HOME
AND NOW YOUR DADDY, GRISSOM. GOOD LAWMEN, ALL OF YOU.
HELL, YOU EVER HAVE A SON, I'LL VOTE FOR HIM, TOO. BUT I JUST CAN'T HAVE THIS BEHAVIOR IN MY FACILITY. YOU UNDERSTAND THAT, DON'T YOU?
I DO.
SHE WANTED IT!
CLEM, YOU ARE THE DEVIL!
DON'T LET HIM GET TO YOU...
Y'ALL HAVE DONE A LOT FOR THIS TOWN, SHERIFF, AND THAT'S WHY WE TOOK HIM, BUT...
THUMP THUMP THUMP THUMP
DAD! STOP KICKING THE GODDAMN DOOR!
THIS IS IT, GRISSOM. I'VE HAD ALL I CAN STAND.
I CAN HEAR HER LIES!
THUMP THUMP THUMP
YOU CAN'T KEEP DOING THIS.

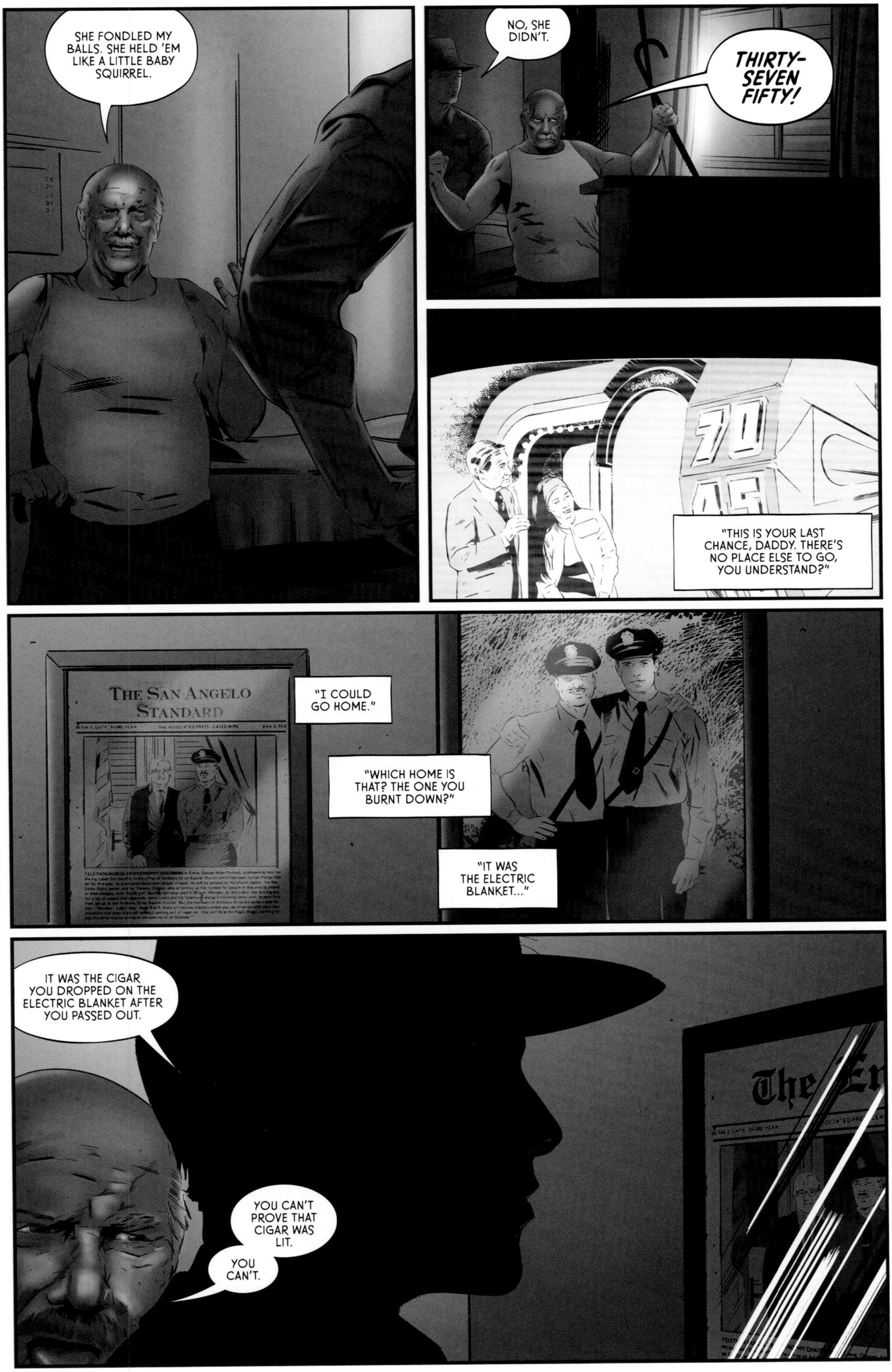

SHE FONDLED MY BALLS. SHE HELD 'EM LIKE A LITTLE BABY SQUIRREL.
NO, SHE DIDN'T.
THIRTY-SEVEN FIFTY!
"THIS IS YOUR LAST CHANCE, DADDY. THERE'S NO PLACE ELSE TO GO, YOU UNDERSTAND?"
THE SAN ANGELO STANDARD
"I COULD GO HOME."
"WHICH HOME IS THAT? THE ONE YOU BURNT DOWN?"
"IT WAS THE ELECTRIC BLANKET..."
IT WAS THE CIGAR YOU DROPPED ON THE ELECTRIC BLANKET AFTER YOU PASSED OUT.
YOU CAN'T PROVE THAT CIGAR WAS LIT.
YOU CAN'T.

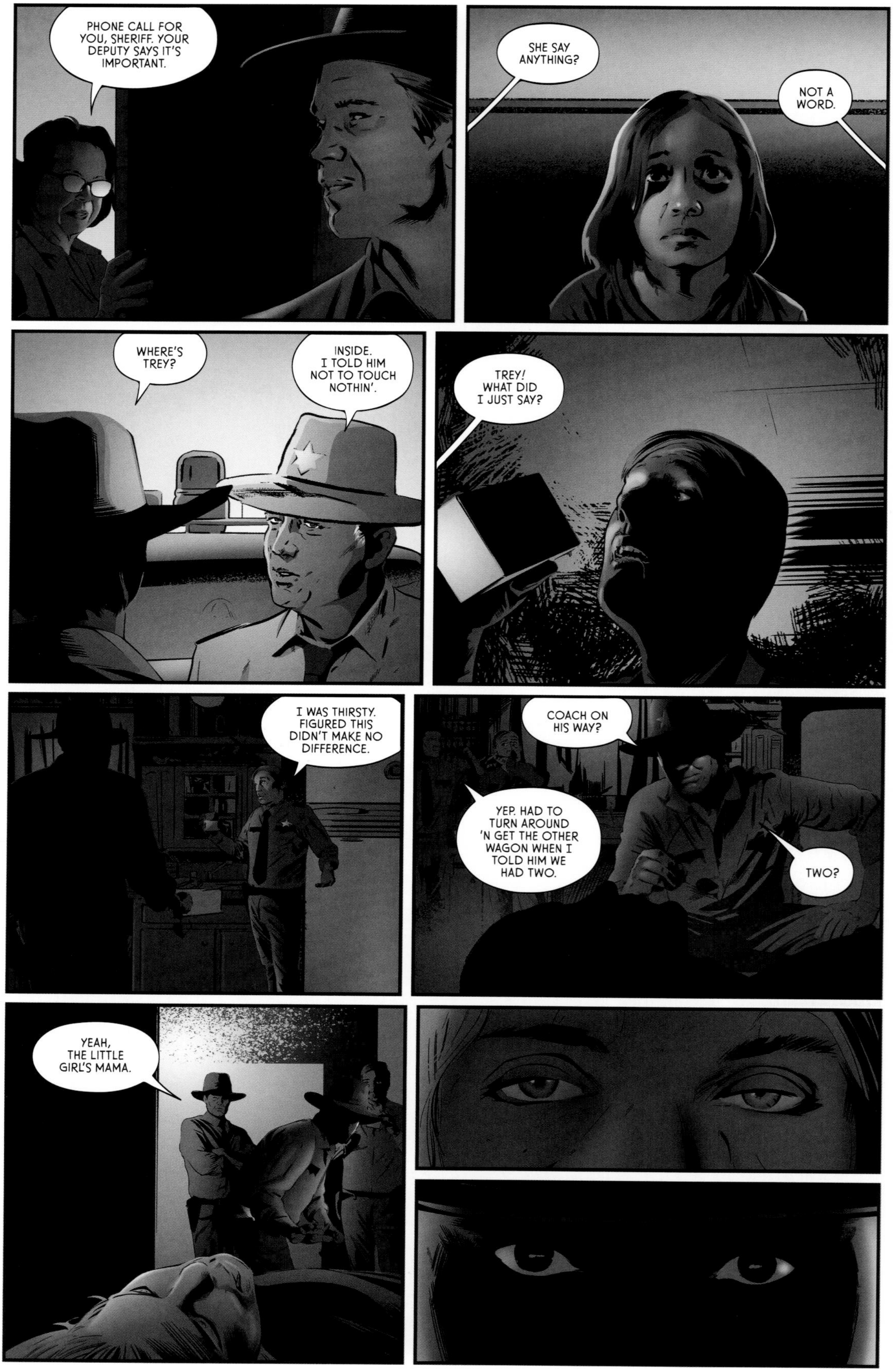
PHONE CALL FOR YOU, SHERIFF. YOUR DEPUTY SAYS IT'S IMPORTANT.
SHE SAY ANYTHING?
NOT A WORD.
WHERE'S TREY?
INSIDE. I TOLD HIM NOT TO TOUCH NOTHIN'.
TREY! WHAT DID I JUST SAY?
I WAS THIRSTY. FIGURED THIS DIDN'T MAKE NO DIFFERENCE.
COACH ON HIS WAY?
YEP. HAD TO TURN AROUND 'N GET THE OTHER WAGON WHEN I TOLD HIM WE HAD TWO.
TWO?
YEAH, THE LITTLE GIRL'S MAMA.

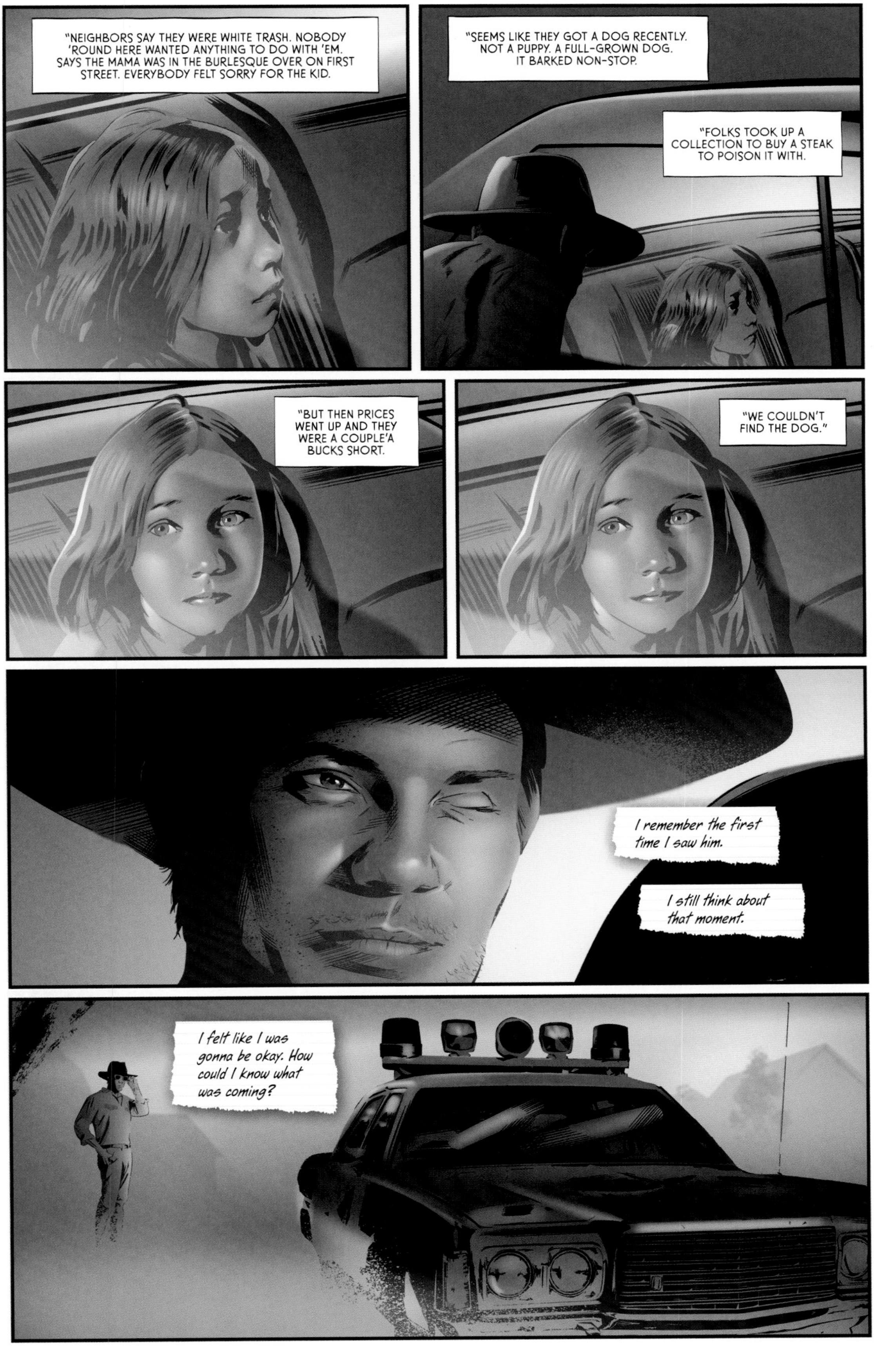
"NEIGHBORS SAY THEY WERE WHITE TRASH. NOBODY 'ROUND HERE WANTED ANYTHING TO DO WITH 'EM. SAYS THE MAMA WAS IN THE BURLESQUE OVER ON FIRST STREET. EVERYBODY FELT SORRY FOR THE KID.
"SEEMS LIKE THEY GOT A DOG RECENTLY. NOT A PUPPY. A FULL-GROWN DOG. IT BARKED NON-STOP.
"FOLKS TOOK UP A COLLECTION TO BUY A STEAK TO POISON IT WITH.
"BUT THEN PRICES WENT UP AND THEY WERE A COUPLE'A BUCKS SHORT.
"WE COULDN'T FIND THE DOG."
I remember the first time I saw him.
I still think about that moment.
I felt like I was gonna be okay. How could I know what was coming?

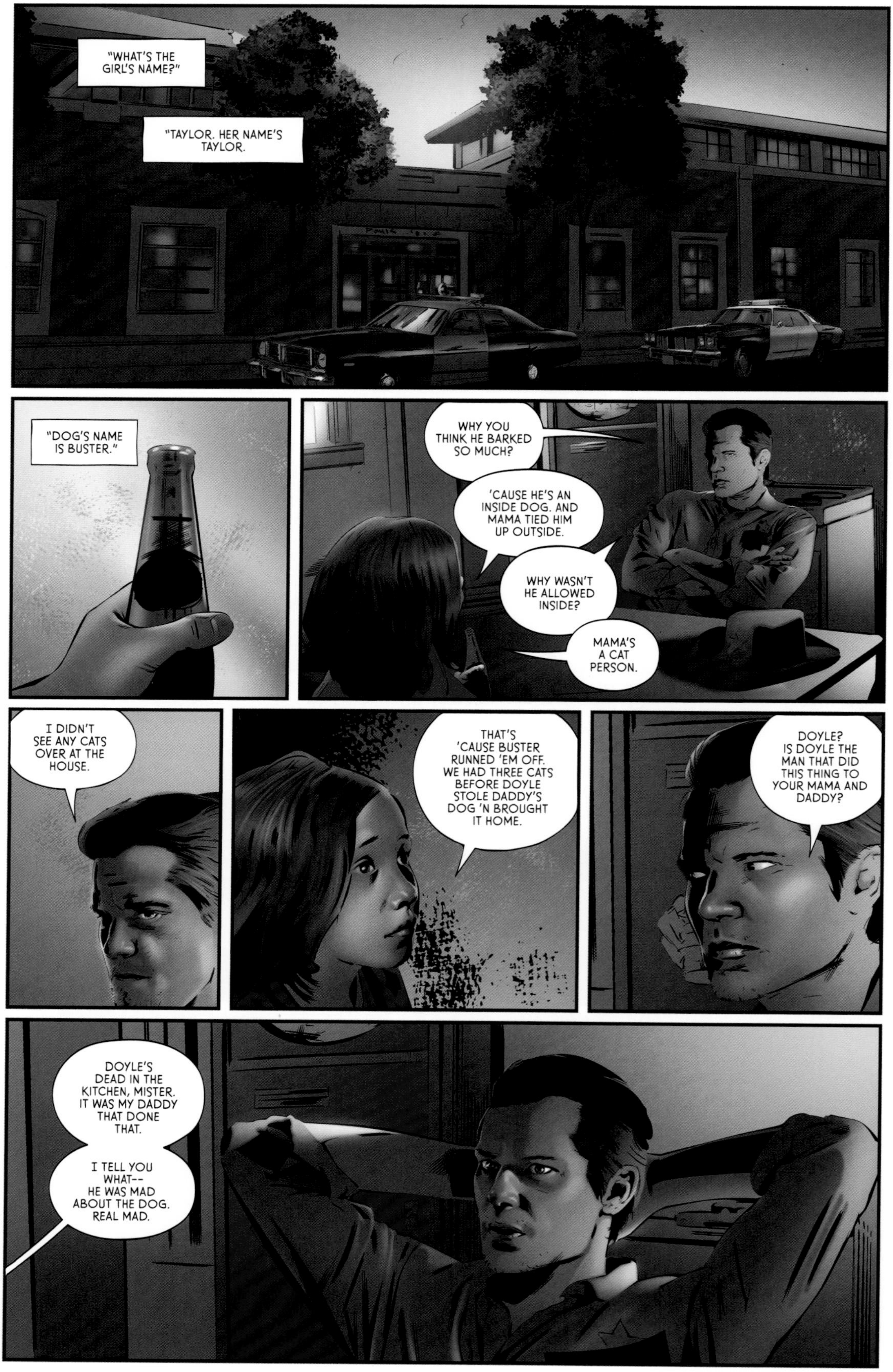
"WHAT'S THE GIRL'S NAME?"
"TAYLOR. HER NAME'S TAYLOR.
"DOG'S NAME IS BUSTER."
WHY YOU THINK HE BARKED SO MUCH?
'CAUSE HE'S AN INSIDE DOG. AND MAMA TIED HIM UP OUTSIDE.
WHY WASN'T HE ALLOWED INSIDE?
MAMA'S A CAT PERSON.
I DIDN'T SEE ANY CATS OVER AT THE HOUSE.
THAT'S 'CAUSE BUSTER RUNNED 'EM OFF. WE HAD THREE CATS BEFORE DOYLE STOLE DADDY'S DOG 'N BROUGHT IT HOME.
DOYLE? IS DOYLE THE MAN THAT DID THIS THING TO YOUR MAMA AND DADDY?
DOYLE'S DEAD IN THE KITCHEN, MISTER. IT WAS MY DADDY THAT DONE THAT.
I TELL YOU WHAT-- HE WAS MAD ABOUT THE DOG. REAL MAD.

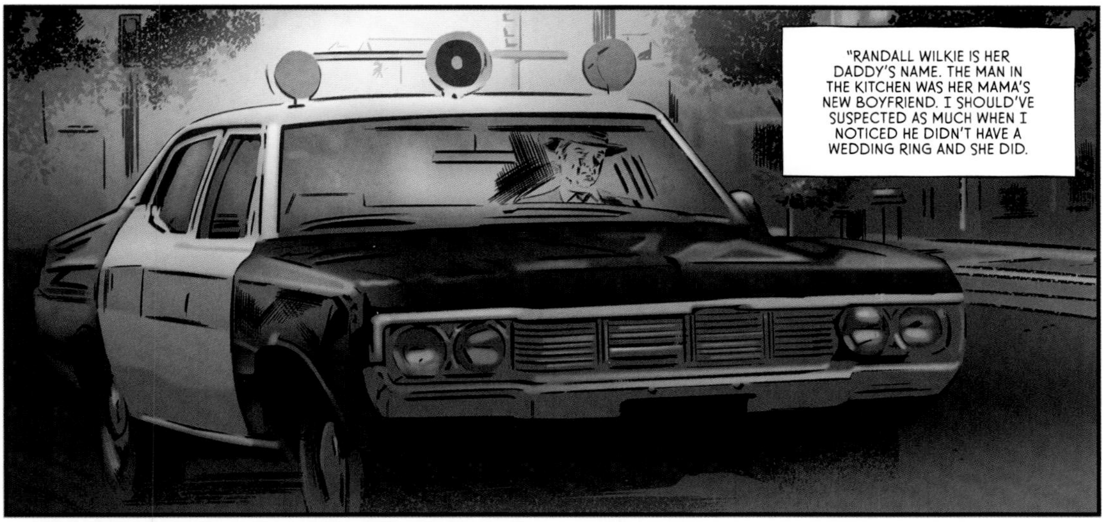
"RANDALL WILKIE IS HER DADDY'S NAME. THE MAN IN THE KITCHEN WAS HER MAMA'S NEW BOYFRIEND. I SHOULD'VE SUSPECTED AS MUCH WHEN I NOTICED HE DIDN'T HAVE A WEDDING RING AND SHE DID.

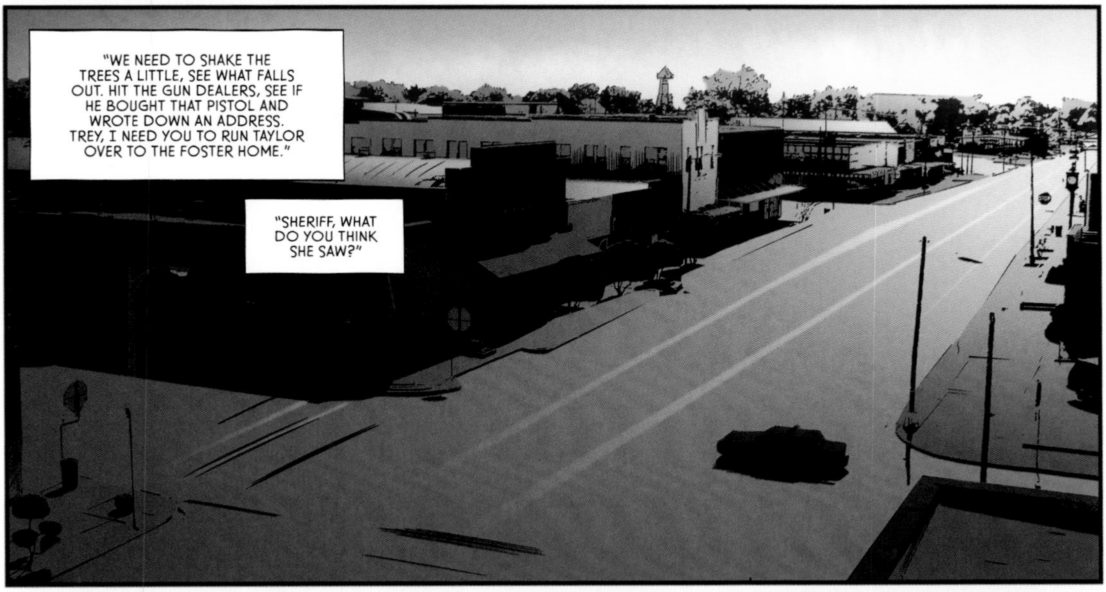
"WE NEED TO SHAKE THE TREES A LITTLE, SEE WHAT FALLS OUT. HIT THE GUN DEALERS, SEE IF HE BOUGHT THAT PISTOL AND WROTE DOWN AN ADDRESS. TREY, I NEED YOU TO RUN TAYLOR OVER TO THE FOSTER HOME."
"SHERIFF, WHAT DO YOU THINK SHE SAW?"

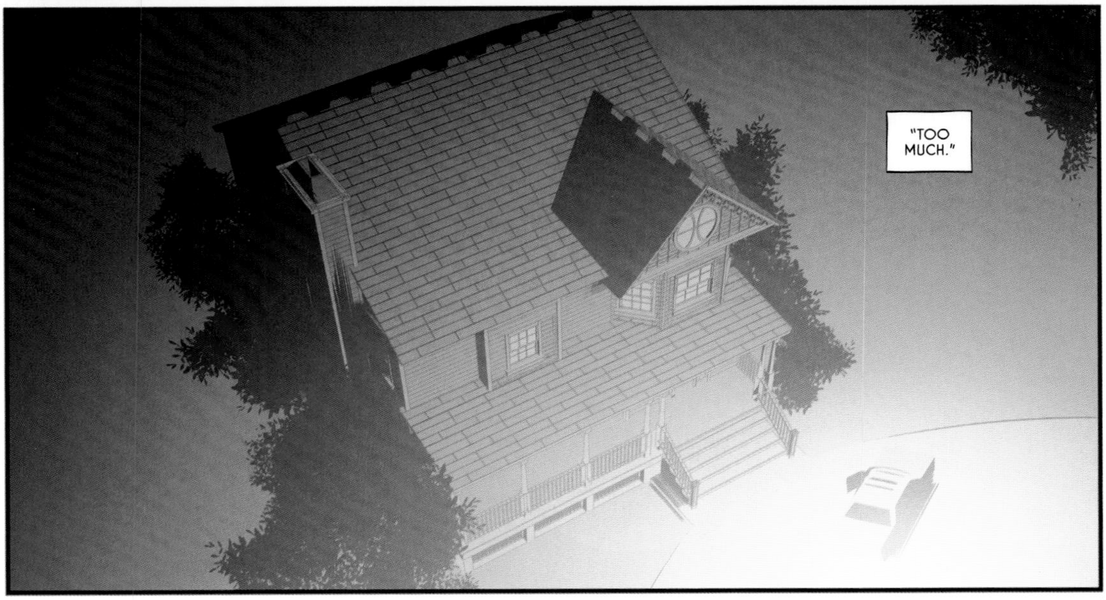
"TOO MUCH."

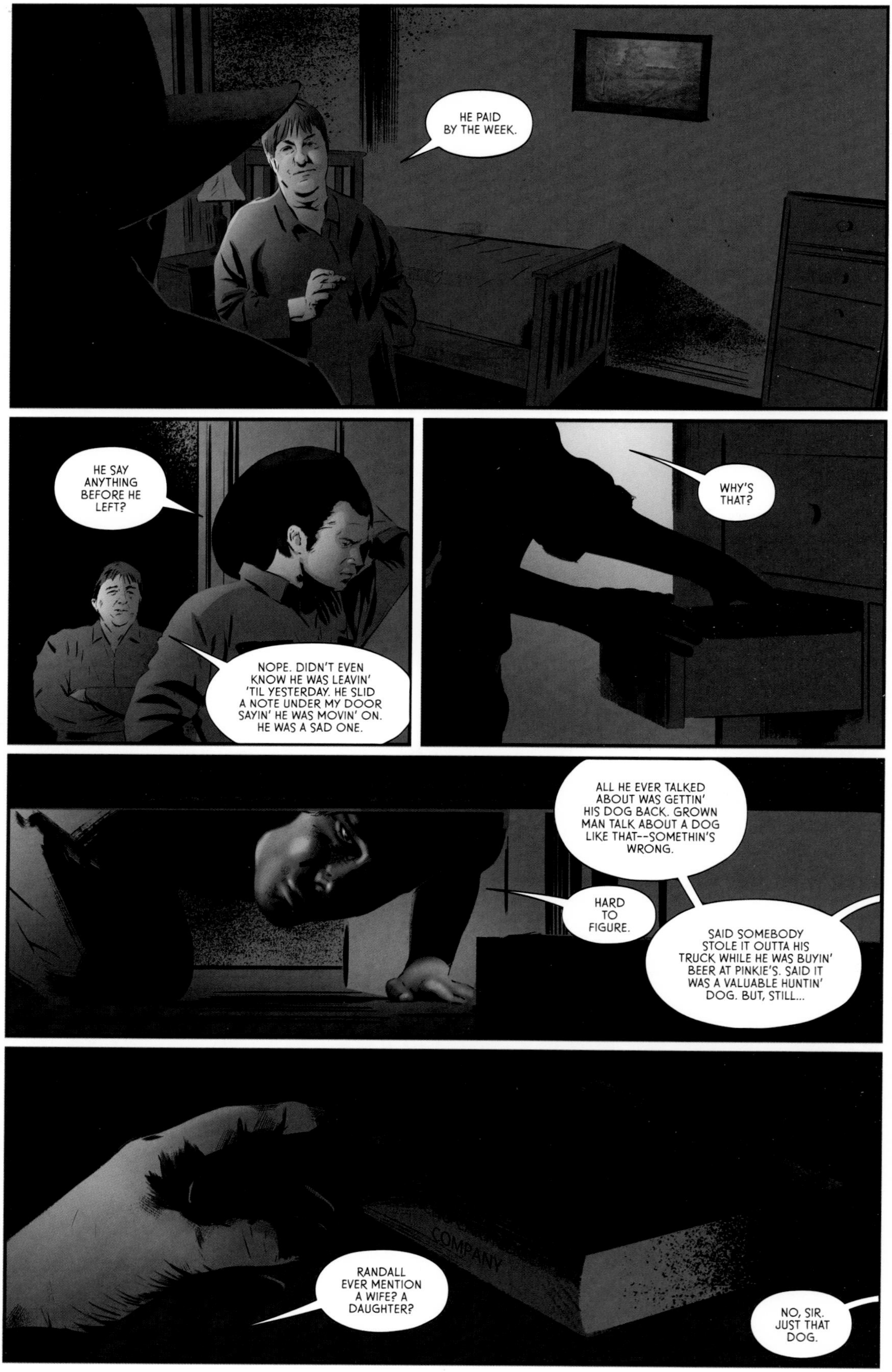
HE PAID BY THE WEEK.
HE SAY ANYTHING BEFORE HE LEFT?
NOPE. DIDN'T EVEN KNOW HE WAS LEAVIN' 'TIL YESTERDAY. HE SLID A NOTE UNDER MY DOOR SAYIN' HE WAS MOVIN' ON. HE WAS A SAD ONE.
WHY'S THAT?
ALL HE EVER TALKED ABOUT WAS GETTIN' HIS DOG BACK. GROWN MAN TALK ABOUT A DOG LIKE THAT--SOMETHIN'S WRONG.
HARD TO FIGURE.
SAID SOMEBODY STOLE IT OUTTA HIS TRUCK WHILE HE WAS BUYIN' BEER AT PINKIE'S. SAID IT WAS A VALUABLE HUNTIN' DOG. BUT, STILL...
COMPANY
RANDALL EVER MENTION A WIFE? A DAUGHTER?
NO, SIR. JUST THAT DOG.

YEP. THIS ONE'S MINE.

BUT IT'S OLD. I DON'T HAND-STAMP 'EM LIKE THAT NO MORE. TOO MUCH WORK.

SO, YOU KNOW RANDALL WILKIE?

SURE. ONE'A MY BEST CUSTOMERS. HE BUYS YEAR ROUND. NOT JUST HUNTIN' SEASON. HAVEN'T SEEN 'IM LATELY THOUGH. HE LOADED UP AT THE END OF THE TURKEY SHOOT IN MAY. HEARD HE WAS HAVIN' A HARD TIME WITH THE WIFE. FIGURED THAT WAS CUTTIN' INTO HIS FUN. HEH.

EVER GO HUNTIN' WITH HIM?

I DON'T MIX BUSINESS WITH PLEASURE. SOME OF THE BOYS AROUND TOWN AT THE GUN SHOPS WILL. YOU KNOW, THEY SEE IT AS A SALES OPPORTUNITY, BUT, HELL, I SELL BULLETS. WHAT'S THERE TO TALK ABOUT?

HOW'S YOUR DADDY?

HE'S FINE. THANKS FOR ASKING.

THINGS JUST HAVEN'T BEEN THE SAME AROUND HERE SINCE HE RETIRED.

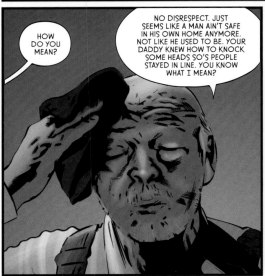

HOW DO YOU MEAN?

NO DISRESPECT. JUST SEEMS LIKE A MAN AIN'T SAFE IN HIS OWN HOME ANYMORE. NOT LIKE HE USED TO BE. YOUR DADDY KNEW HOW TO KNOCK SOME HEADS SO'S PEOPLE STAYED IN LINE. YOU KNOW WHAT I MEAN?

YEAH. YEAH, I DO.

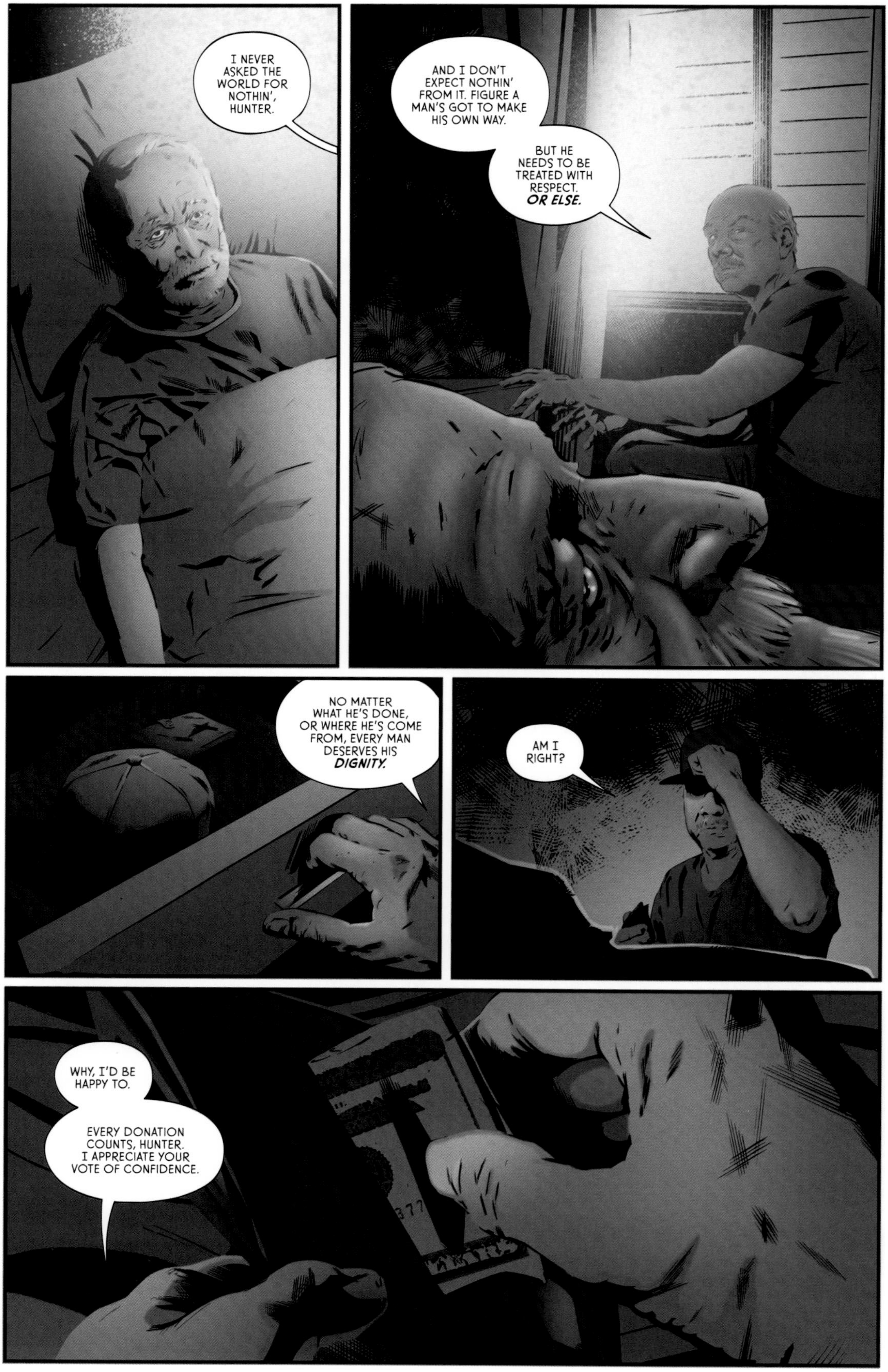
I NEVER ASKED THE WORLD FOR NOTHIN', HUNTER.
AND I DON'T EXPECT NOTHIN' FROM IT. FIGURE A MAN'S GOT TO MAKE HIS OWN WAY.
BUT HE NEEDS TO BE TREATED WITH RESPECT. ***OR ELSE.***
NO MATTER WHAT HE'S DONE, OR WHERE HE'S COME FROM, EVERY MAN DESERVES HIS ***DIGNITY.***
AM I RIGHT?
WHY, I'D BE HAPPY TO.
EVERY DONATION COUNTS, HUNTER. I APPRECIATE YOUR VOTE OF CONFIDENCE.

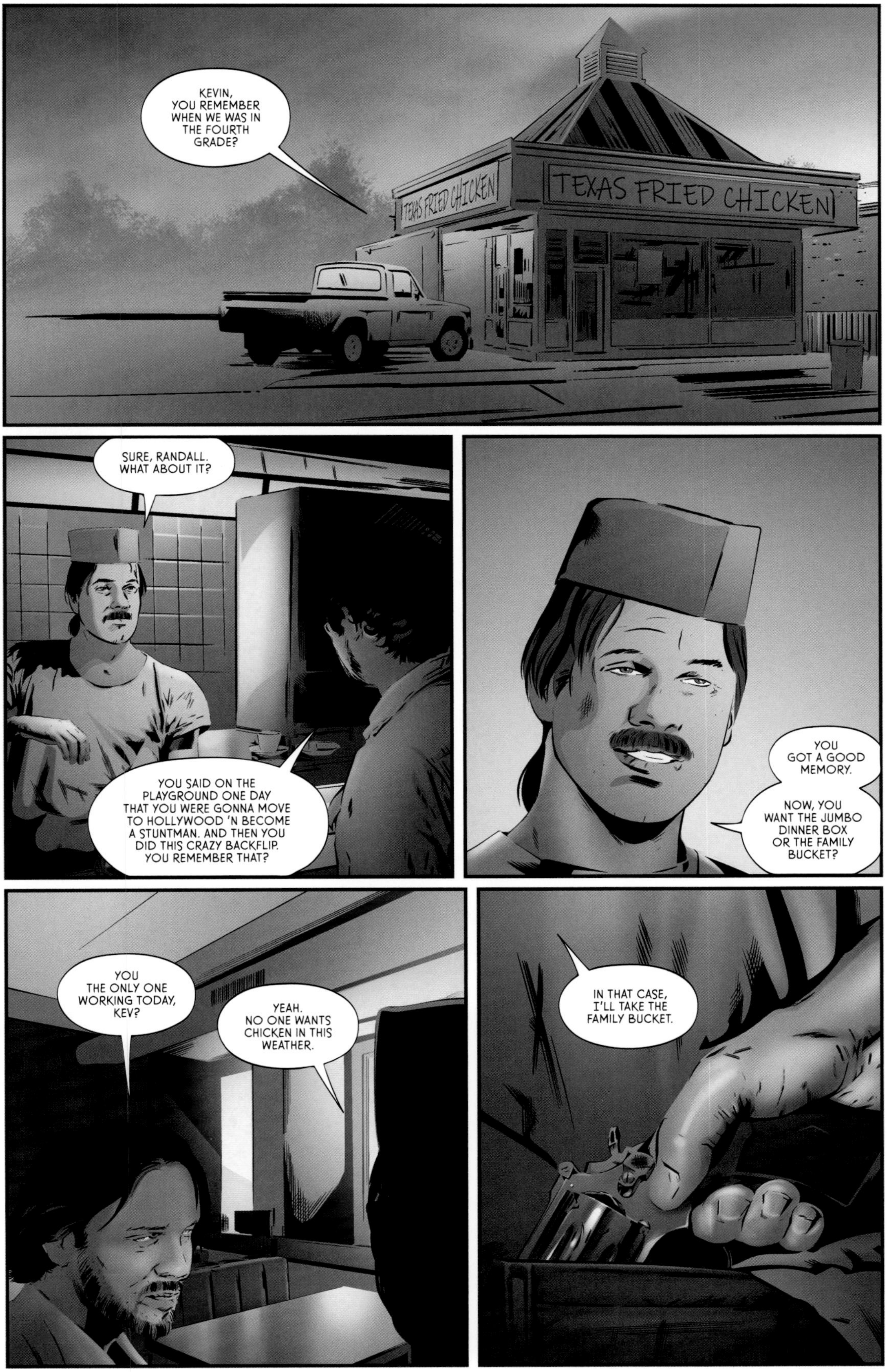
KEVIN, YOU REMEMBER WHEN WE WAS IN THE FOURTH GRADE?
TEXAS FRIED CHICKEN
TEXAS FRIED CHICKEN
SURE, RANDALL. WHAT ABOUT IT?
YOU SAID ON THE PLAYGROUND ONE DAY THAT YOU WERE GONNA MOVE TO HOLLYWOOD 'N BECOME A STUNTMAN. AND THEN YOU DID THIS CRAZY BACKFLIP. YOU REMEMBER THAT?
YOU GOT A GOOD MEMORY.
NOW, YOU WANT THE JUMBO DINNER BOX OR THE FAMILY BUCKET?
YOU THE ONLY ONE WORKING TODAY, KEV?
YEAH. NO ONE WANTS CHICKEN IN THIS WEATHER.
IN THAT CASE, I'LL TAKE THE FAMILY BUCKET.

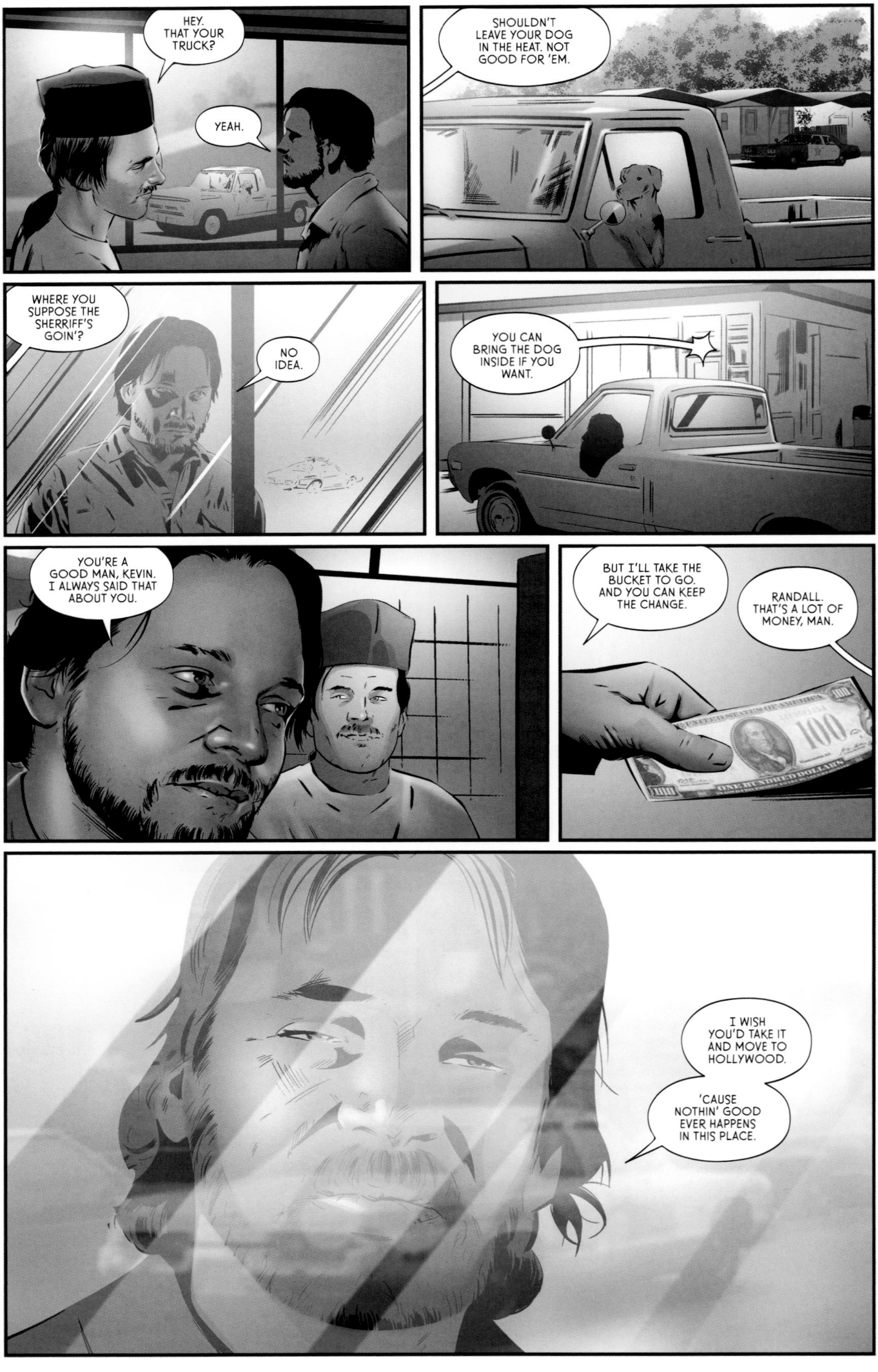
HEY. THAT YOUR TRUCK?
YEAH.
SHOULDN'T LEAVE YOUR DOG IN THE HEAT. NOT GOOD FOR 'EM.
WHERE YOU SUPPOSE THE SHERRIFF'S GOIN'?
NO IDEA.
YOU CAN BRING THE DOG INSIDE IF YOU WANT.
YOU'RE A GOOD MAN, KEVIN. I ALWAYS SAID THAT ABOUT YOU.
BUT I'LL TAKE THE BUCKET TO GO. AND YOU CAN KEEP THE CHANGE.
RANDALL. THAT'S A LOT OF MONEY, MAN.
100
ONE HUNDRED DOLLARS
I WISH YOU'D TAKE IT AND MOVE TO HOLLYWOOD.
'CAUSE NOTHIN' GOOD EVER HAPPENS IN THIS PLACE.

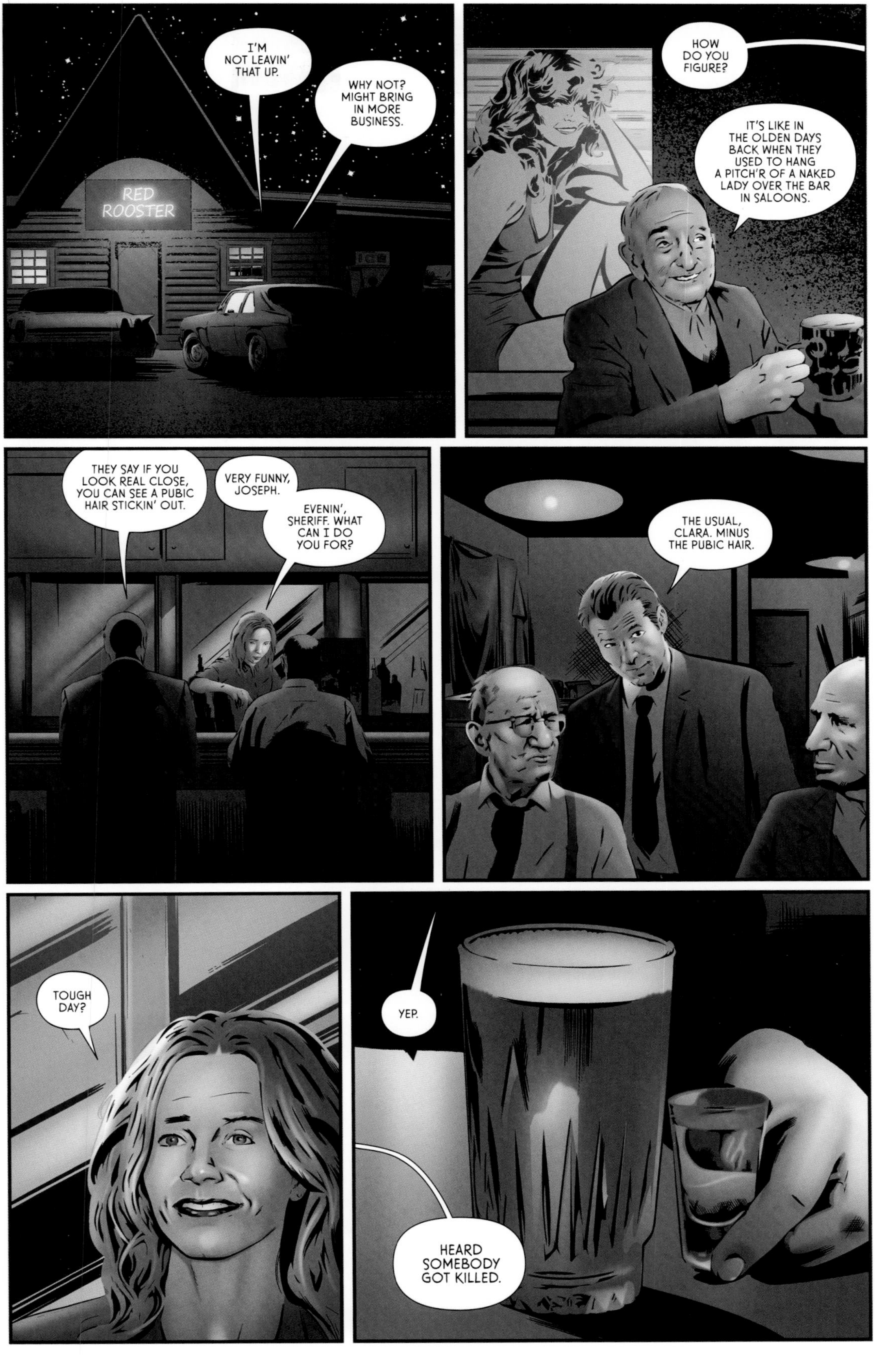
RED ROOSTER
I'M NOT LEAVIN' THAT UP.
WHY NOT? MIGHT BRING IN MORE BUSINESS.
HOW DO YOU FIGURE?
IT'S LIKE IN THE OLDEN DAYS BACK WHEN THEY USED TO HANG A PITCH'R OF A NAKED LADY OVER THE BAR IN SALOONS.
THEY SAY IF YOU LOOK REAL CLOSE, YOU CAN SEE A PUBIC HAIR STICKIN' OUT.
VERY FUNNY, JOSEPH.
EVENIN', SHERIFF. WHAT CAN I DO YOU FOR?
THE USUAL, CLARA. MINUS THE PUBIC HAIR.
TOUGH DAY?
YEP.
HEARD SOMEBODY GOT KILLED.

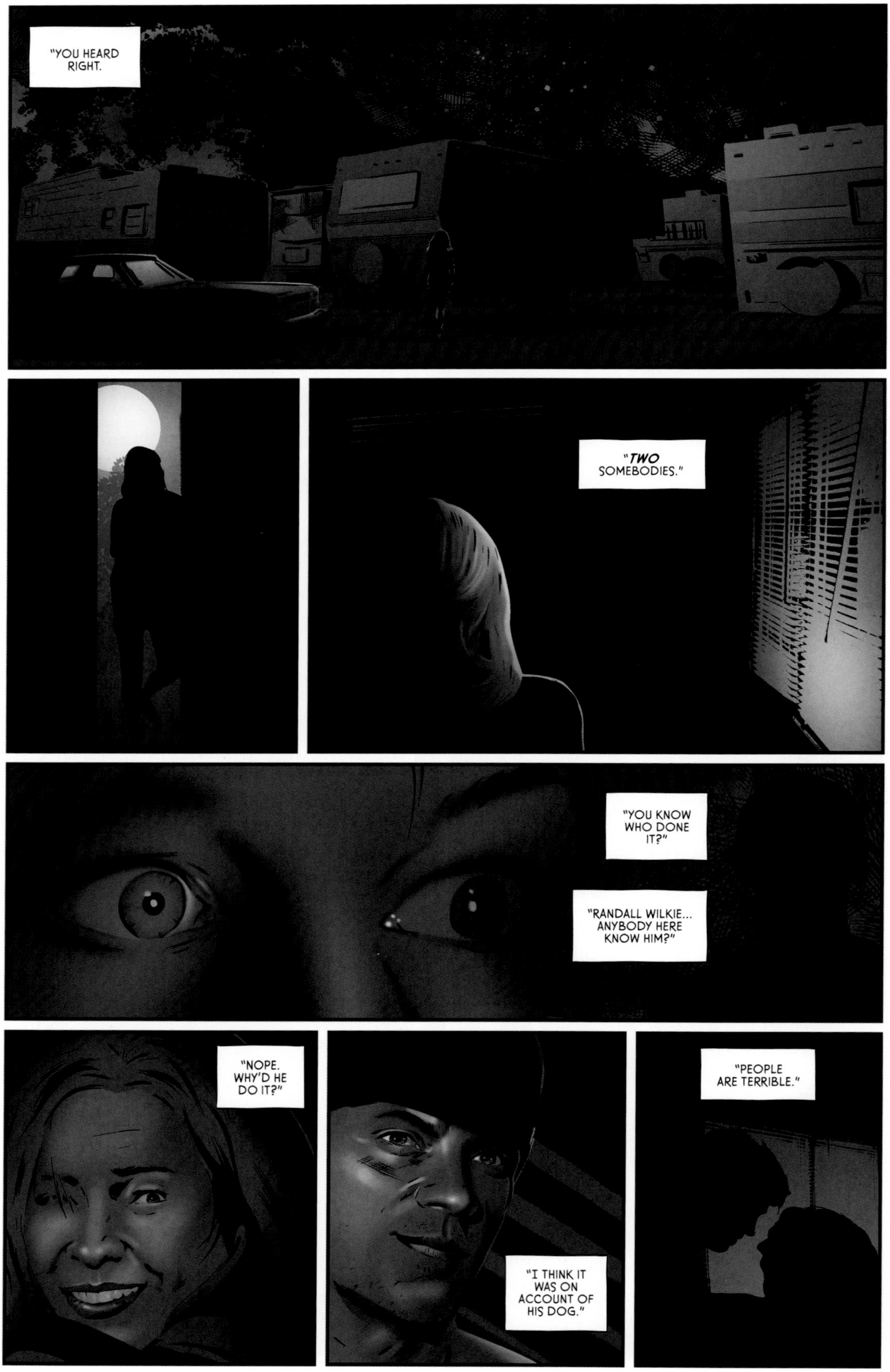
"YOU HEARD RIGHT.
"*TWO* SOMEBODIES."
"YOU KNOW WHO DONE IT?"
"RANDALL WILKIE... ANYBODY HERE KNOW HIM?"
"NOPE. WHY'D HE DO IT?"
"I THINK IT WAS ON ACCOUNT OF HIS DOG."
"PEOPLE ARE TERRIBLE."

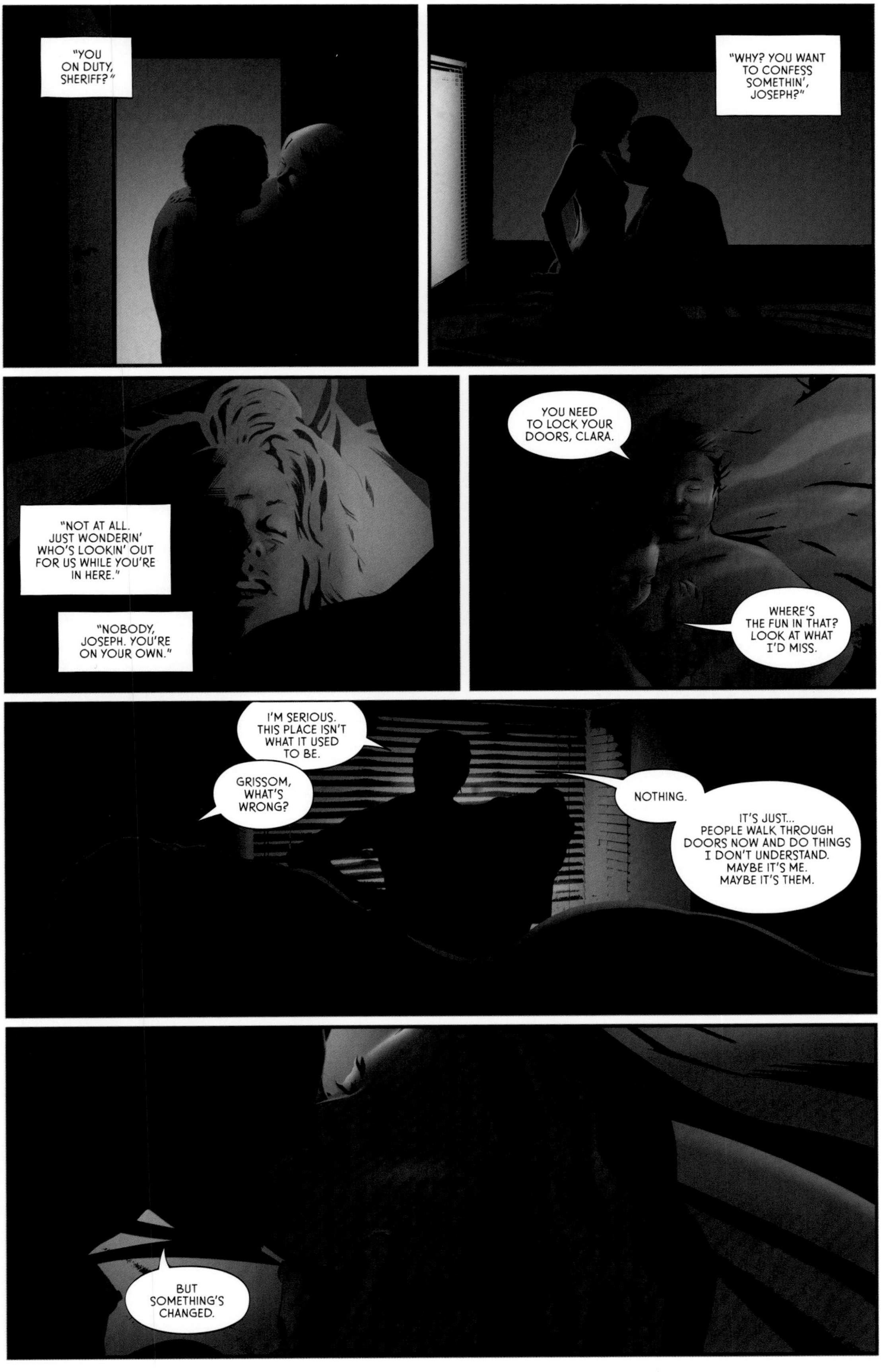
"YOU ON DUTY, SHERIFF?"
"WHY? YOU WANT TO CONFESS SOMETHIN', JOSEPH?"
"NOT AT ALL. JUST WONDERIN' WHO'S LOOKIN' OUT FOR US WHILE YOU'RE IN HERE."
"NOBODY, JOSEPH. YOU'RE ON YOUR OWN."
YOU NEED TO LOCK YOUR DOORS, CLARA.
WHERE'S THE FUN IN THAT? LOOK AT WHAT I'D MISS.
I'M SERIOUS. THIS PLACE ISN'T WHAT IT USED TO BE.
GRISSOM, WHAT'S WRONG?
NOTHING.
IT'S JUST... PEOPLE WALK THROUGH DOORS NOW AND DO THINGS I DON'T UNDERSTAND. MAYBE IT'S ME. MAYBE IT'S THEM.
BUT SOMETHING'S CHANGED.

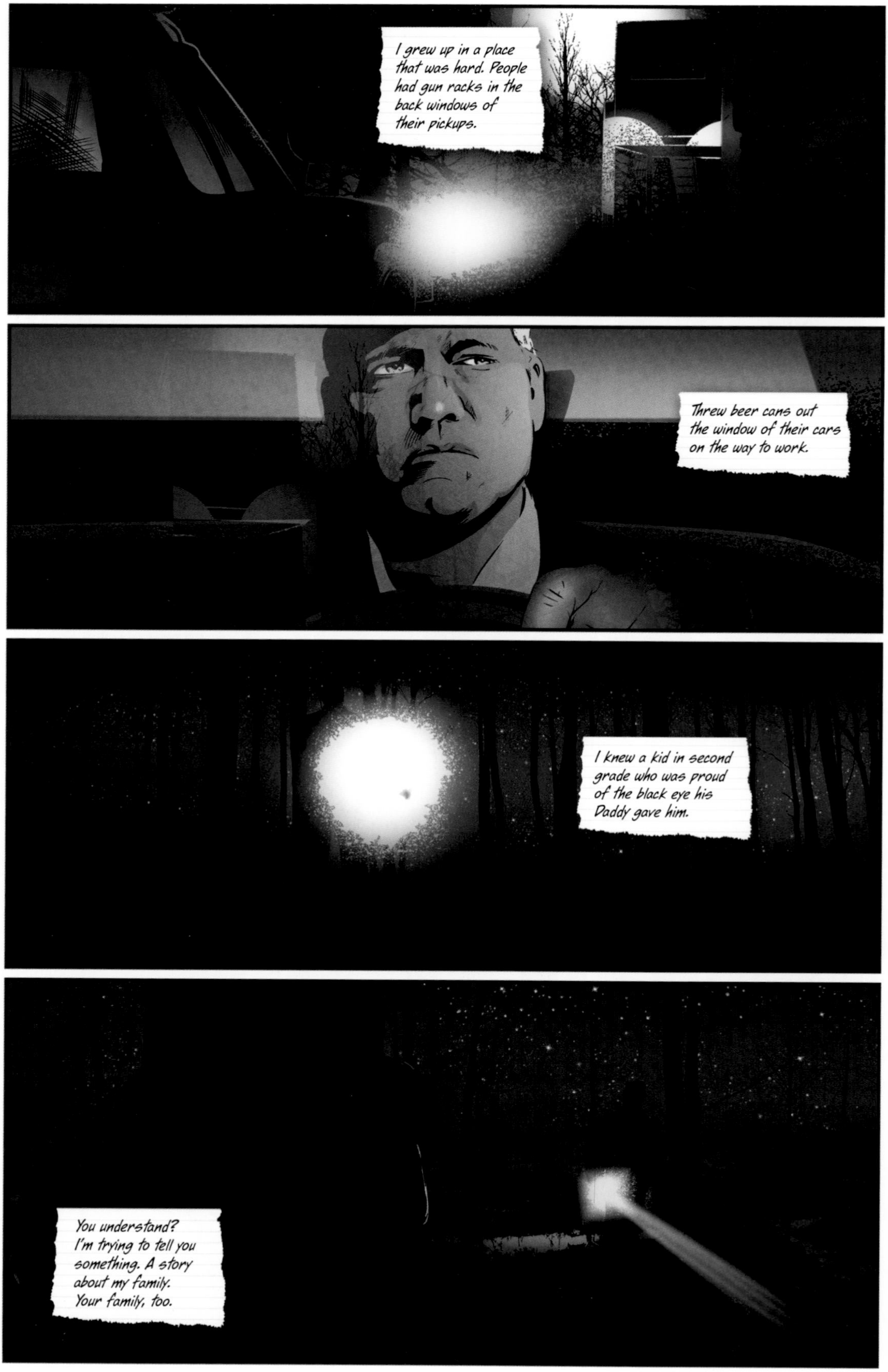
I grew up in a place that was hard. People had gun racks in the back windows of their pickups.
Threw beer cans out the window of their cars on the way to work.
I knew a kid in second grade who was proud of the black eye his Daddy gave him.
You understand? I'm trying to tell you something. A story about my family. Your family, too.

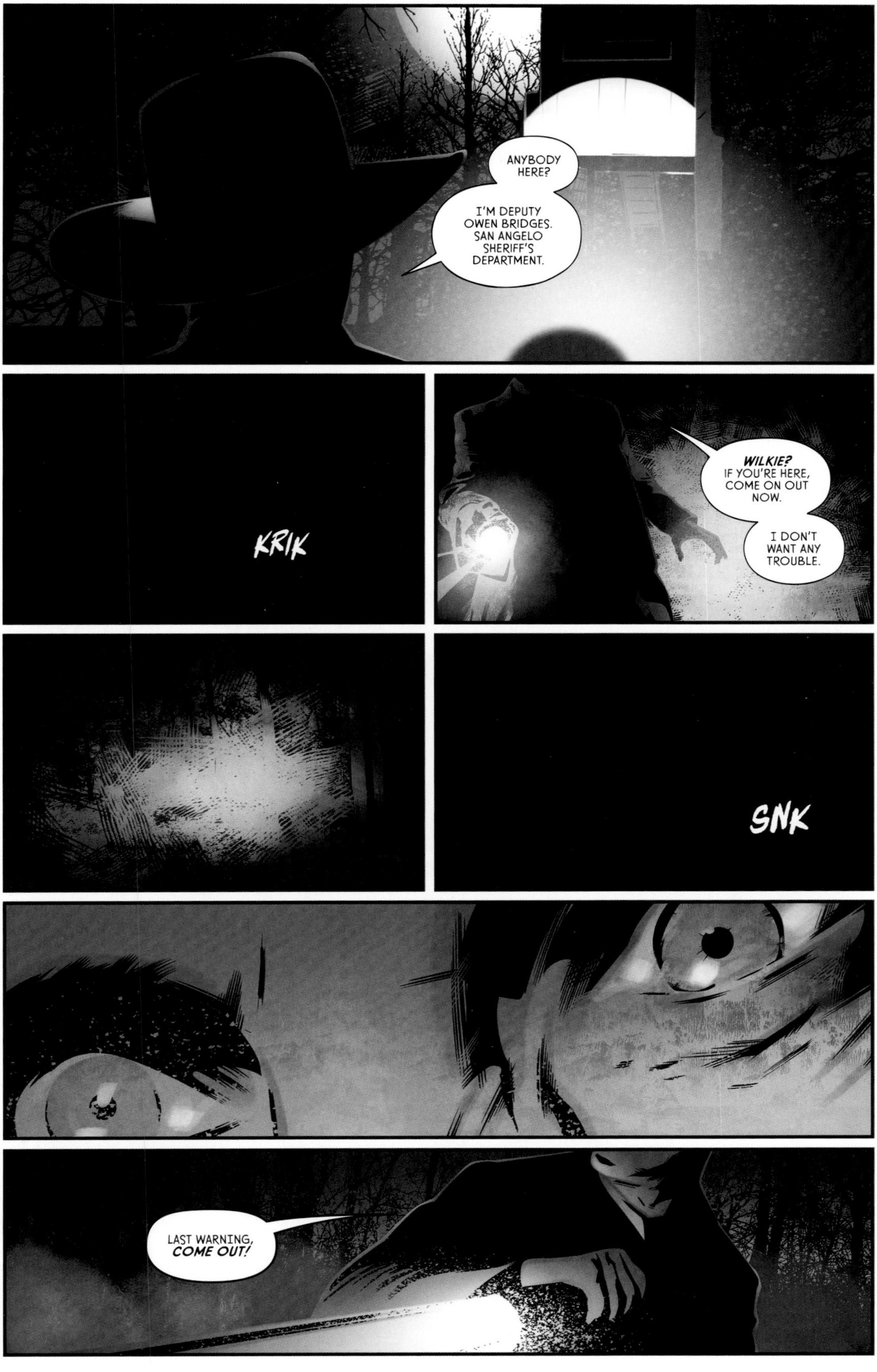
ANYBODY HERE?
I'M DEPUTY OWEN BRIDGES. SAN ANGELO SHERIFF'S DEPARTMENT.
KRIK
WILKIE? IF YOU'RE HERE, COME ON OUT NOW.
I DON'T WANT ANY TROUBLE.
SNK
LAST WARNING, *COME OUT!*

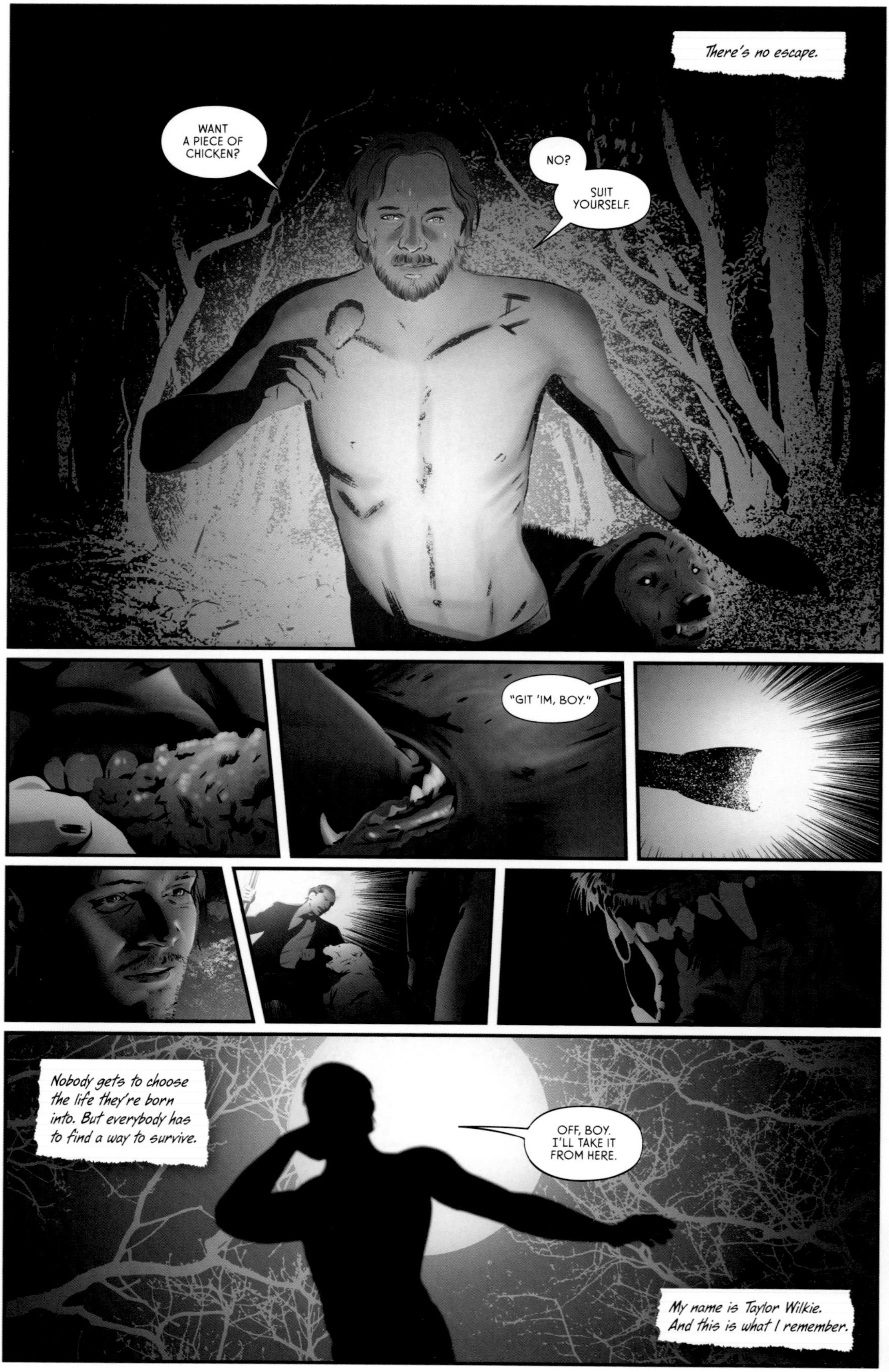
There's no escape.
WANT A PIECE OF CHICKEN?
NO?
SUIT YOURSELF.
"GIT 'IM, BOY."
Nobody gets to choose the life they're born into. But everybody has to find a way to survive.
OFF, BOY. I'LL TAKE IT FROM HERE.
My name is Taylor Wilkie. And this is what I remember.

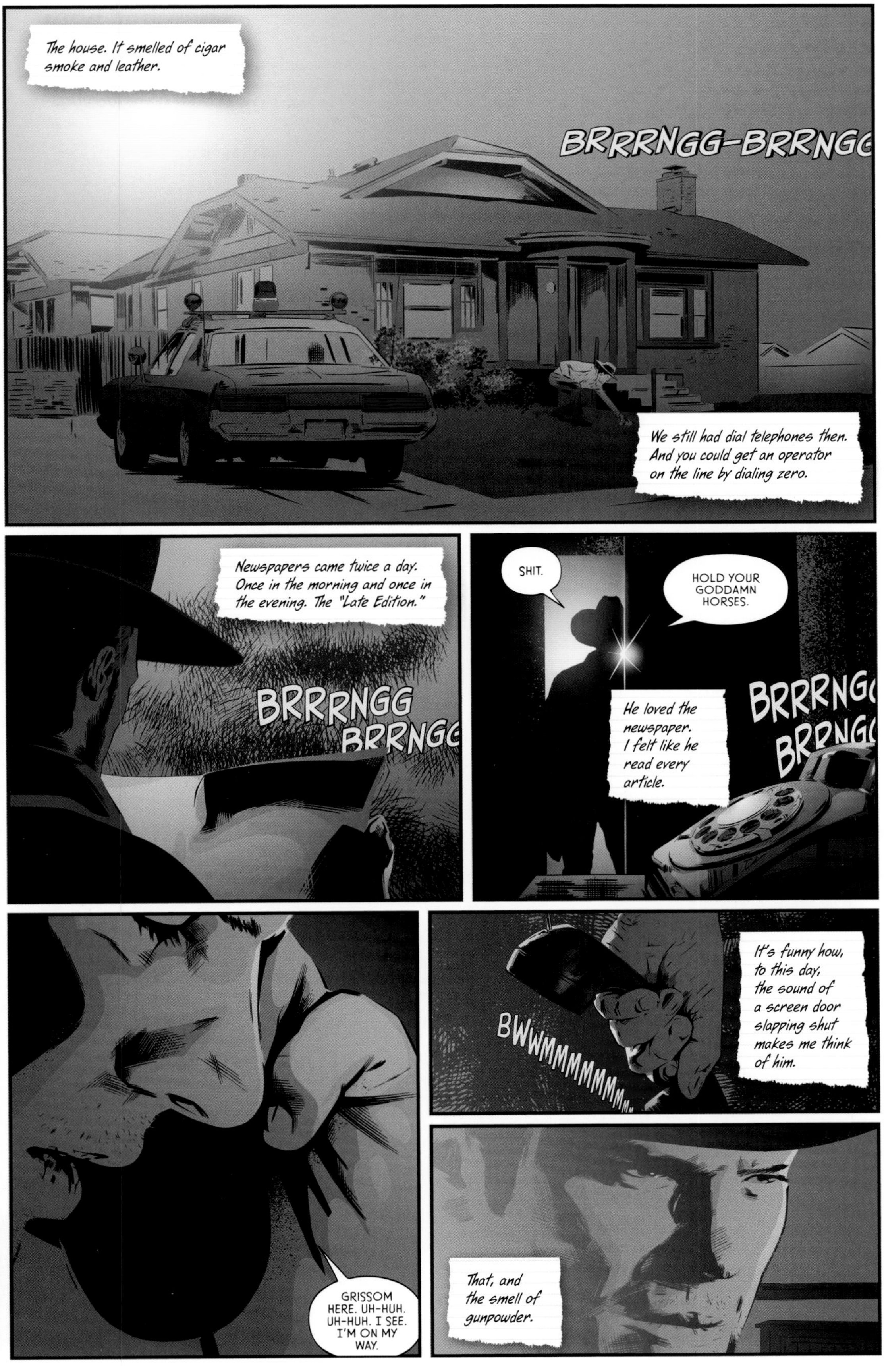
The house. It smelled of cigar smoke and leather.
BRRRNGG-BRRNGG
We still had dial telephones then. And you could get an operator on the line by dialing zero.
Newspapers came twice a day. Once in the morning and once in the evening. The "Late Edition."
BRRRNGG BRRNGG
SHIT.
HOLD YOUR GODDAMN HORSES.
He loved the newspaper. I felt like he read every article.
BRRRNGG BRRNGG
GRISSOM HERE. UH-HUH. UH-HUH. I SEE. I'M ON MY WAY.
It's funny how, to this day, the sound of a screen door slapping shut makes me think of him.
BWWMMMMMMMMm
That, and the smell of gunpowder.

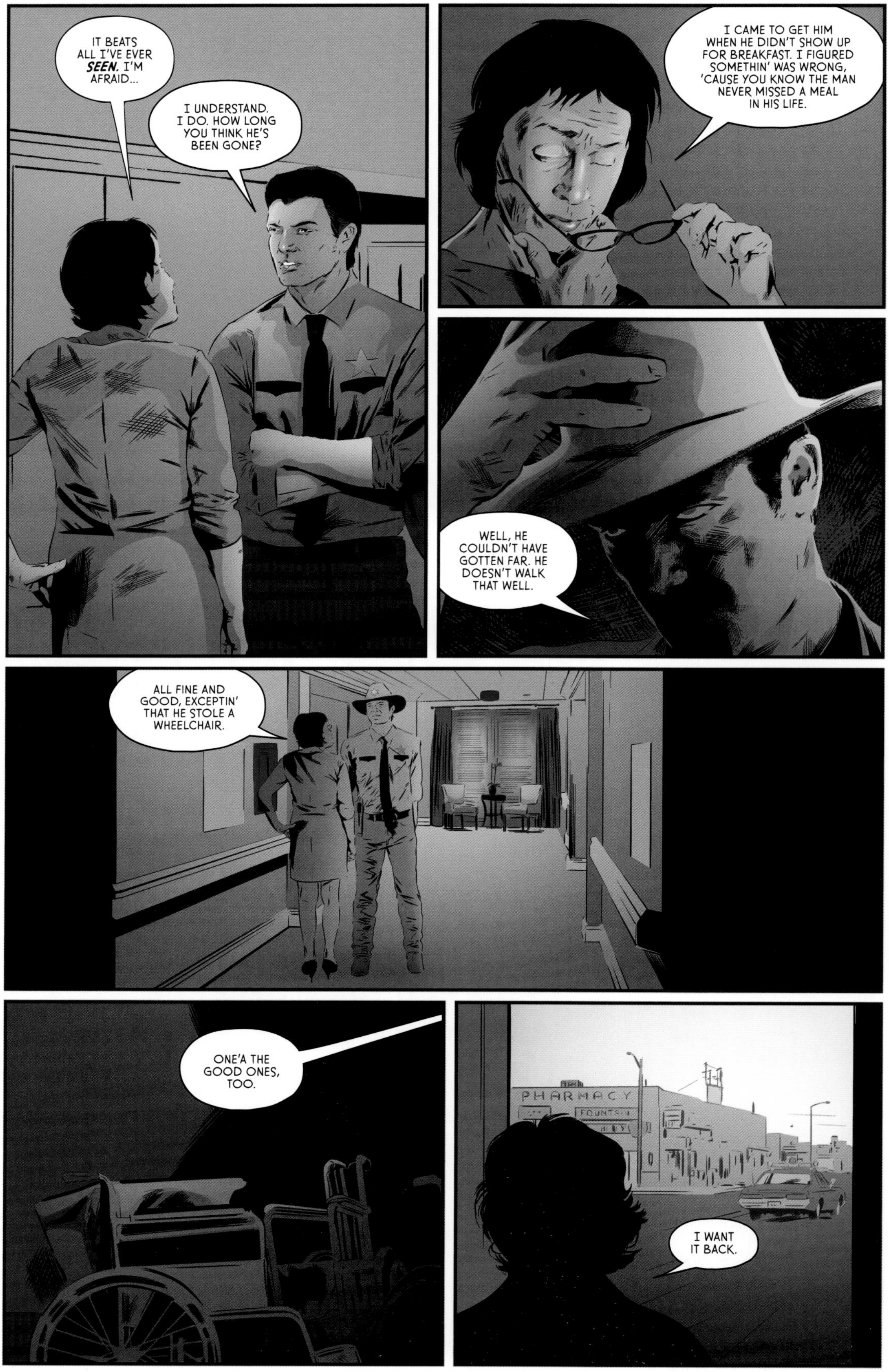

IT BEATS ALL I'VE EVER ***SEEN.*** I'M AFRAID...
I UNDERSTAND. I DO. HOW LONG YOU THINK HE'S BEEN GONE?
I CAME TO GET HIM WHEN HE DIDN'T SHOW UP FOR BREAKFAST. I FIGURED SOMETHIN' WAS WRONG, 'CAUSE YOU KNOW THE MAN NEVER MISSED A MEAL IN HIS LIFE.
WELL, HE COULDN'T HAVE GOTTEN FAR. HE DOESN'T WALK THAT WELL.
ALL FINE AND GOOD, EXCEPTIN' THAT HE STOLE A WHEELCHAIR.
ONE'A THE GOOD ONES, TOO.
PHARMACY
FOUNTAIN
I WANT IT BACK.

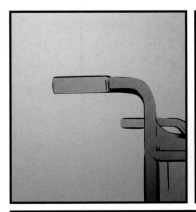

WEDDING OR FUNERAL?

FUNERAL.

FOR WHO?

BIG FOOT JOHNSON.

WHY DON'T YOU GET IN? I'LL DRIVE YOU.

IT'S ON FRIDAY.

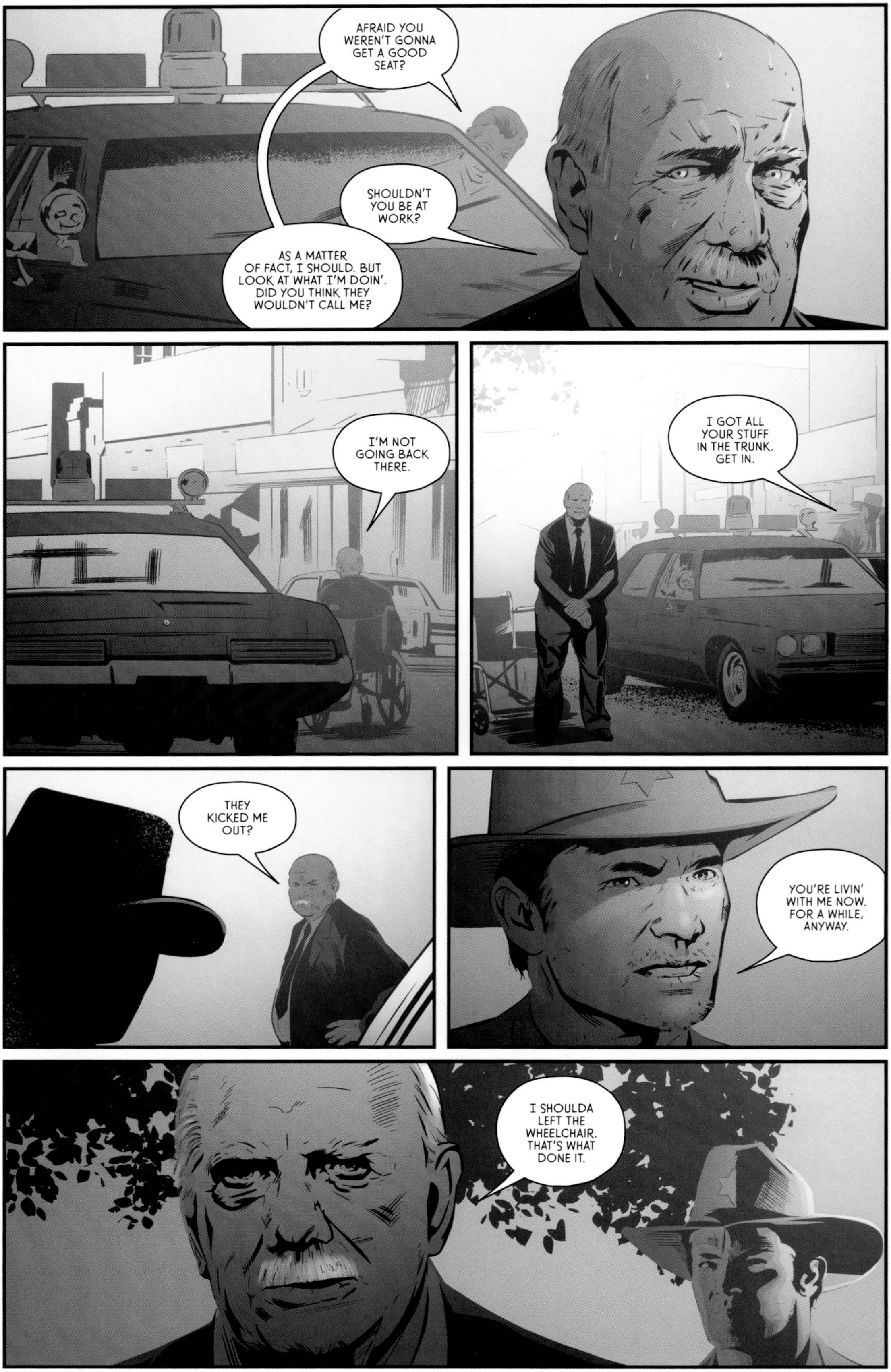
AFRAID YOU WEREN'T GONNA GET A GOOD SEAT?
SHOULDN'T YOU BE AT WORK?
AS A MATTER OF FACT, I SHOULD. BUT LOOK AT WHAT I'M DOIN'. DID YOU THINK THEY WOULDN'T CALL ME?
I'M NOT GOING BACK THERE.
I GOT ALL YOUR STUFF IN THE TRUNK. GET IN.
THEY KICKED ME OUT?
YOU'RE LIVIN' WITH ME NOW. FOR A WHILE, ANYWAY.
I SHOULDA LEFT THE WHEELCHAIR. THAT'S WHAT DONE IT.

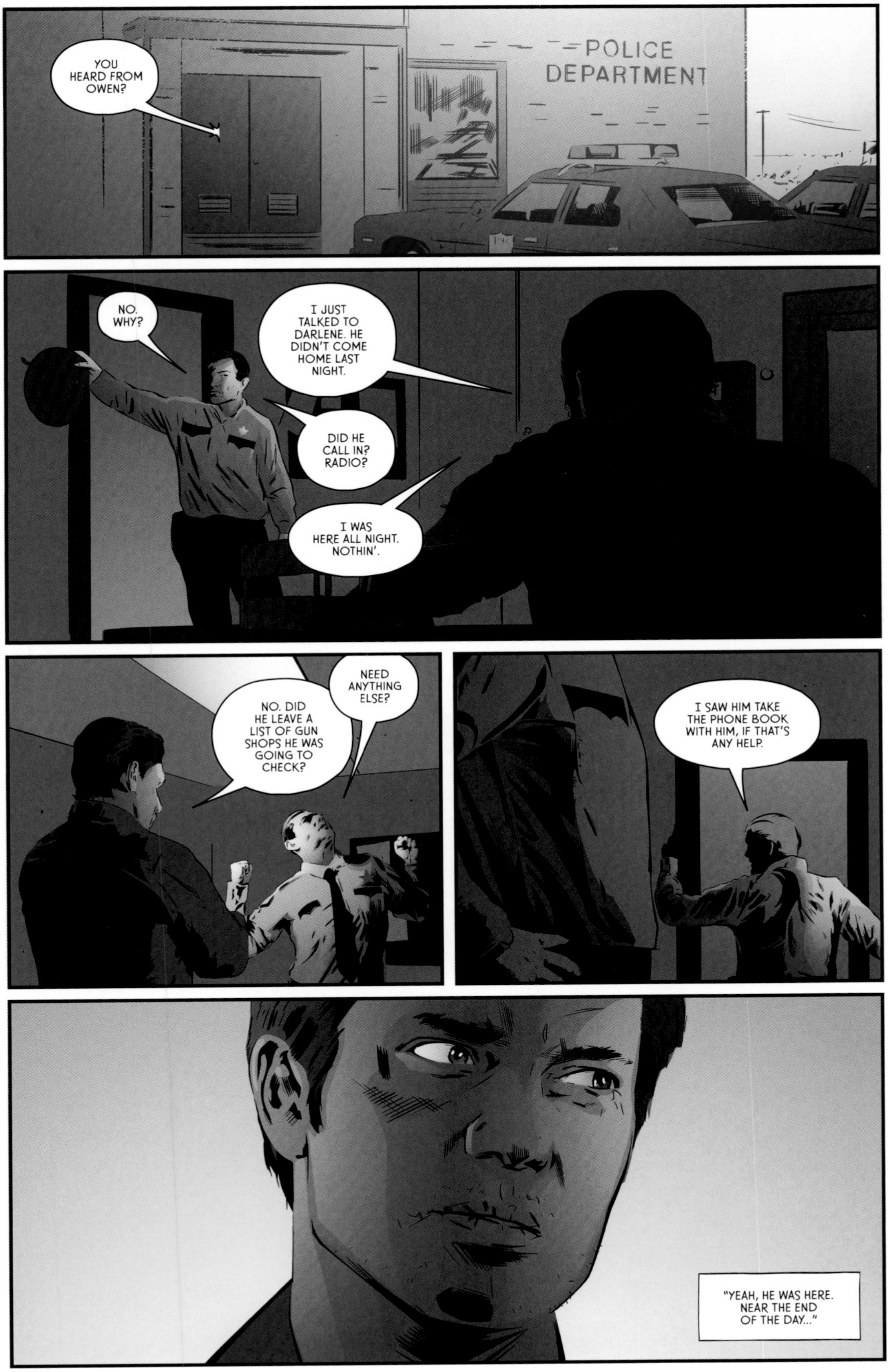
POLICE DEPARTMENT
YOU HEARD FROM OWEN?
NO. WHY?
I JUST TALKED TO DARLENE. HE DIDN'T COME HOME LAST NIGHT.
DID HE CALL IN? RADIO?
I WAS HERE ALL NIGHT. NOTHIN'.
NO. DID HE LEAVE A LIST OF GUN SHOPS HE WAS GOING TO CHECK?
NEED ANYTHING ELSE?
I SAW HIM TAKE THE PHONE BOOK WITH HIM, IF THAT'S ANY HELP.
"YEAH, HE WAS HERE. NEAR THE END OF THE DAY..."

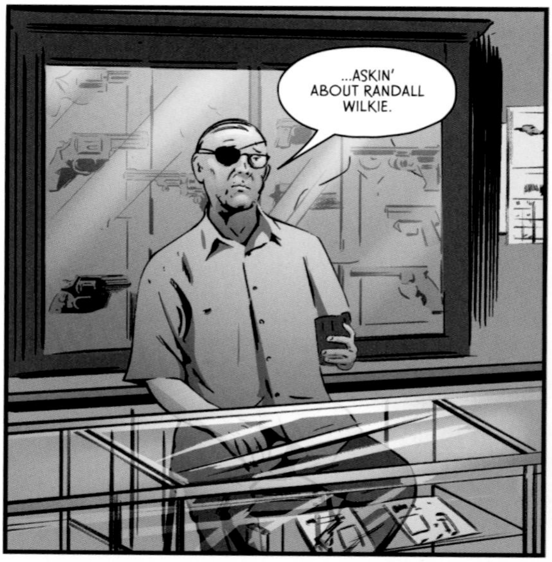
...ASKIN' ABOUT RANDALL WILKIE.

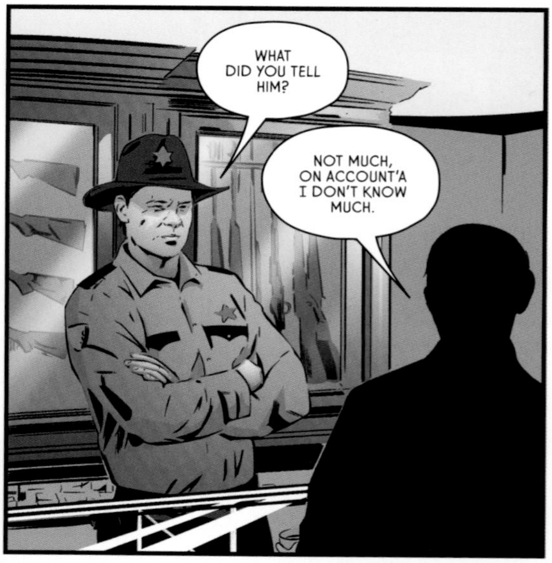
WHAT DID YOU TELL HIM?
NOT MUCH, ON ACCOUNT'A I DON'T KNOW MUCH.

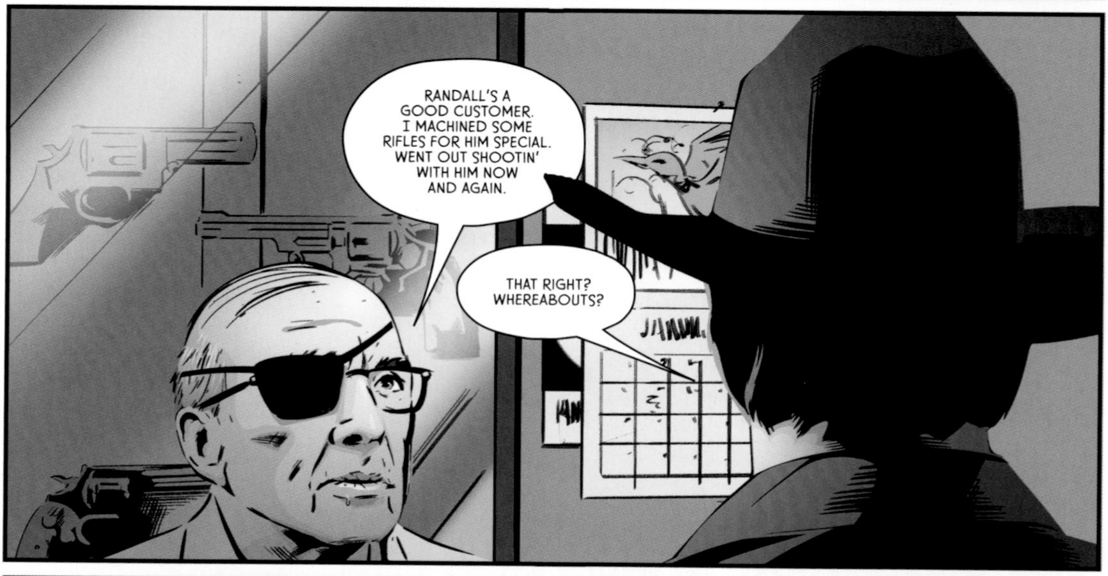
RANDALL'S A GOOD CUSTOMER. I MACHINED SOME RIFLES FOR HIM SPECIAL. WENT OUT SHOOTIN' WITH HIM NOW AND AGAIN.
THAT RIGHT? WHEREABOUTS?

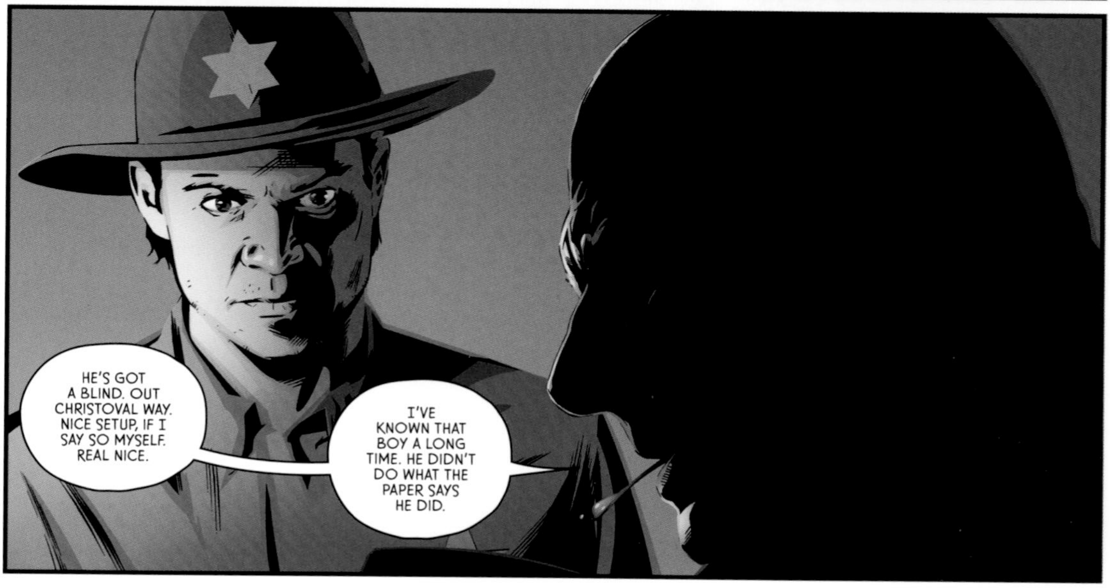
HE'S GOT A BLIND. OUT CHRISTOVAL WAY. NICE SETUP, IF I SAY SO MYSELF. REAL NICE.
I'VE KNOWN THAT BOY A LONG TIME. HE DIDN'T DO WHAT THE PAPER SAYS HE DID.

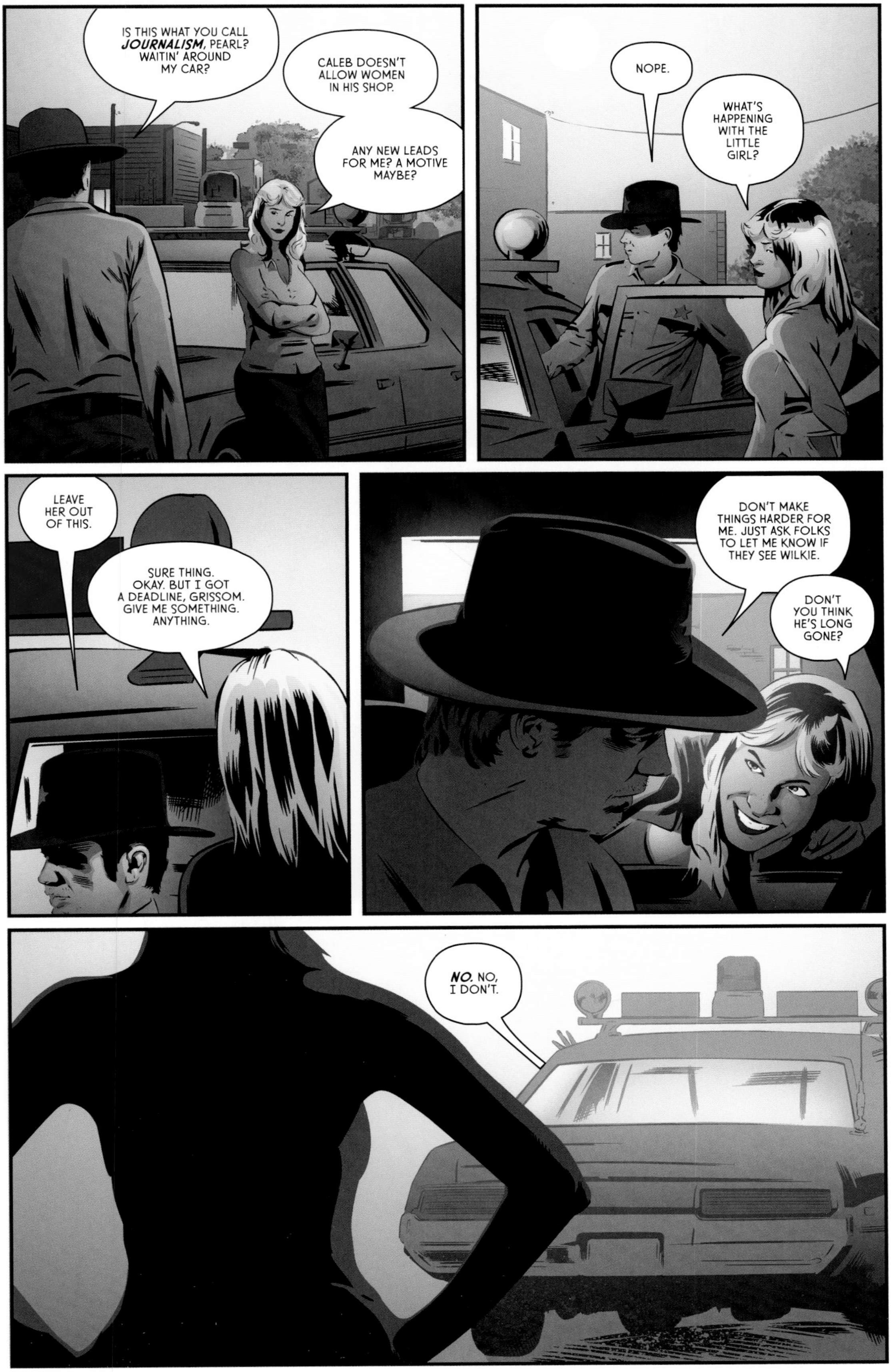

IS THIS WHAT YOU CALL ***JOURNALISM,*** PEARL? WAITIN' AROUND MY CAR?
CALEB DOESN'T ALLOW WOMEN IN HIS SHOP.
ANY NEW LEADS FOR ME? A MOTIVE MAYBE?
NOPE.
WHAT'S HAPPENING WITH THE LITTLE GIRL?
LEAVE HER OUT OF THIS.
SURE THING. OKAY. BUT I GOT A DEADLINE, GRISSOM. GIVE ME SOMETHING. ANYTHING.
DON'T MAKE THINGS HARDER FOR ME. JUST ASK FOLKS TO LET ME KNOW IF THEY SEE WILKIE.
DON'T YOU THINK HE'S LONG GONE?
NO. NO, I DON'T.

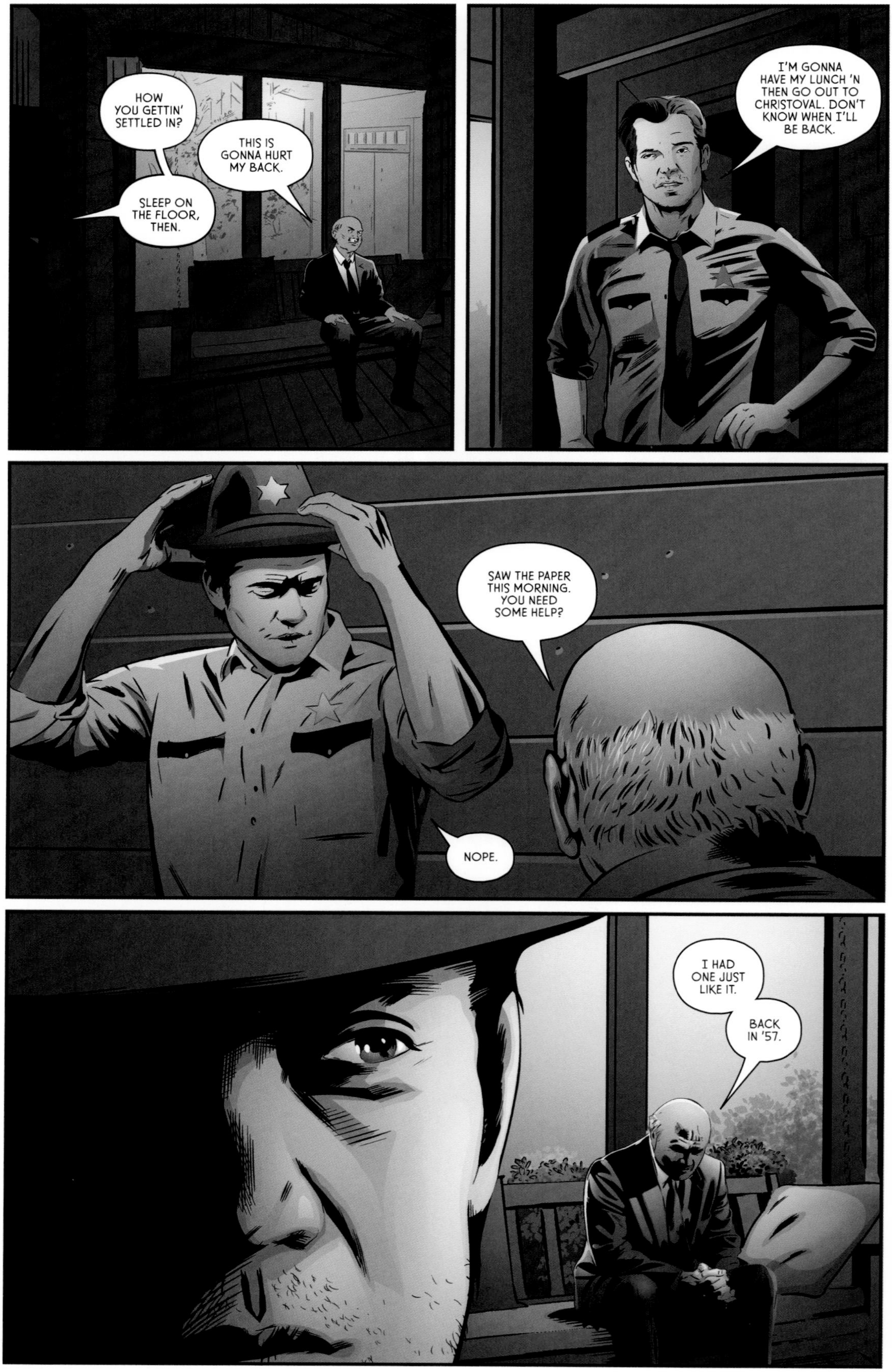
HOW YOU GETTIN' SETTLED IN?
THIS IS GONNA HURT MY BACK.
SLEEP ON THE FLOOR, THEN.
I'M GONNA HAVE MY LUNCH 'N THEN GO OUT TO CHRISTOVAL. DON'T KNOW WHEN I'LL BE BACK.
SAW THE PAPER THIS MORNING. YOU NEED SOME HELP?
NOPE.
I HAD ONE JUST LIKE IT.
BACK IN '57.

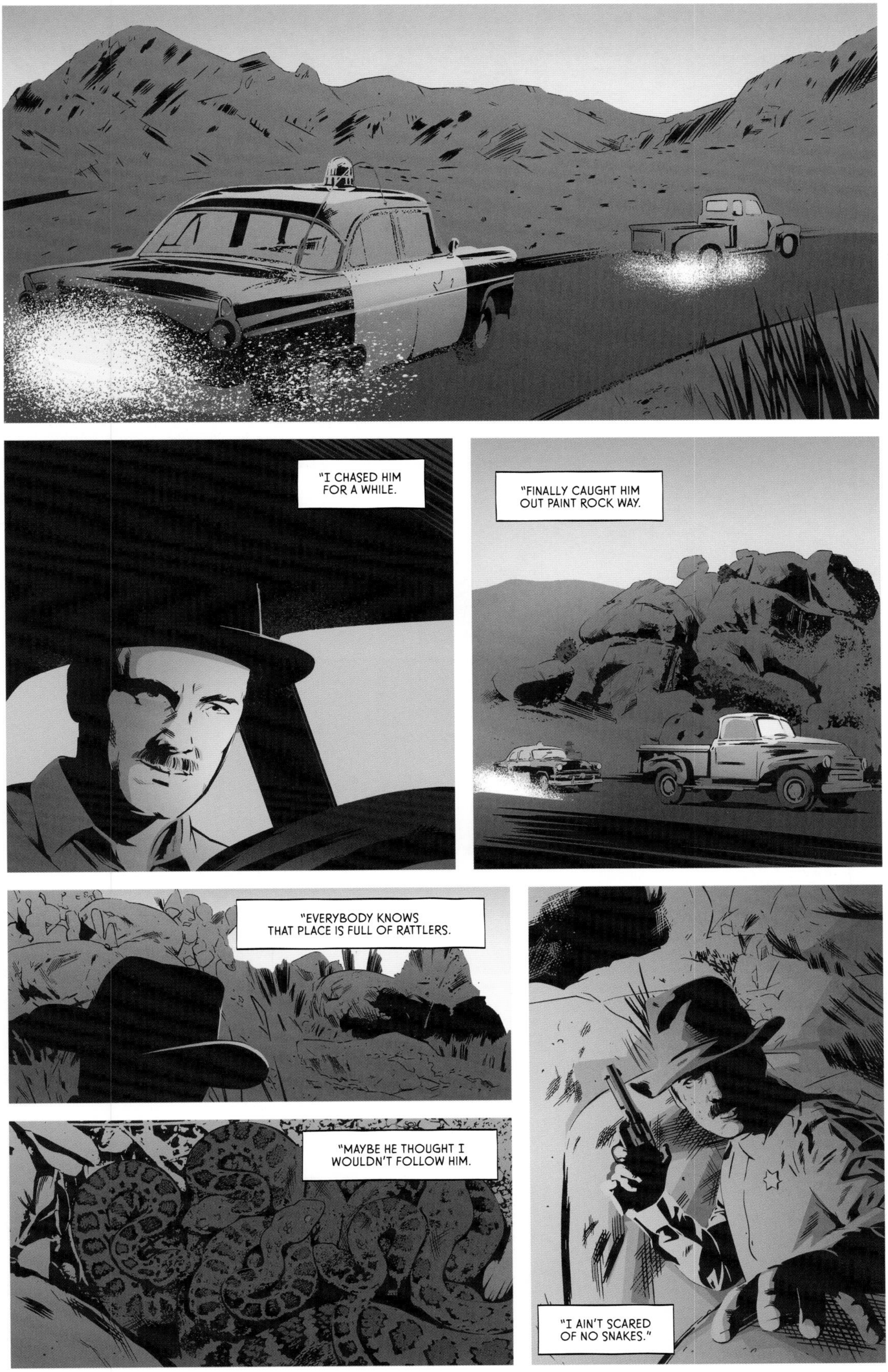
"I CHASED HIM FOR A WHILE.
"FINALLY CAUGHT HIM OUT PAINT ROCK WAY.
"EVERYBODY KNOWS THAT PLACE IS FULL OF RATTLERS.
"MAYBE HE THOUGHT I WOULDN'T FOLLOW HIM.
"I AIN'T SCARED OF NO SNAKES."

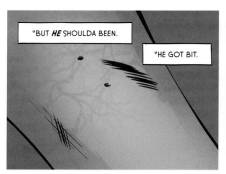

"BUT *HE* SHOULDA BEEN.

"HE GOT BIT.

"BIT *REAL BAD.*

"I HELD MY GUN ON HIM FOR AN HOUR OR SO.

"LET THE POISON SINK IN.

"THEY HAD TO TAKE THAT ARM OFF.

"EVENTUALLY."

YOU BE CAREFUL OUT THERE.

I WILL.

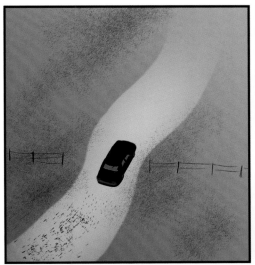

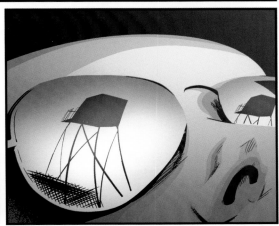

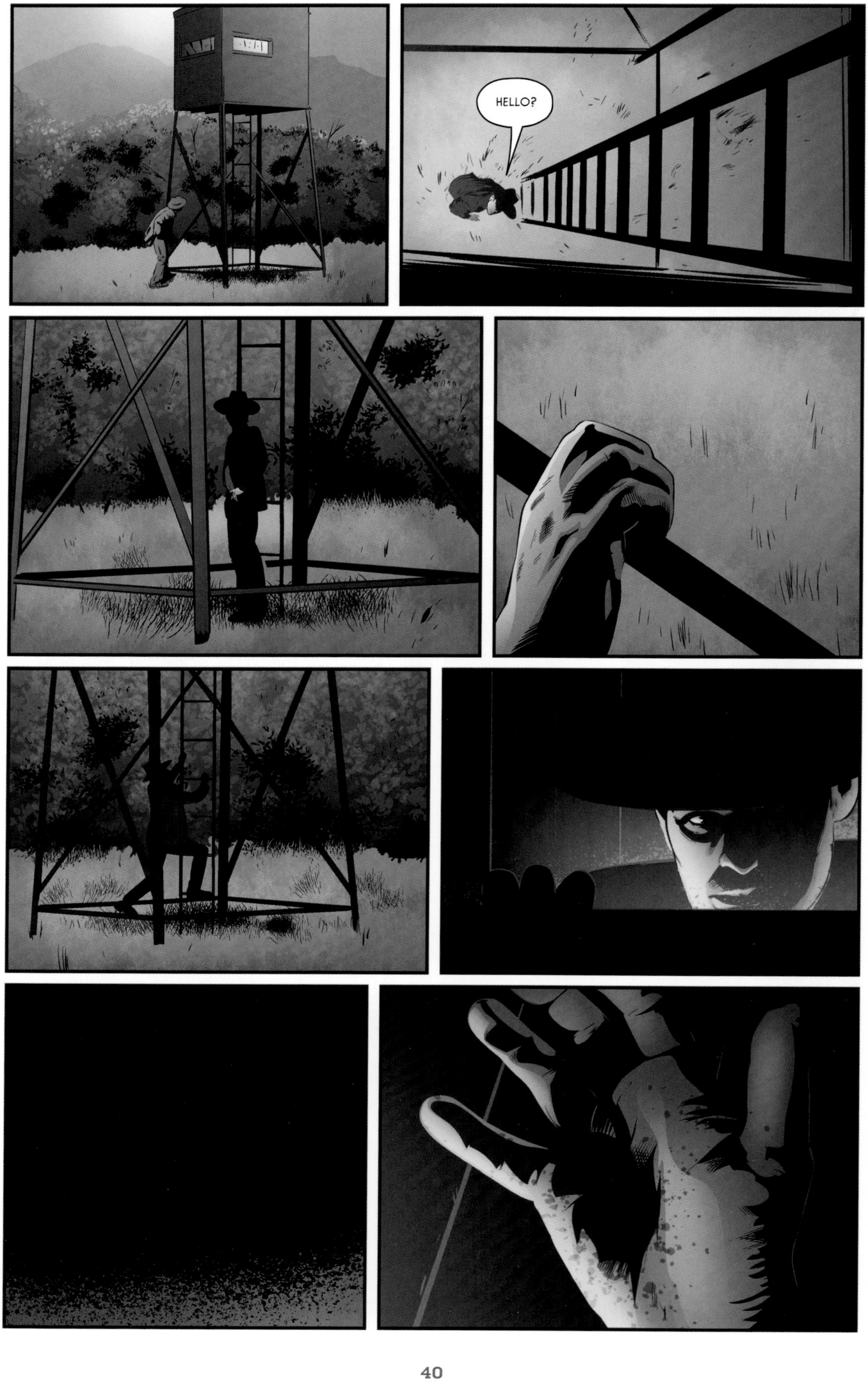
HELLO?

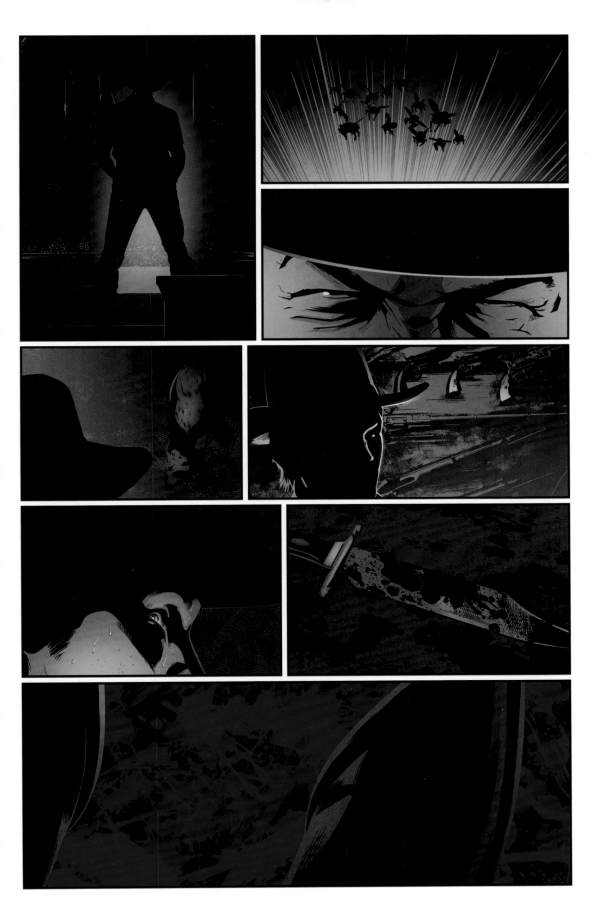

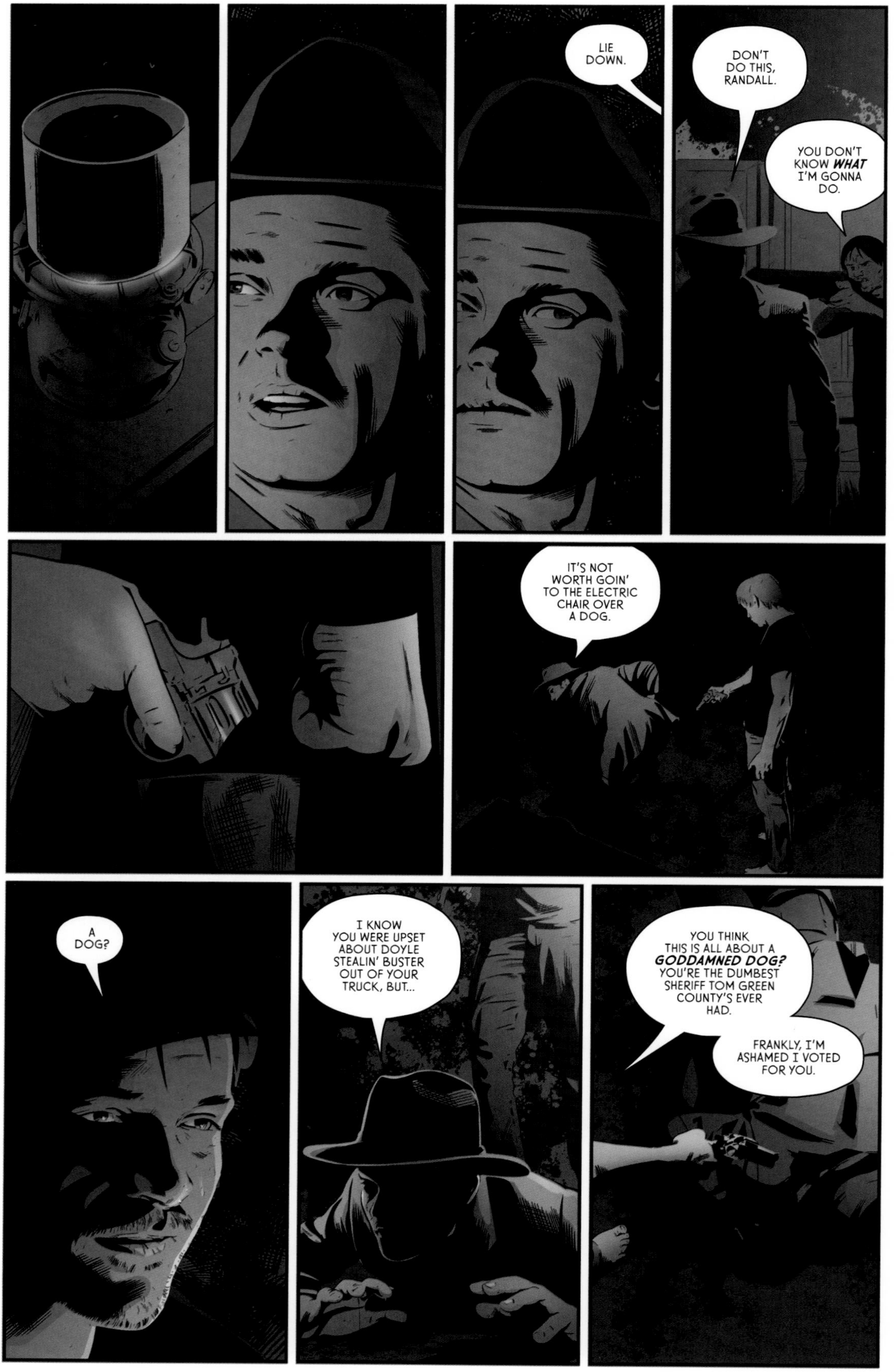
LIE DOWN.
DON'T DO THIS, RANDALL.
YOU DON'T KNOW ***WHAT*** I'M GONNA DO.
IT'S NOT WORTH GOIN' TO THE ELECTRIC CHAIR OVER A DOG.
A DOG?
I KNOW YOU WERE UPSET ABOUT DOYLE STEALIN' BUSTER OUT OF YOUR TRUCK, BUT...
YOU THINK THIS IS ALL ABOUT A ***GODDAMNED DOG?*** YOU'RE THE DUMBEST SHERIFF TOM GREEN COUNTY'S EVER HAD.
FRANKLY, I'M ASHAMED I VOTED FOR YOU.

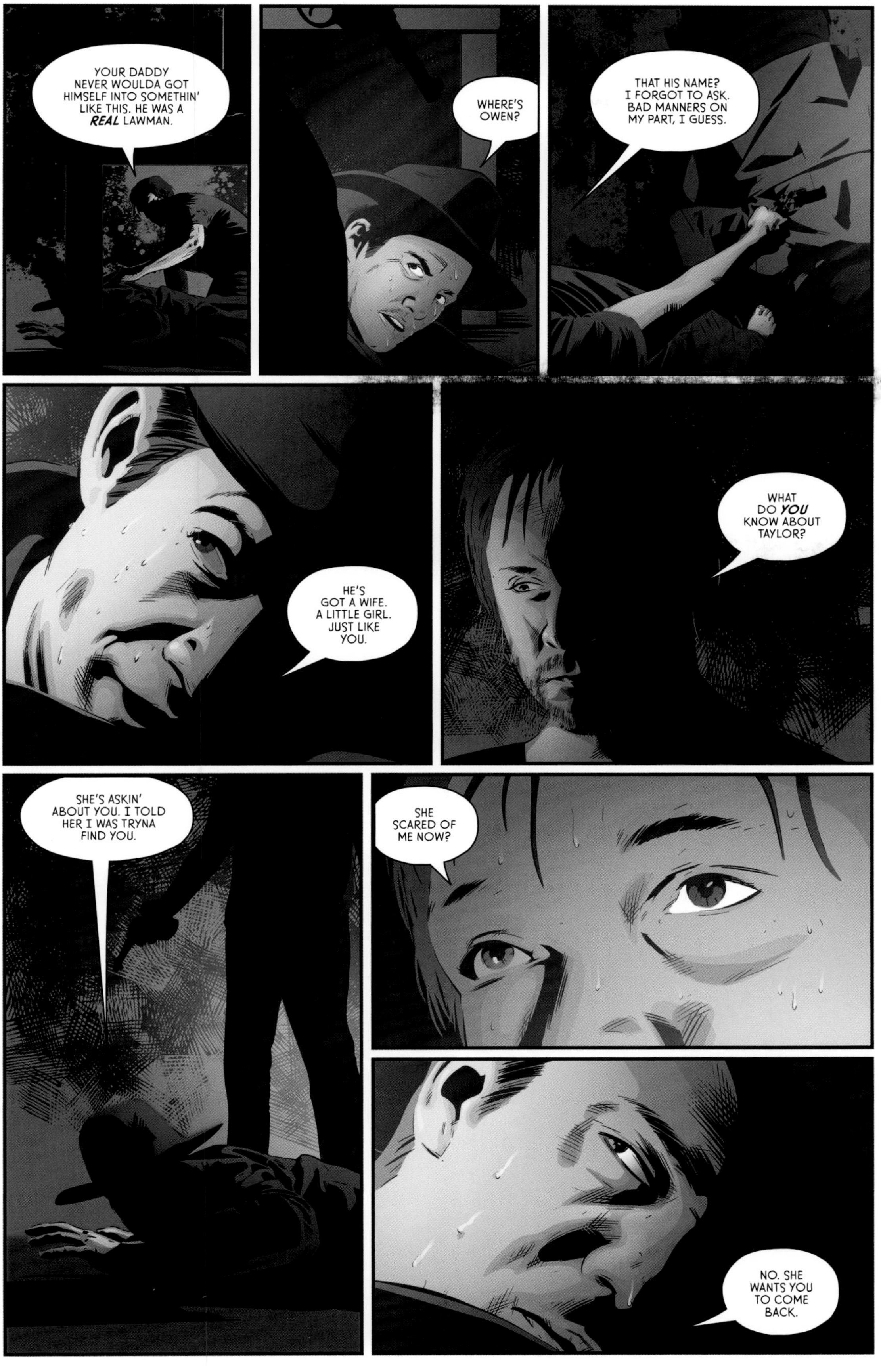
YOUR DADDY NEVER WOULDA GOT HIMSELF INTO SOMETHIN' LIKE THIS. HE WAS A *REAL* LAWMAN.
WHERE'S OWEN?
THAT HIS NAME? I FORGOT TO ASK. BAD MANNERS ON MY PART, I GUESS.
HE'S GOT A WIFE. A LITTLE GIRL. JUST LIKE YOU.
WHAT DO *YOU* KNOW ABOUT TAYLOR?
SHE'S ASKIN' ABOUT YOU. I TOLD HER I WAS TRYNA FIND YOU.
SHE SCARED OF ME NOW?
NO. SHE WANTS YOU TO COME BACK.

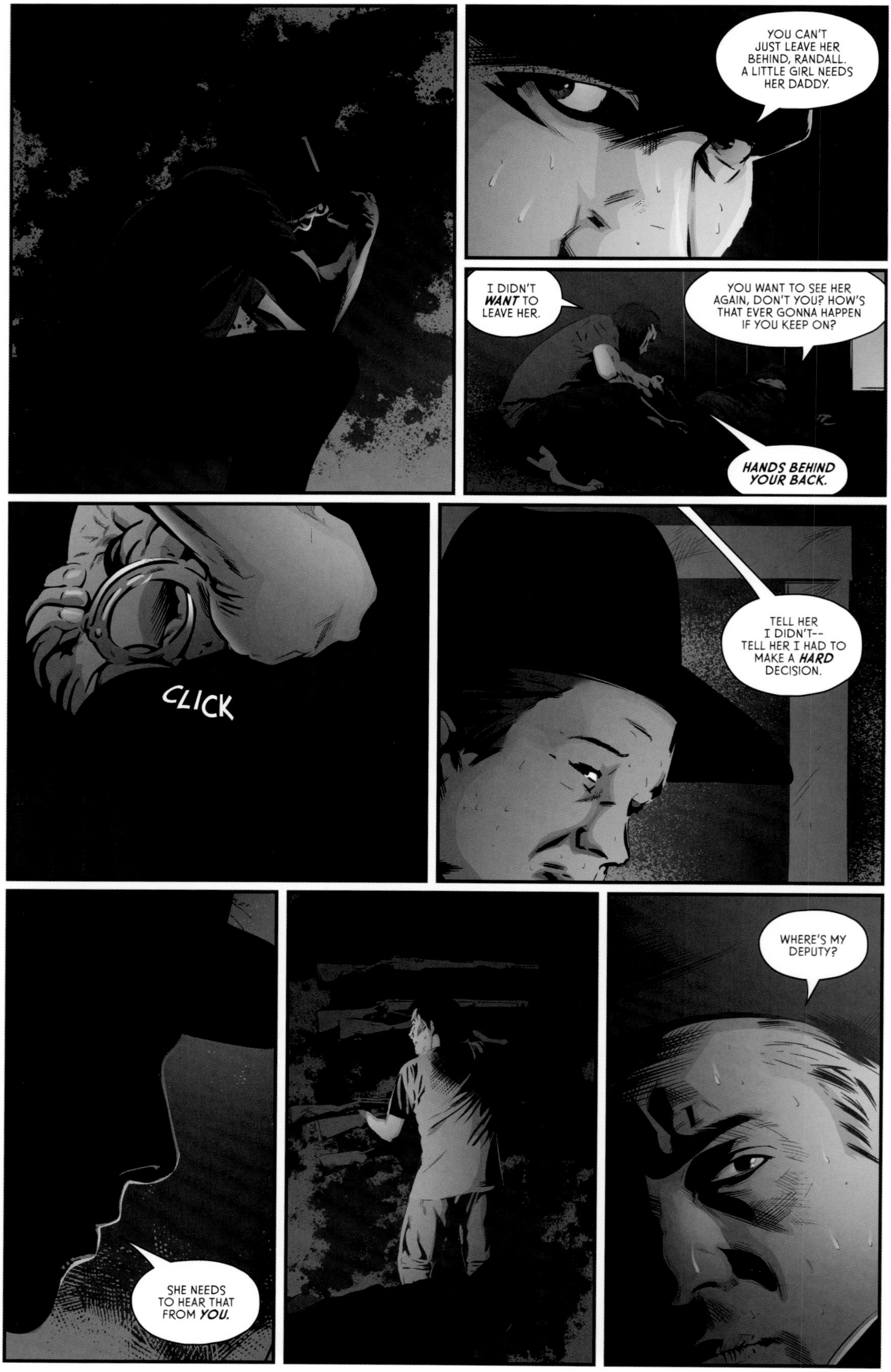
YOU CAN'T JUST LEAVE HER BEHIND, RANDALL. A LITTLE GIRL NEEDS HER DADDY.
I DIDN'T *WANT* TO LEAVE HER.
YOU WANT TO SEE HER AGAIN, DON'T YOU? HOW'S THAT EVER GONNA HAPPEN IF YOU KEEP ON?
HANDS BEHIND YOUR BACK.
CLICK
TELL HER I DIDN'T-- TELL HER I HAD TO MAKE A *HARD* DECISION.
SHE NEEDS TO HEAR THAT FROM *YOU.*
WHERE'S MY DEPUTY?

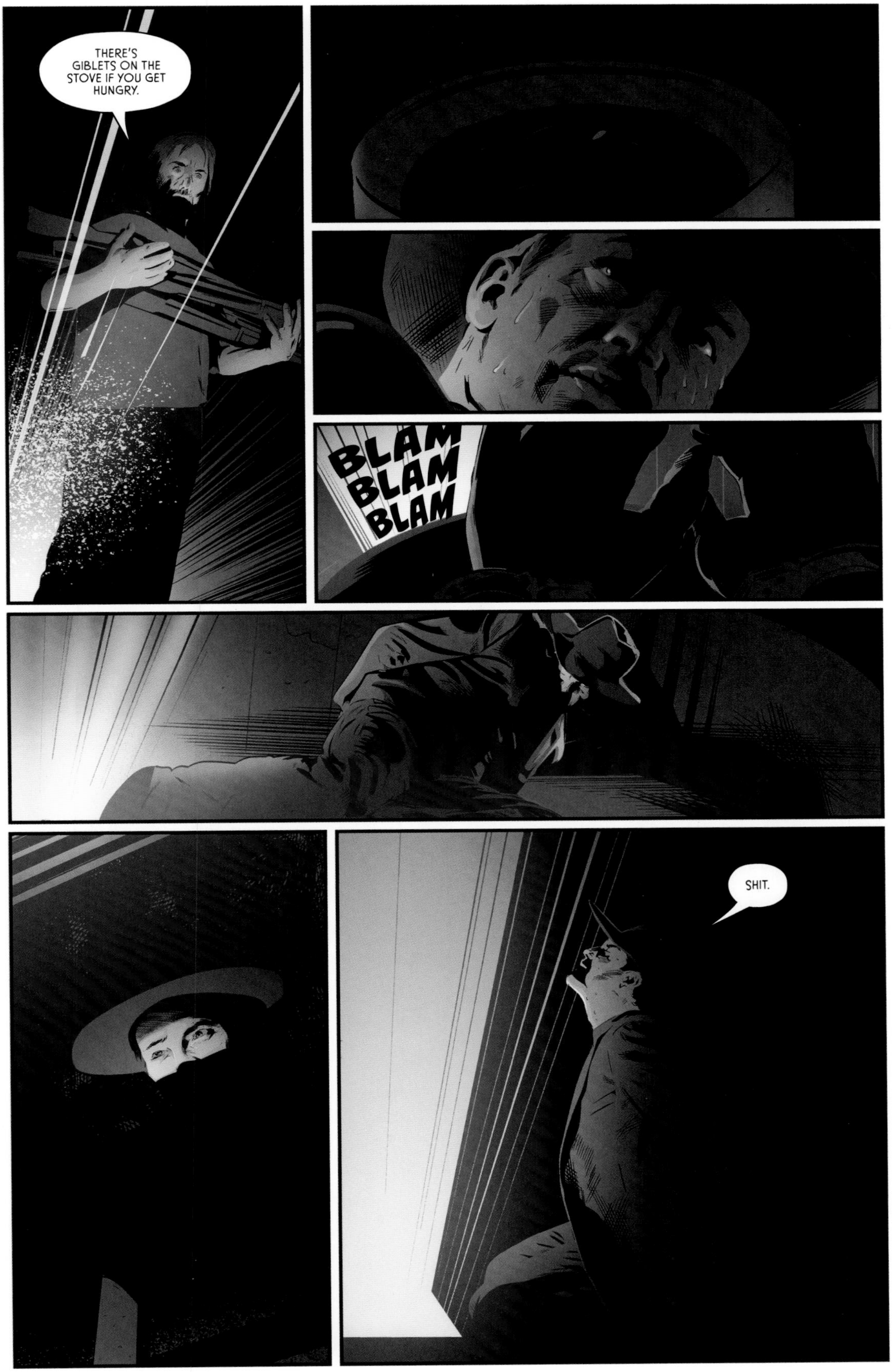
THERE'S GIBLETS ON THE STOVE IF YOU GET HUNGRY.
BLAM
BLAM
BLAM
SHIT.

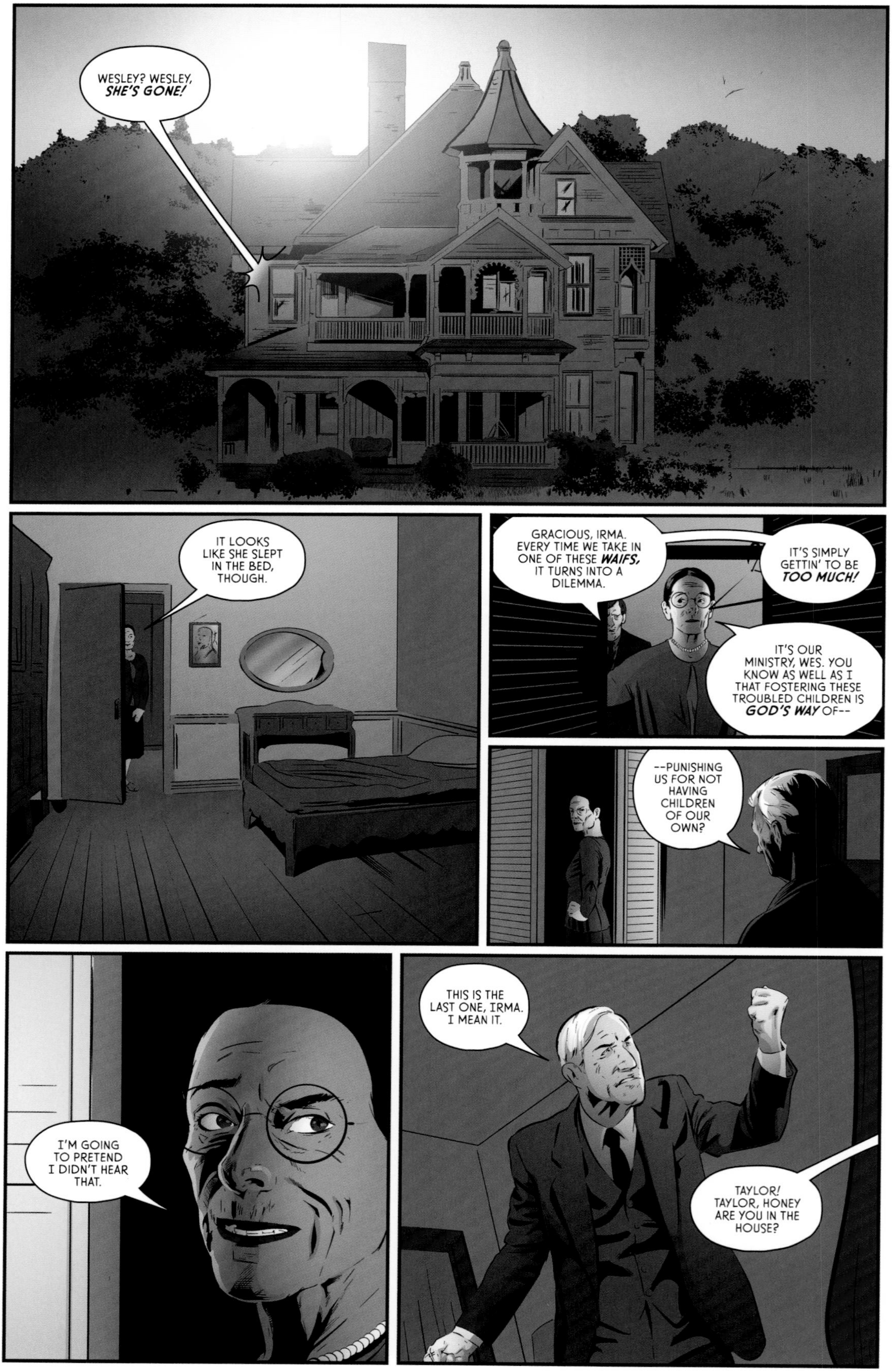
WESLEY? WESLEY, SHE'S GONE!
IT LOOKS LIKE SHE SLEPT IN THE BED, THOUGH.
GRACIOUS, IRMA. EVERY TIME WE TAKE IN ONE OF THESE WAIFS, IT TURNS INTO A DILEMMA.
IT'S SIMPLY GETTIN' TO BE TOO MUCH!
IT'S OUR MINISTRY, WES. YOU KNOW AS WELL AS I THAT FOSTERING THESE TROUBLED CHILDREN IS GOD'S WAY OF--
--PUNISHING US FOR NOT HAVING CHILDREN OF OUR OWN?
I'M GOING TO PRETEND I DIDN'T HEAR THAT.
THIS IS THE LAST ONE, IRMA. I MEAN IT.
TAYLOR! TAYLOR, HONEY ARE YOU IN THE HOUSE?

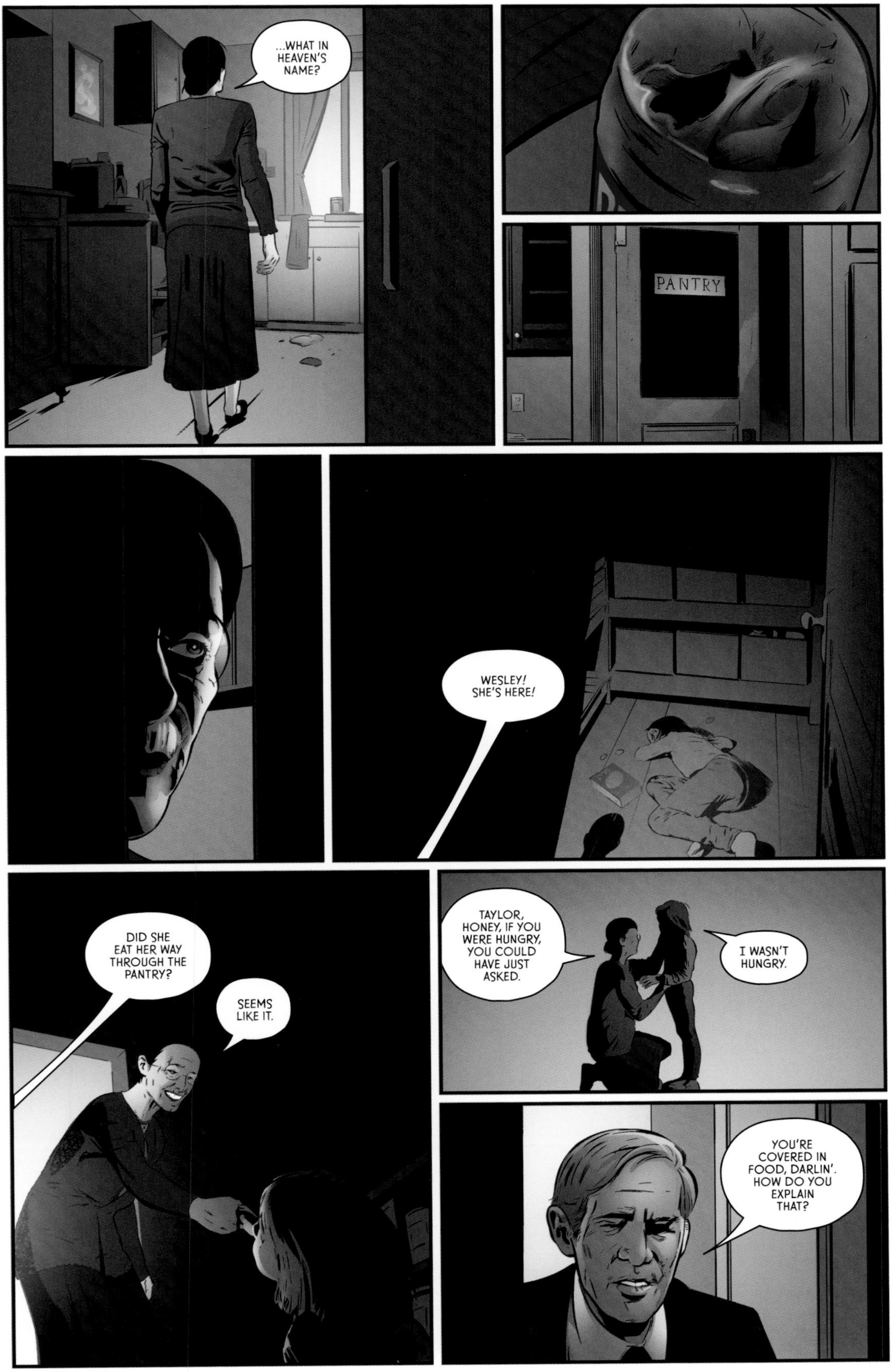
...WHAT IN HEAVEN'S NAME?
PANTRY
WESLEY! SHE'S HERE!
DID SHE EAT HER WAY THROUGH THE PANTRY?
SEEMS LIKE IT.
TAYLOR, HONEY, IF YOU WERE HUNGRY, YOU COULD HAVE JUST ASKED.
I WASN'T HUNGRY.
YOU'RE COVERED IN FOOD, DARLIN'. HOW DO YOU EXPLAIN THAT?

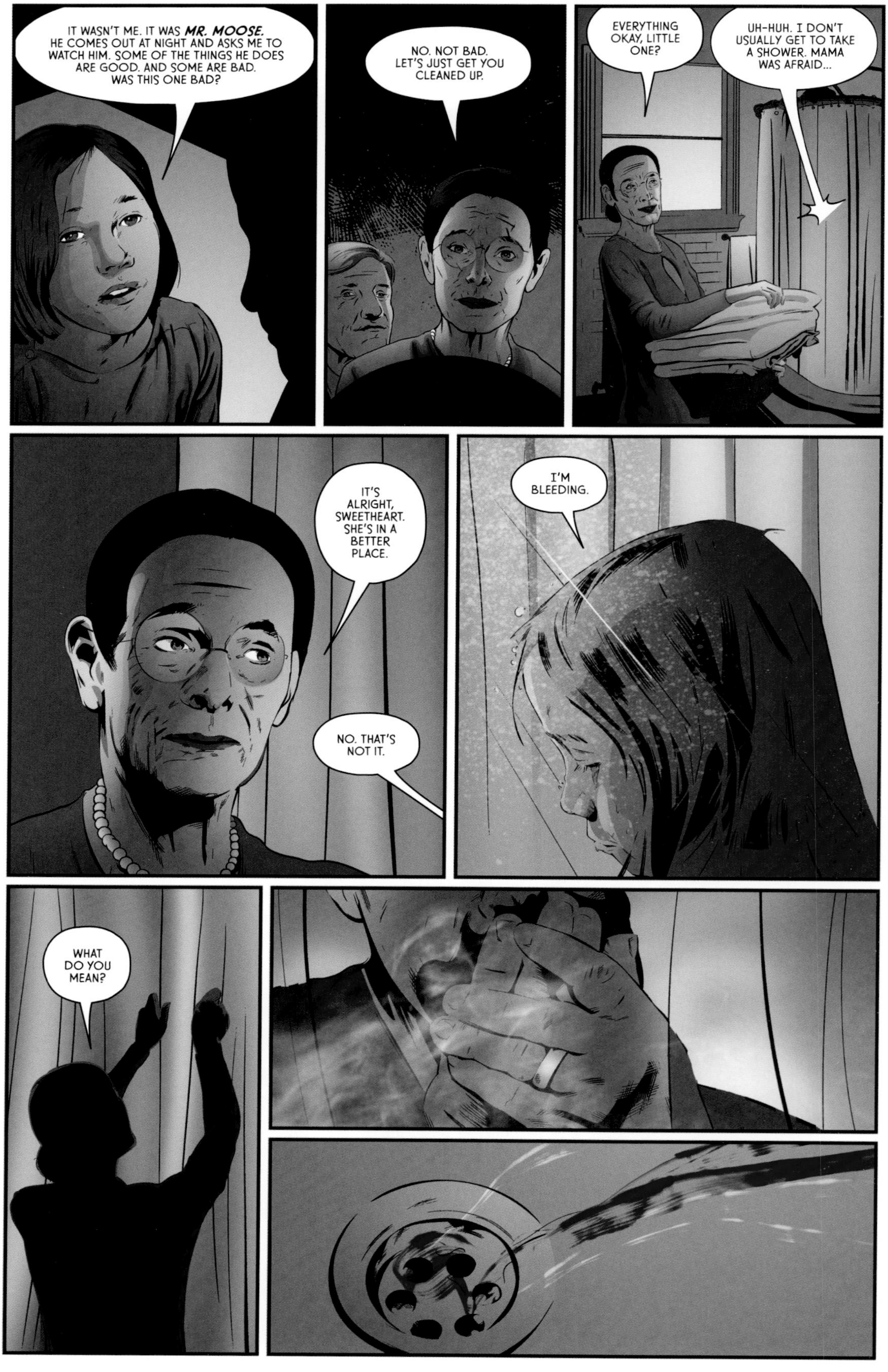
IT WASN'T ME. IT WAS MR. MOOSE. HE COMES OUT AT NIGHT AND ASKS ME TO WATCH HIM. SOME OF THE THINGS HE DOES ARE GOOD. AND SOME ARE BAD. WAS THIS ONE BAD?
NO. NOT BAD. LET'S JUST GET YOU CLEANED UP.
EVERYTHING OKAY, LITTLE ONE?
UH-HUH. I DON'T USUALLY GET TO TAKE A SHOWER. MAMA WAS AFRAID...
IT'S ALRIGHT, SWEETHEART. SHE'S IN A BETTER PLACE.
NO. THAT'S NOT IT.
I'M BLEEDING.
WHAT DO YOU MEAN?

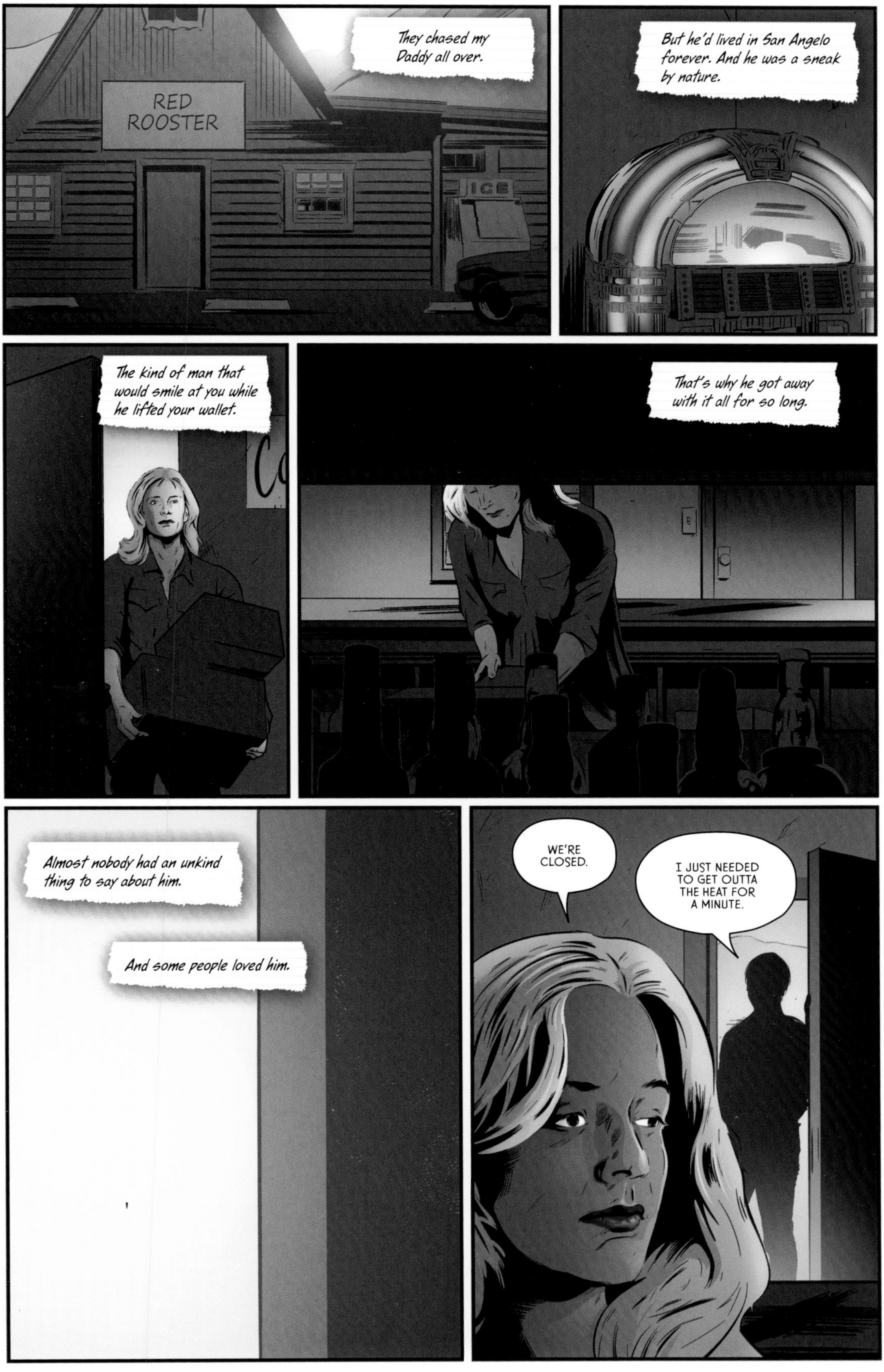
RED ROOSTER
They chased my Daddy all over.
ICE
But he'd lived in San Angelo forever. And he was a sneak by nature.
The kind of man that would smile at you while he lifted your wallet.
That's why he got away with it all for so long.
Almost nobody had an unkind thing to say about him.
And some people loved him.
WE'RE CLOSED.
I JUST NEEDED TO GET OUTTA THE HEAT FOR A MINUTE.

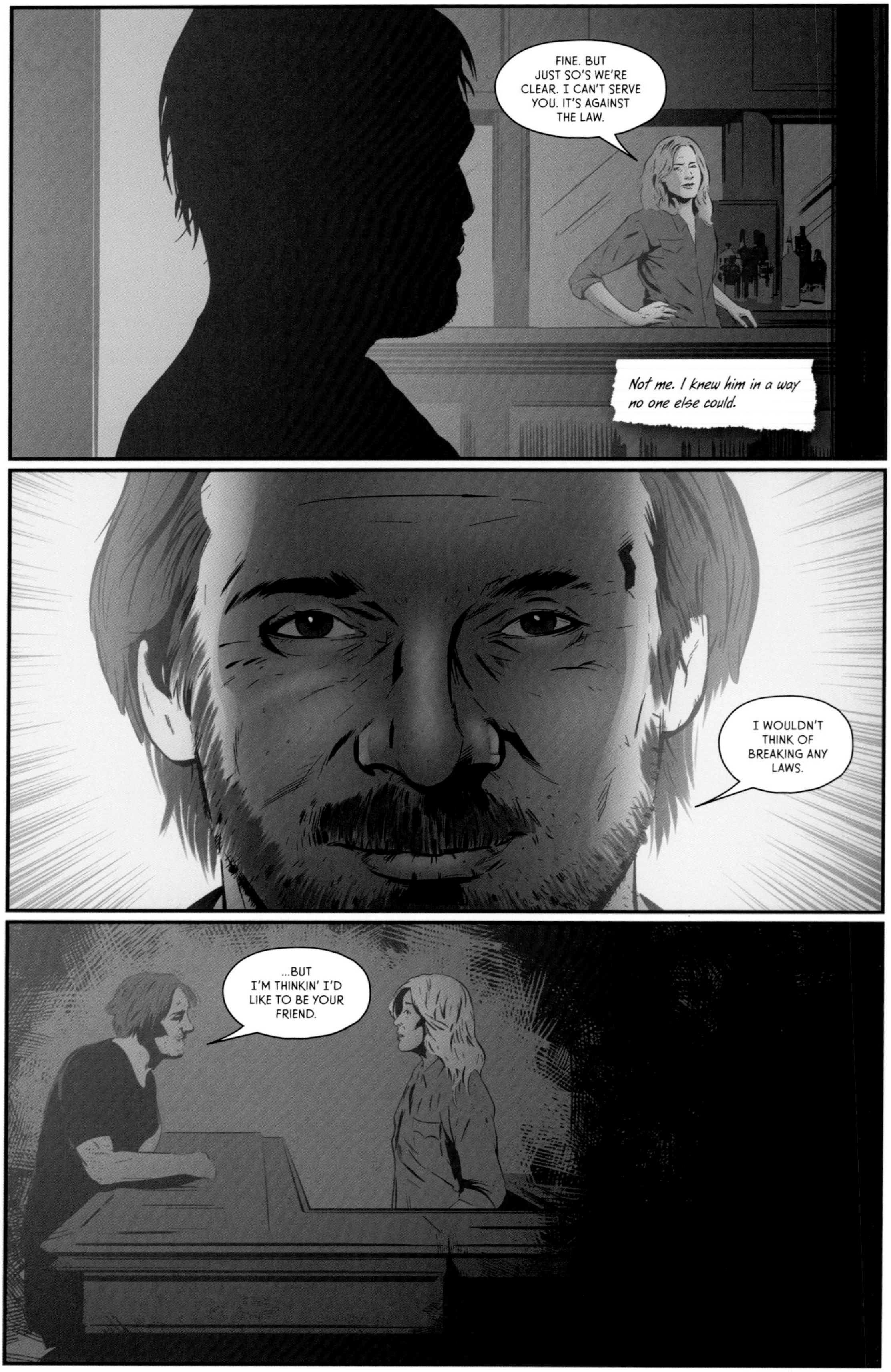
FINE. BUT JUST SO'S WE'RE CLEAR. I CAN'T SERVE YOU. IT'S AGAINST THE LAW.
Not me. I knew him in a way no one else could.
I WOULDN'T THINK OF BREAKING ANY LAWS.
...BUT I'M THINKIN' I'D LIKE TO BE YOUR FRIEND.

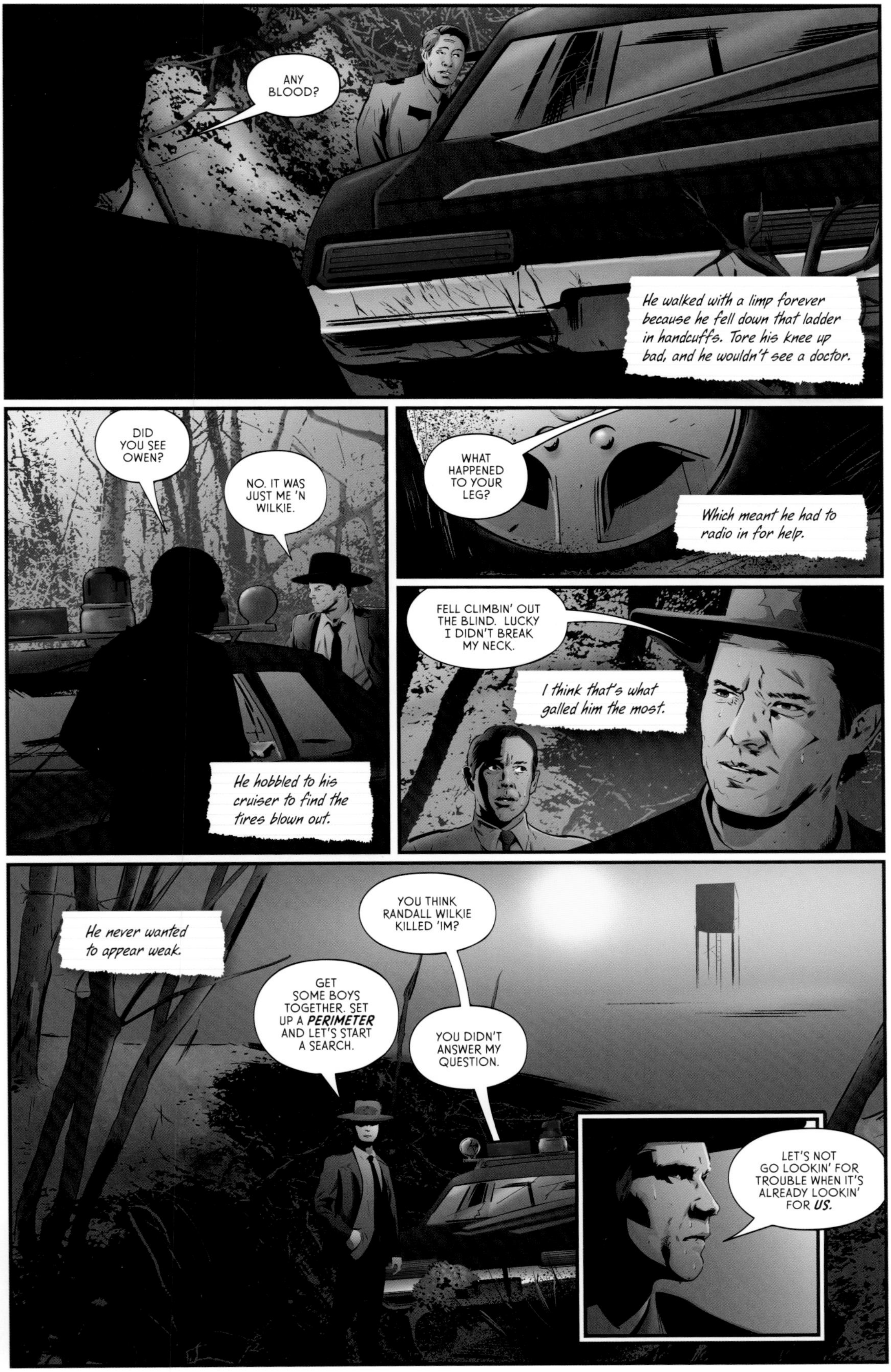
ANY BLOOD?
He walked with a limp forever because he fell down that ladder in handcuffs. Tore his knee up bad, and he wouldn't see a doctor.
DID YOU SEE OWEN?
NO. IT WAS JUST ME 'N WILKIE.
He hobbled to his cruiser to find the tires blown out.
WHAT HAPPENED TO YOUR LEG?
Which meant he had to radio in for help.
FELL CLIMBIN' OUT THE BLIND. LUCKY I DIDN'T BREAK MY NECK.
I think that's what galled him the most.
He never wanted to appear weak.
YOU THINK RANDALL WILKIE KILLED 'IM?
GET SOME BOYS TOGETHER. SET UP A **PERIMETER** AND LET'S START A SEARCH.
YOU DIDN'T ANSWER MY QUESTION.
LET'S NOT GO LOOKIN' FOR TROUBLE WHEN IT'S ALREADY LOOKIN' FOR **US.**

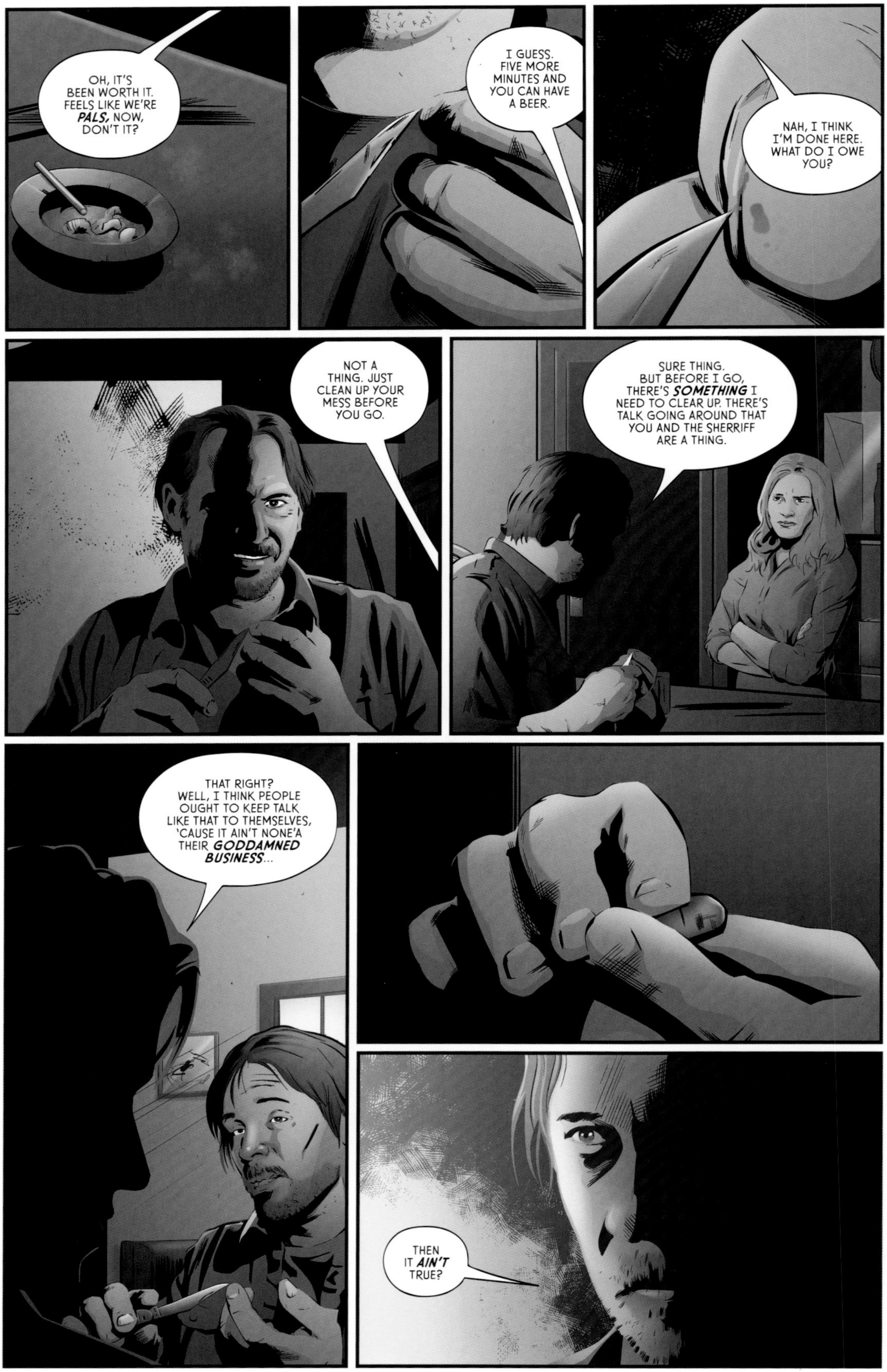
OH, IT'S BEEN WORTH IT. FEELS LIKE WE'RE PALS, NOW, DON'T IT?
I GUESS. FIVE MORE MINUTES AND YOU CAN HAVE A BEER.
NAH, I THINK I'M DONE HERE. WHAT DO I OWE YOU?
NOT A THING. JUST CLEAN UP YOUR MESS BEFORE YOU GO.
SURE THING. BUT BEFORE I GO, THERE'S SOMETHING I NEED TO CLEAR UP. THERE'S TALK GOING AROUND THAT YOU AND THE SHERRIFF ARE A THING.
THAT RIGHT? WELL, I THINK PEOPLE OUGHT TO KEEP TALK LIKE THAT TO THEMSELVES, 'CAUSE IT AIN'T NONE'A THEIR GODDAMNED BUSINESS...
THEN IT AIN'T TRUE?

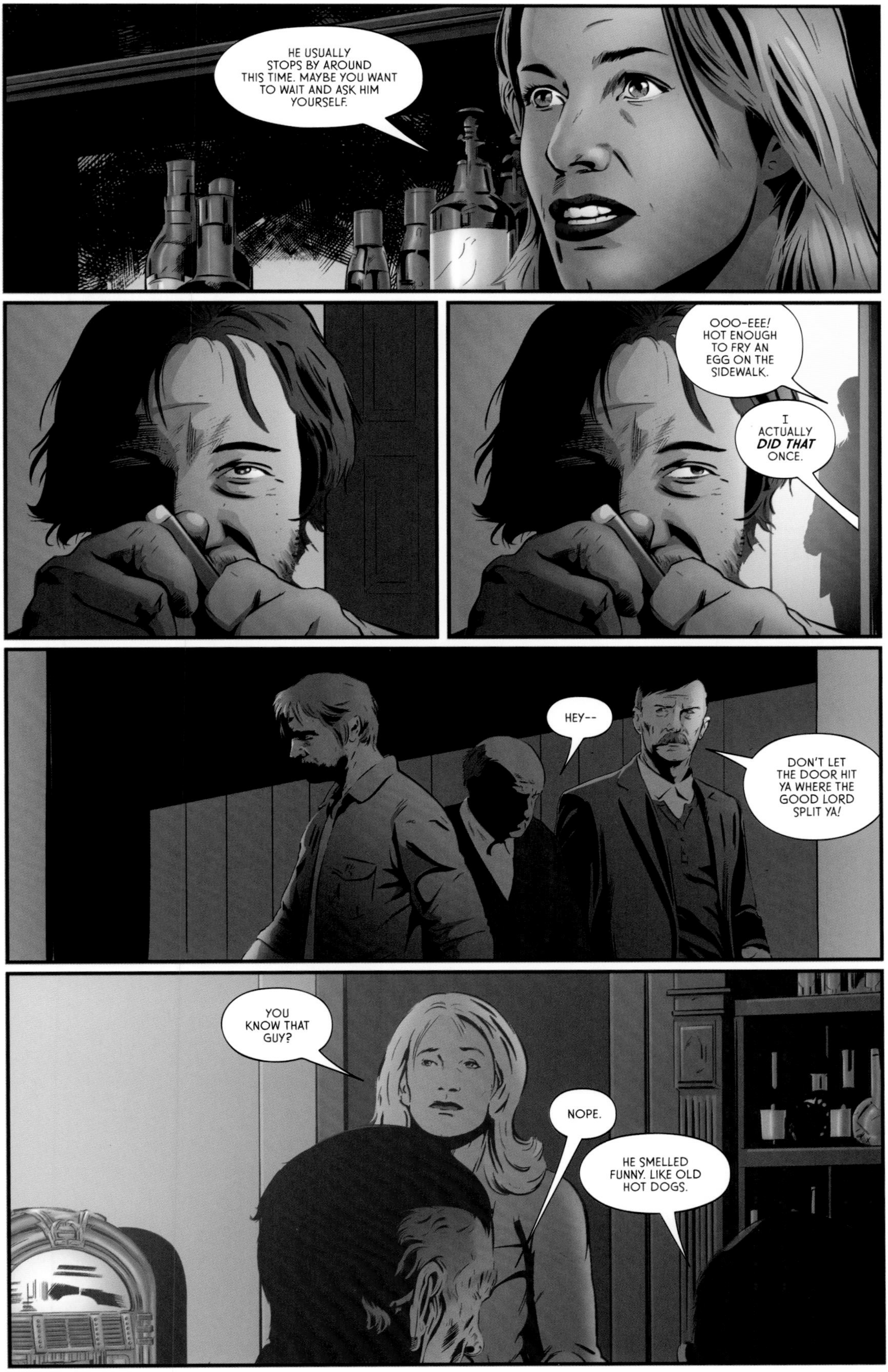
HE USUALLY STOPS BY AROUND THIS TIME. MAYBE YOU WANT TO WAIT AND ASK HIM YOURSELF.
OOO-EEE! HOT ENOUGH TO FRY AN EGG ON THE SIDEWALK.
I ACTUALLY *DID THAT* ONCE.
HEY--
DON'T LET THE DOOR HIT YA WHERE THE GOOD LORD SPLIT YA!
YOU KNOW THAT GUY?
NOPE.
HE SMELLED FUNNY. LIKE OLD HOT DOGS.

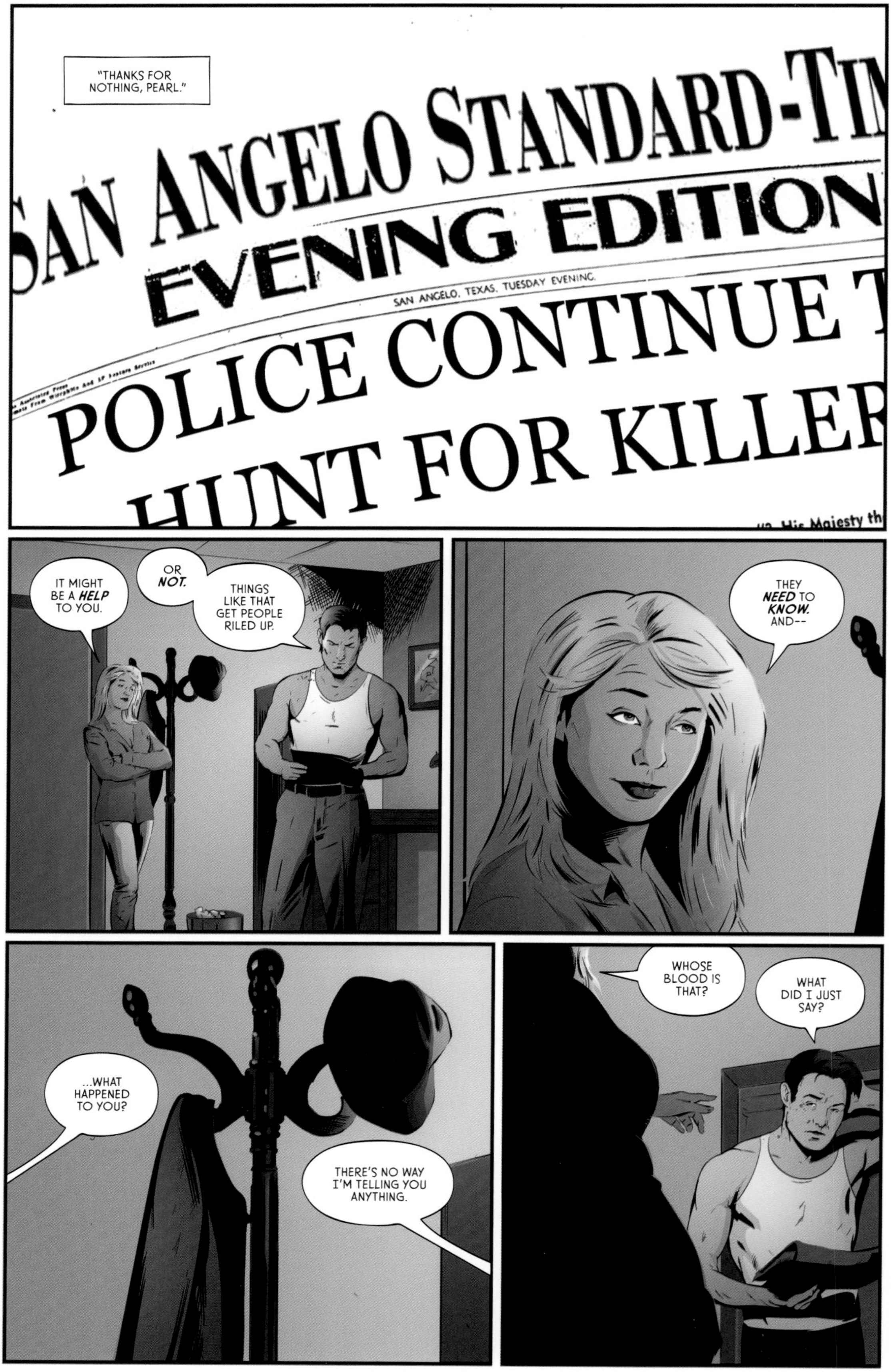
"THANKS FOR NOTHING, PEARL."
SAN ANGELO STANDARD-TIM
EVENING EDITION
SAN ANGELO, TEXAS, TUESDAY EVENING.
POLICE CONTINUE T
HUNT FOR KILLER
IT MIGHT BE A *HELP* TO YOU.
OR ***NOT.***
THINGS LIKE THAT GET PEOPLE RILED UP.
THEY ***NEED*** TO ***KNOW.*** AND--
...WHAT HAPPENED TO YOU?
THERE'S NO WAY I'M TELLING YOU ANYTHING.
WHOSE BLOOD IS THAT?
WHAT DID I JUST SAY?

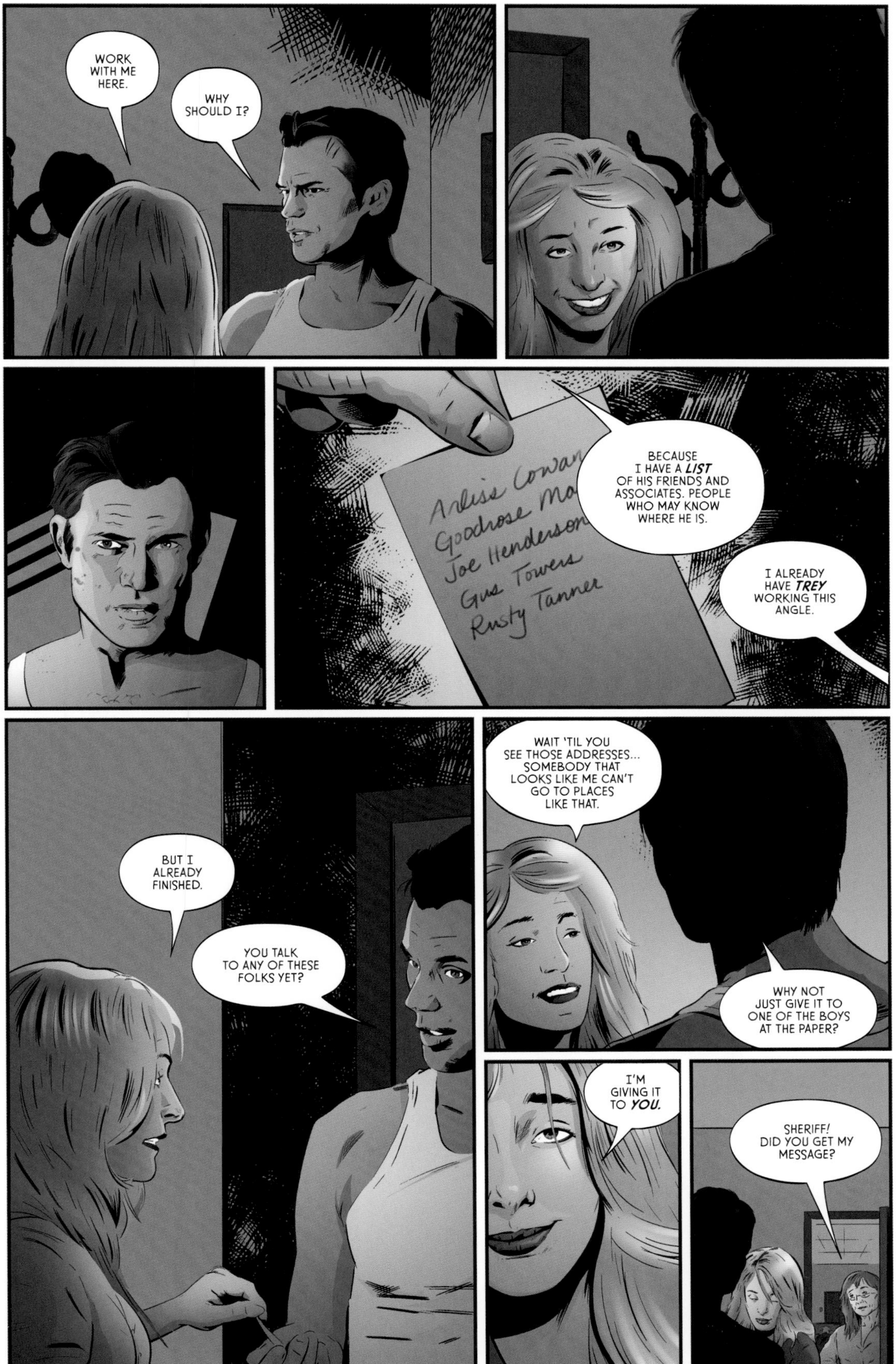
WORK WITH ME HERE.
WHY SHOULD I?
Arliss Cowan
Joe Henderson
Gus Towers
Rusty Tanner
BECAUSE I HAVE A ***LIST*** OF HIS FRIENDS AND ASSOCIATES. PEOPLE WHO MAY KNOW WHERE HE IS.
I ALREADY HAVE ***TREY*** WORKING THIS ANGLE.
BUT I ALREADY FINISHED.
YOU TALK TO ANY OF THESE FOLKS YET?
WAIT 'TIL YOU SEE THOSE ADDRESSES... SOMEBODY THAT LOOKS LIKE ME CAN'T GO TO PLACES LIKE THAT.
WHY NOT JUST GIVE IT TO ONE OF THE BOYS AT THE PAPER?
I'M GIVING IT TO ***YOU.***
SHERIFF! DID YOU GET MY MESSAGE?

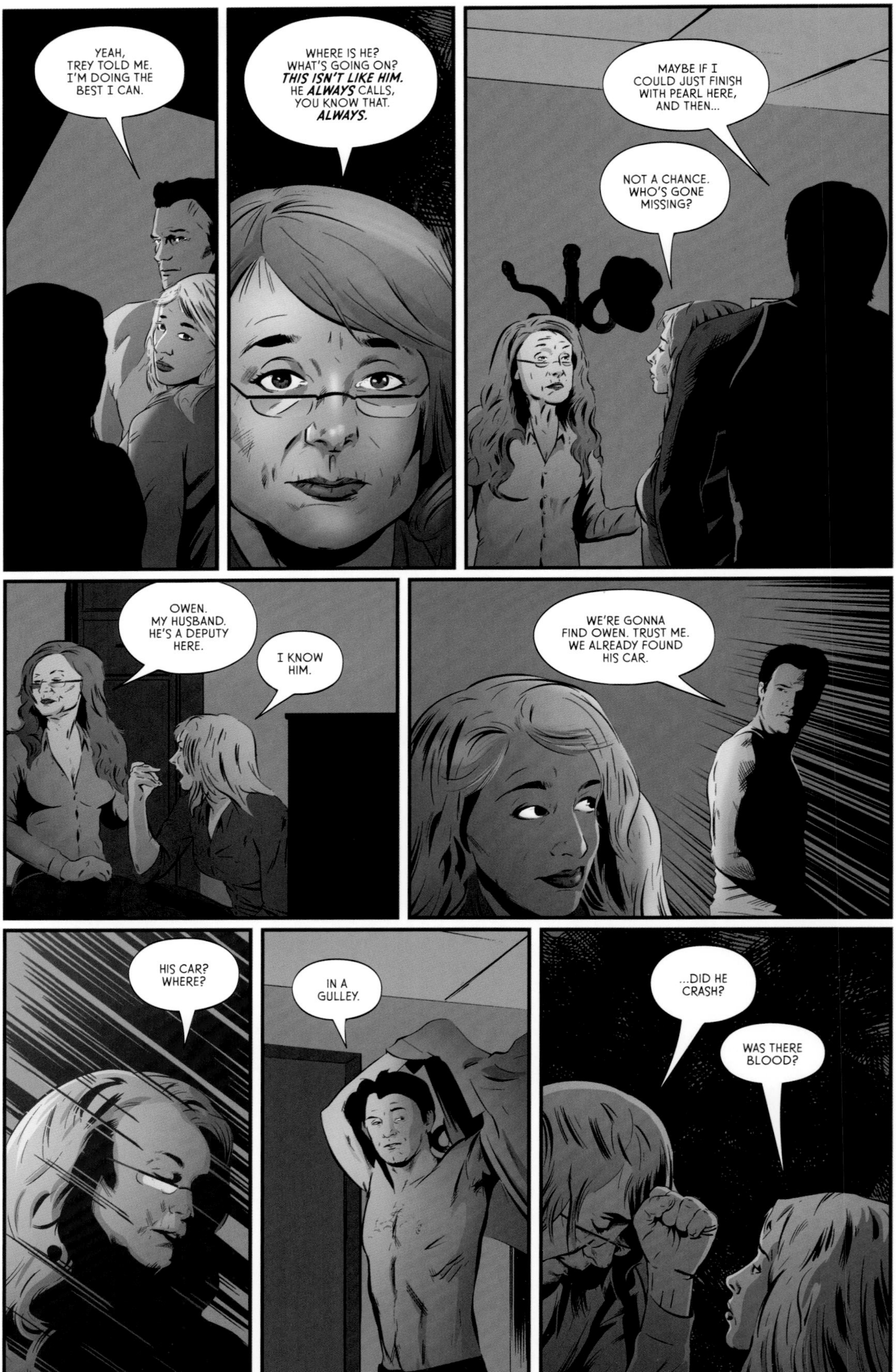
YEAH, TREY TOLD ME. I'M DOING THE BEST I CAN.
WHERE IS HE? WHAT'S GOING ON? **THIS ISN'T LIKE HIM.** HE **ALWAYS** CALLS, YOU KNOW THAT. **ALWAYS.**
MAYBE IF I COULD JUST FINISH WITH PEARL HERE, AND THEN...
NOT A CHANCE. WHO'S GONE MISSING?
OWEN. MY HUSBAND. HE'S A DEPUTY HERE.
I KNOW HIM.
WE'RE GONNA FIND OWEN. TRUST ME. WE ALREADY FOUND HIS CAR.
HIS CAR? WHERE?
IN A GULLEY.
...DID HE CRASH?
WAS THERE BLOOD?

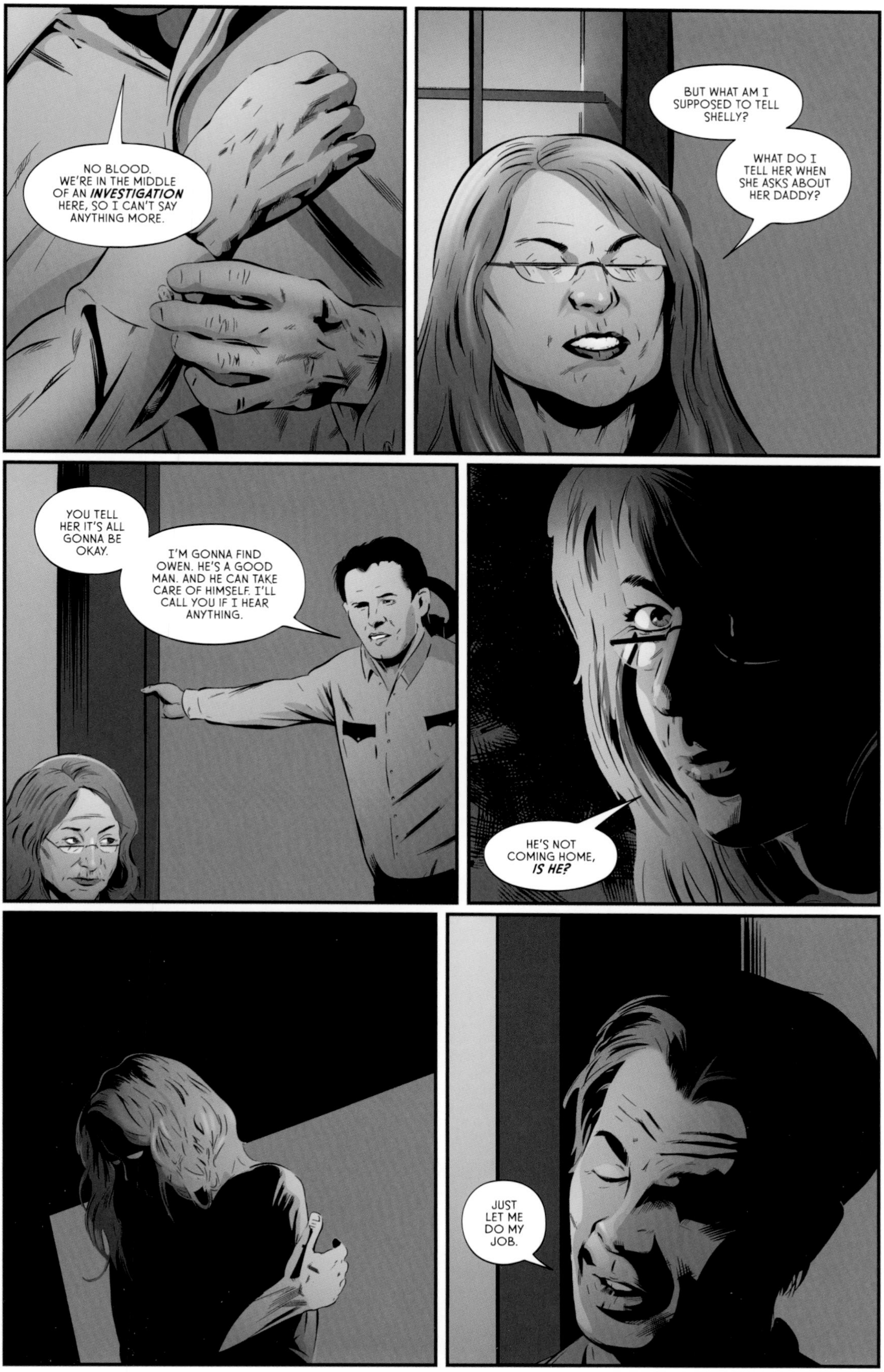
NO BLOOD. WE'RE IN THE MIDDLE OF AN ***INVESTIGATION*** HERE, SO I CAN'T SAY ANYTHING MORE.
BUT WHAT AM I SUPPOSED TO TELL SHELLY?
WHAT DO I TELL HER WHEN SHE ASKS ABOUT HER DADDY?
YOU TELL HER IT'S ALL GONNA BE OKAY.
I'M GONNA FIND OWEN. HE'S A GOOD MAN. AND HE CAN TAKE CARE OF HIMSELF. I'LL CALL YOU IF I HEAR ANYTHING.
HE'S NOT COMING HOME, ***IS HE?***
JUST LET ME DO MY JOB.

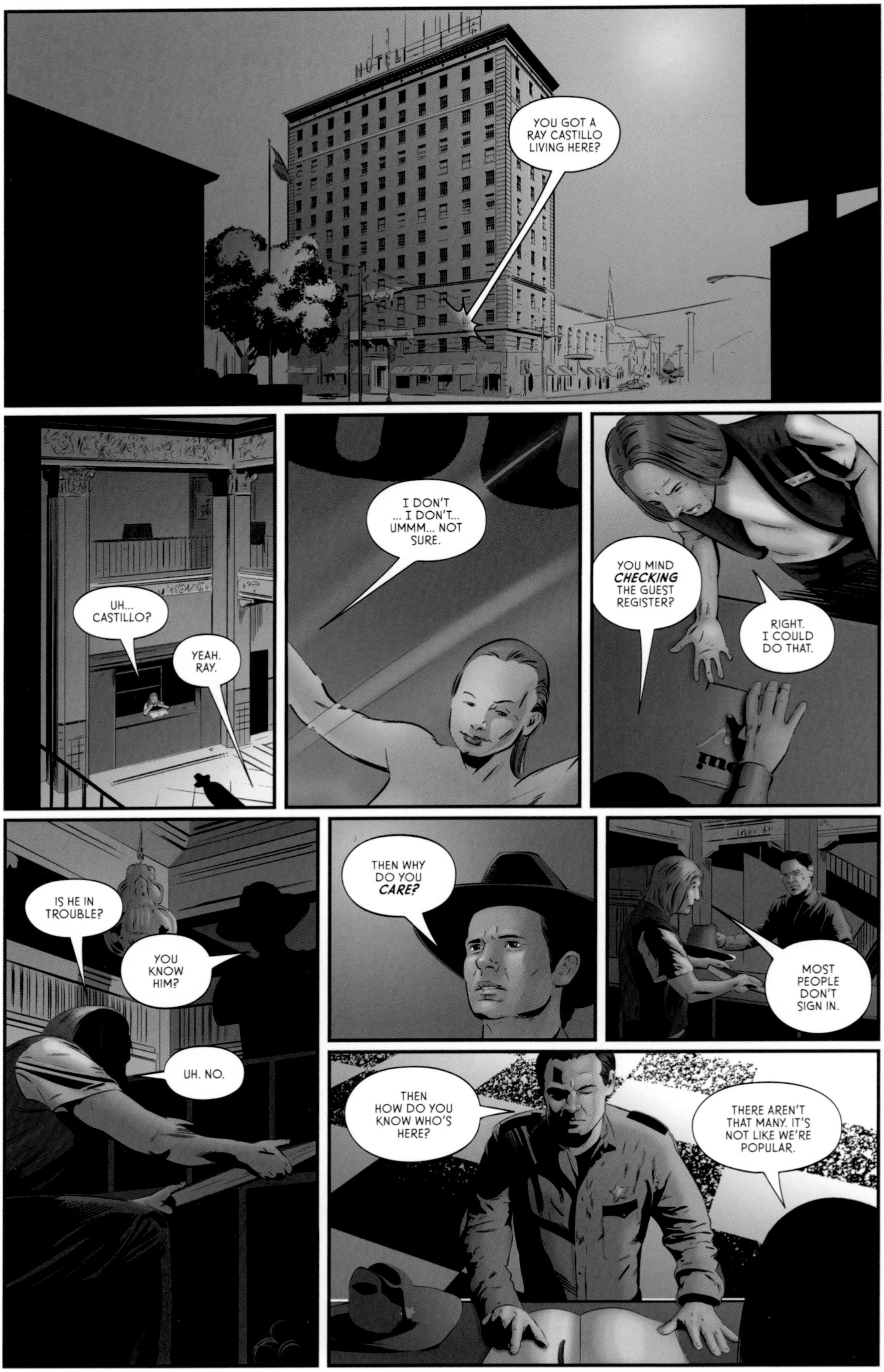
NOTEL
YOU GOT A RAY CASTILLO LIVING HERE?
UH... CASTILLO?
YEAH. RAY.
I DON'T ... I DON'T... UMMM... NOT SURE.
YOU MIND *CHECKING* THE GUEST REGISTER?
RIGHT. I COULD DO THAT.
IS HE IN TROUBLE?
YOU KNOW HIM?
UH. NO.
THEN WHY DO YOU *CARE?*
MOST PEOPLE DON'T SIGN IN.
THEN HOW DO YOU KNOW WHO'S HERE?
THERE AREN'T THAT MANY. IT'S NOT LIKE WE'RE POPULAR.

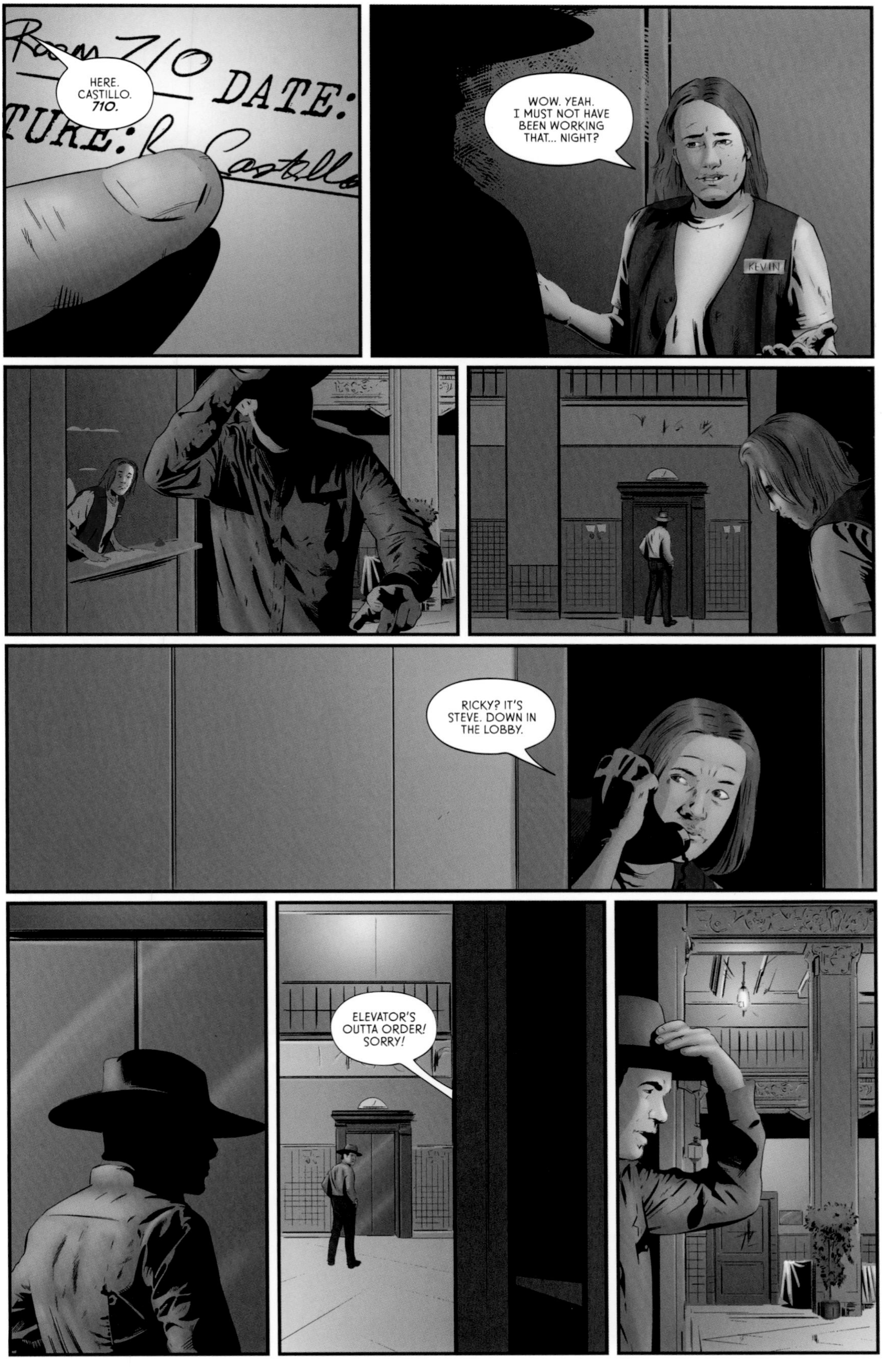
Room 710
DATE:
TURE:
HERE. CASTILLO. *710.*
WOW. YEAH. I MUST NOT HAVE BEEN WORKING THAT... NIGHT?
KEVIN
RICKY? IT'S STEVE. DOWN IN THE LOBBY.
ELEVATOR'S OUTTA ORDER! SORRY!

5TH FLOOR

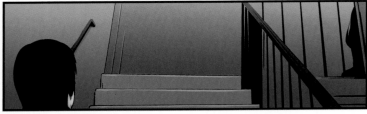

HEY, RAY.

WHAT'S THE HURRY?

AAH!

710

WHAT'S IN THE BAG?

62

NOTHIN', MAN. WHAT'S ALL THIS? WHAT DID I DO?

I DON'T KNOW. WHAT *DID* YOU DO? YOU SEEM TO BE IN A HURRY.

AW, MAN.

HAVE A SEAT. LET'S SEE WHAT'S IN THE BAG.

THAT'S NOT MINE.

RIGHT.

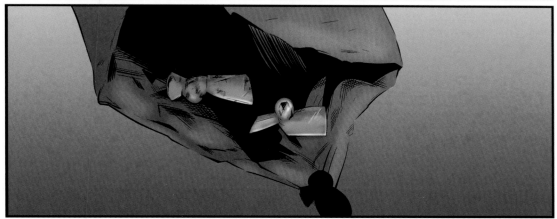

THOSE AREN'T MINE. RICKY'S THE ONE YOU WANT. MY BROTHER.

WOW. DON'T MAKE ME TWIST YOUR ARM.

I ALREADY SERVED SEVEN IN HUNTSVILLE. I CAN'T GO BACK. I'LL GO CRAZY.

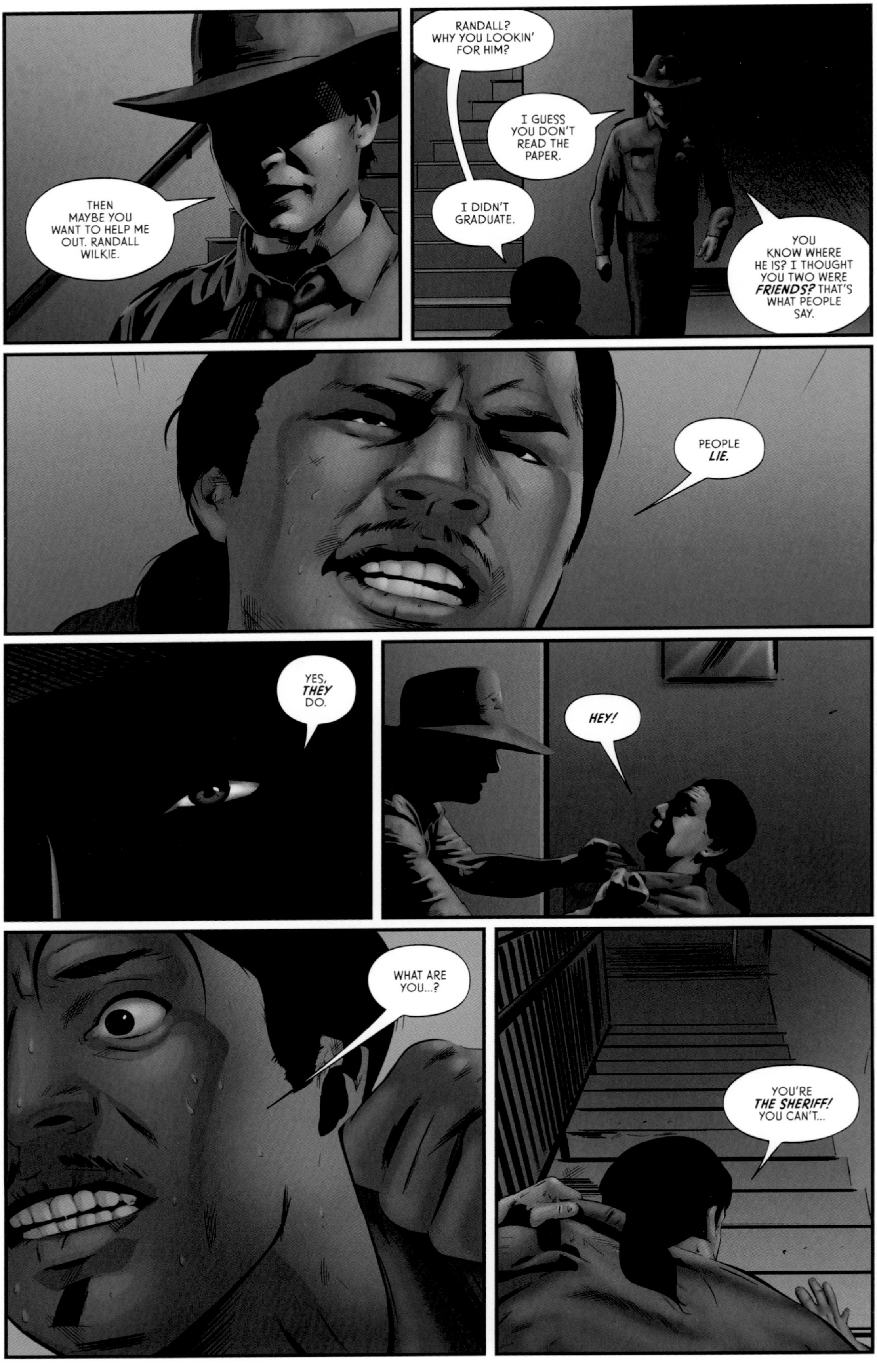
THEN MAYBE YOU WANT TO HELP ME OUT. RANDALL WILKIE.
RANDALL? WHY YOU LOOKIN' FOR HIM?
I GUESS YOU DON'T READ THE PAPER.
I DIDN'T GRADUATE.
YOU KNOW WHERE HE IS? I THOUGHT YOU TWO WERE ***FRIENDS?*** THAT'S WHAT PEOPLE SAY.
PEOPLE ***LIE.***
YES, ***THEY*** DO.
HEY!
WHAT ARE YOU...?
YOU'RE ***THE SHERIFF!*** YOU CAN'T...

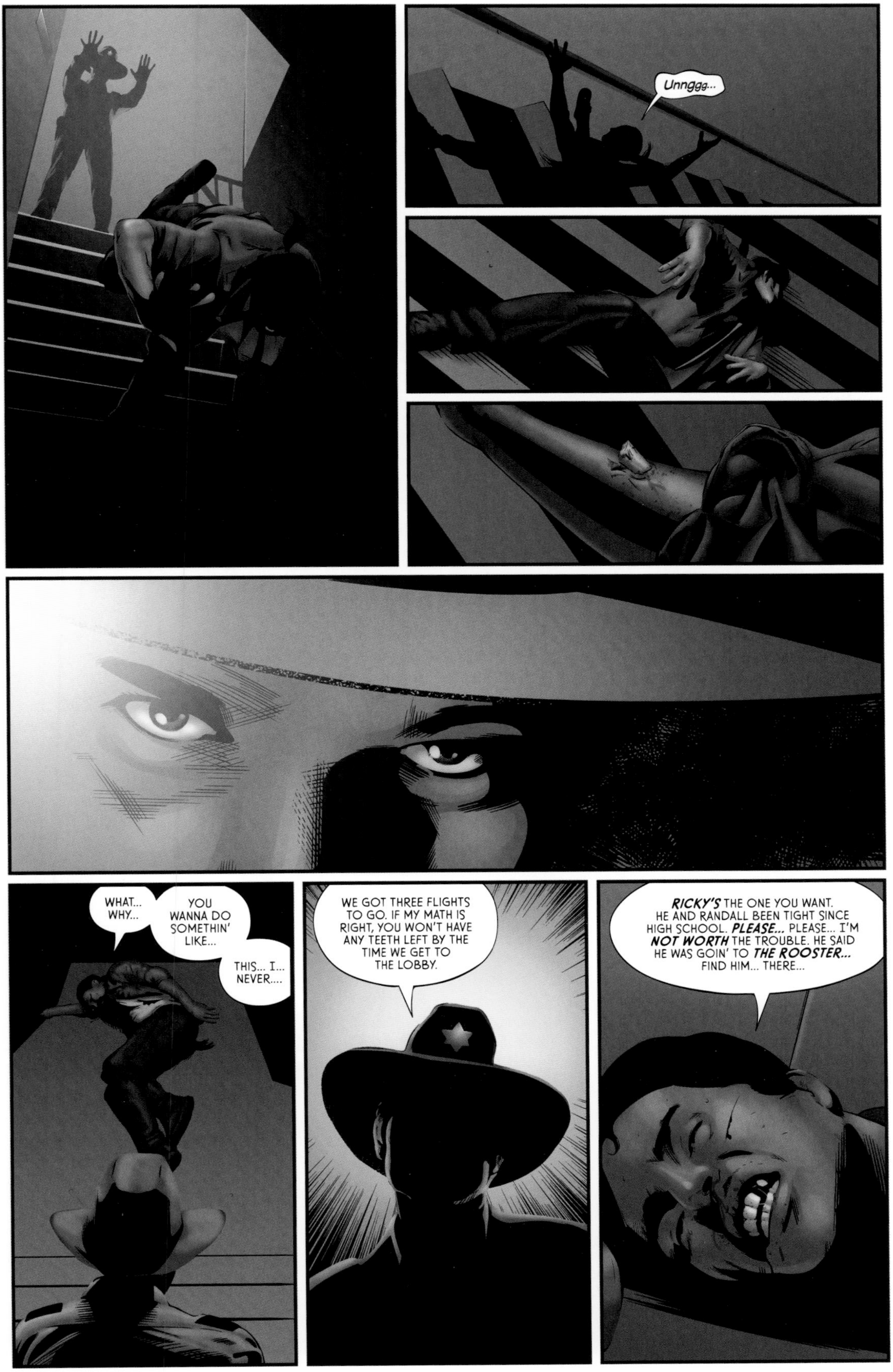
Unnggg...
WHAT... WHY...
YOU WANNA DO SOMETHIN' LIKE...
THIS... I... NEVER....
WE GOT THREE FLIGHTS TO GO. IF MY MATH IS RIGHT, YOU WON'T HAVE ANY TEETH LEFT BY THE TIME WE GET TO THE LOBBY.
RICKY'S THE ONE YOU WANT. HE AND RANDALL BEEN TIGHT SINCE HIGH SCHOOL. PLEASE... PLEASE... I'M NOT WORTH THE TROUBLE. HE SAID HE WAS GOIN' TO THE ROOSTER... FIND HIM... THERE...

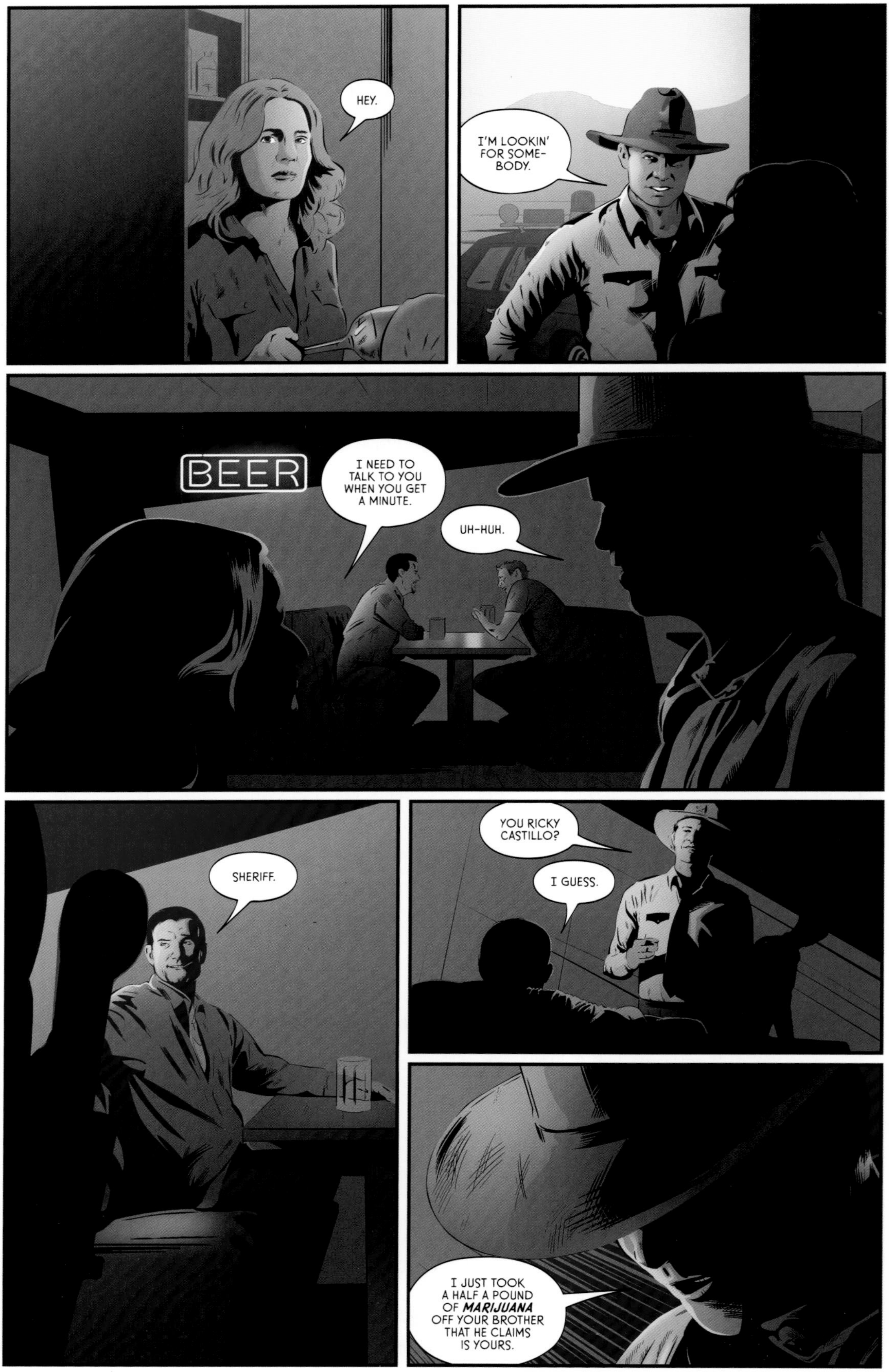
HEY.
I'M LOOKIN' FOR SOME-BODY.
BEER
I NEED TO TALK TO YOU WHEN YOU GET A MINUTE.
UH-HUH.
SHERIFF.
YOU RICKY CASTILLO?
I GUESS.
I JUST TOOK A HALF A POUND OF ***MARIJUANA*** OFF YOUR BROTHER THAT HE CLAIMS IS YOURS.

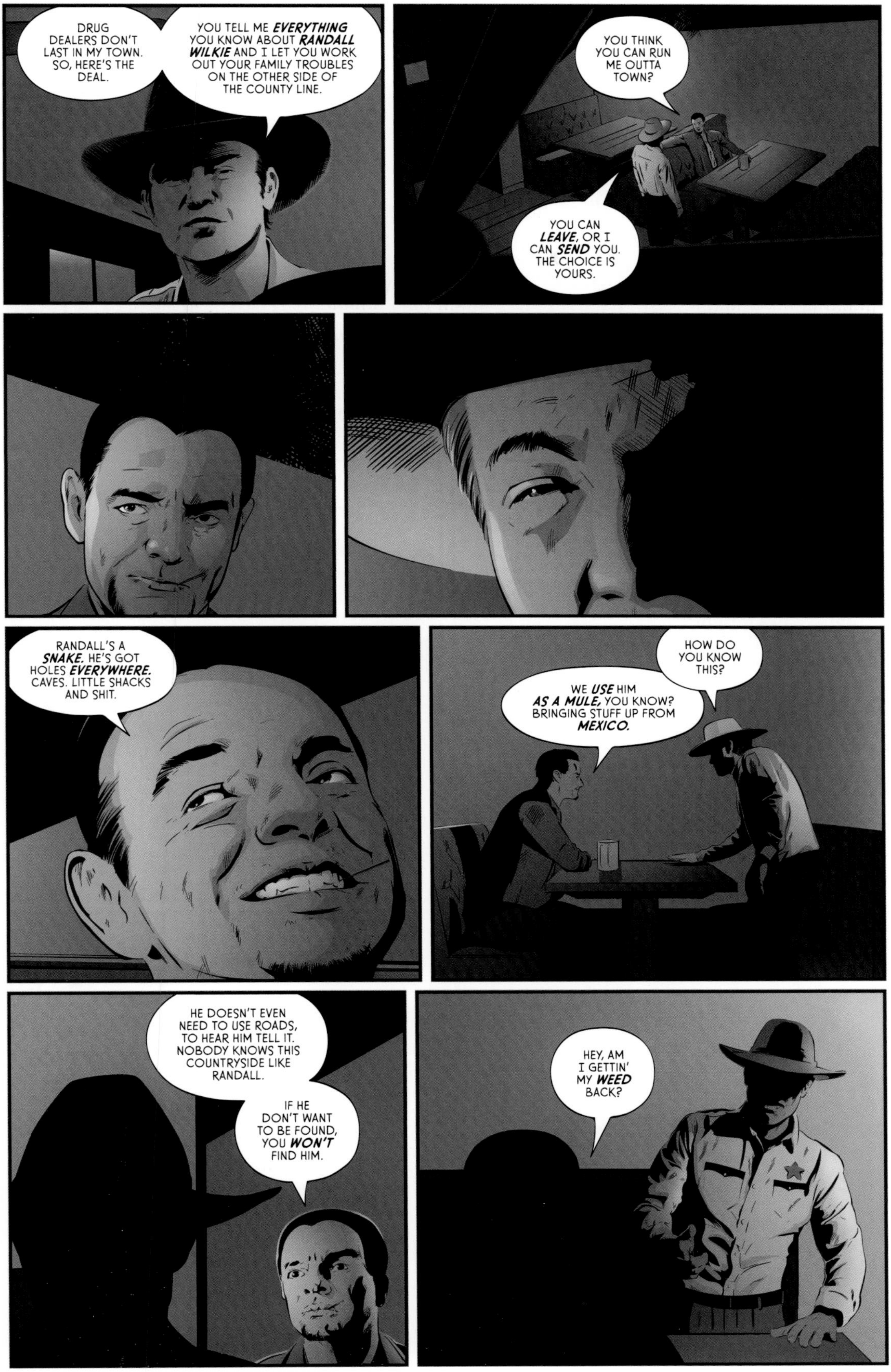
DRUG DEALERS DON'T LAST IN MY TOWN. SO, HERE'S THE DEAL.
YOU TELL ME EVERYTHING YOU KNOW ABOUT RANDALL WILKIE AND I LET YOU WORK OUT YOUR FAMILY TROUBLES ON THE OTHER SIDE OF THE COUNTY LINE.
YOU THINK YOU CAN RUN ME OUTTA TOWN?
YOU CAN LEAVE, OR I CAN SEND YOU. THE CHOICE IS YOURS.
RANDALL'S A SNAKE. HE'S GOT HOLES EVERYWHERE. CAVES. LITTLE SHACKS AND SHIT.
HOW DO YOU KNOW THIS?
WE USE HIM AS A MULE, YOU KNOW? BRINGING STUFF UP FROM MEXICO.
HE DOESN'T EVEN NEED TO USE ROADS, TO HEAR HIM TELL IT. NOBODY KNOWS THIS COUNTRYSIDE LIKE RANDALL.
IF HE DON'T WANT TO BE FOUND, YOU WON'T FIND HIM.
HEY, AM I GETTIN' MY WEED BACK?

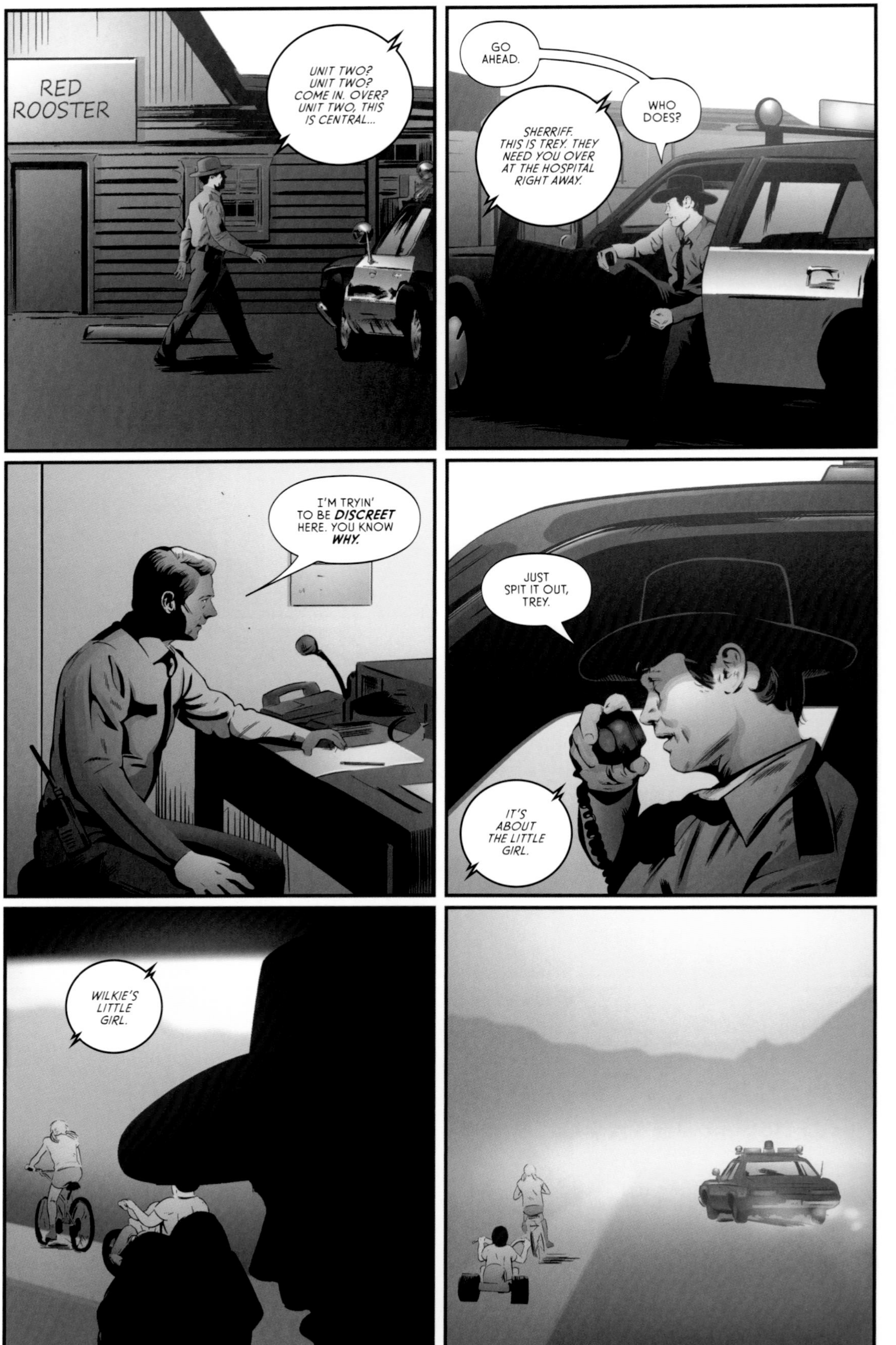
RED ROOSTER
UNIT TWO? UNIT TWO? COME IN. OVER? UNIT TWO, THIS IS CENTRAL...
GO AHEAD.
SHERRIFF. THIS IS TREY. THEY NEED YOU OVER AT THE HOSPITAL RIGHT AWAY.
WHO DOES?
I'M TRYIN' TO BE DISCREET HERE. YOU KNOW WHY.
JUST SPIT IT OUT, TREY.
IT'S ABOUT THE LITTLE GIRL.
WILKIE'S LITTLE GIRL.

IT'S PART OF THE PROCEDURE, YOU SEE.

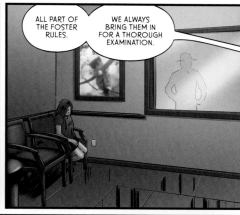

ALL PART OF THE FOSTER RULES.

WE ALWAYS BRING THEM IN FOR A THOROUGH EXAMINATION.

THIS IS THE FIRST TIME WE'VE ENCOUNTERED ANYTHING LIKE *THIS.* I WAS SCARED TO *DEATH.*

OF WHAT? *WHAT'S* THE PROBLEM?

SHE'S BEEN *RAPED.* MULTIPLE TIMES I'D SAY.

RECENTLY?

WITHIN THE *LAST WEEK.* SHE DIDN'T WANT ME...

LET'S JUST SAY SHE WASN'T *COOPERATIVE.* UNDERSTANDABLE. I DID MY BEST BUT...

SHE DOESN'T WANT TO TALK ABOUT IT.

SINCE THESE THINGS *USUALLY* INVOLVE A FAMILY MEMBER OR FRIEND...

...IT'S *COMPLICATED* FOR A CHILD.

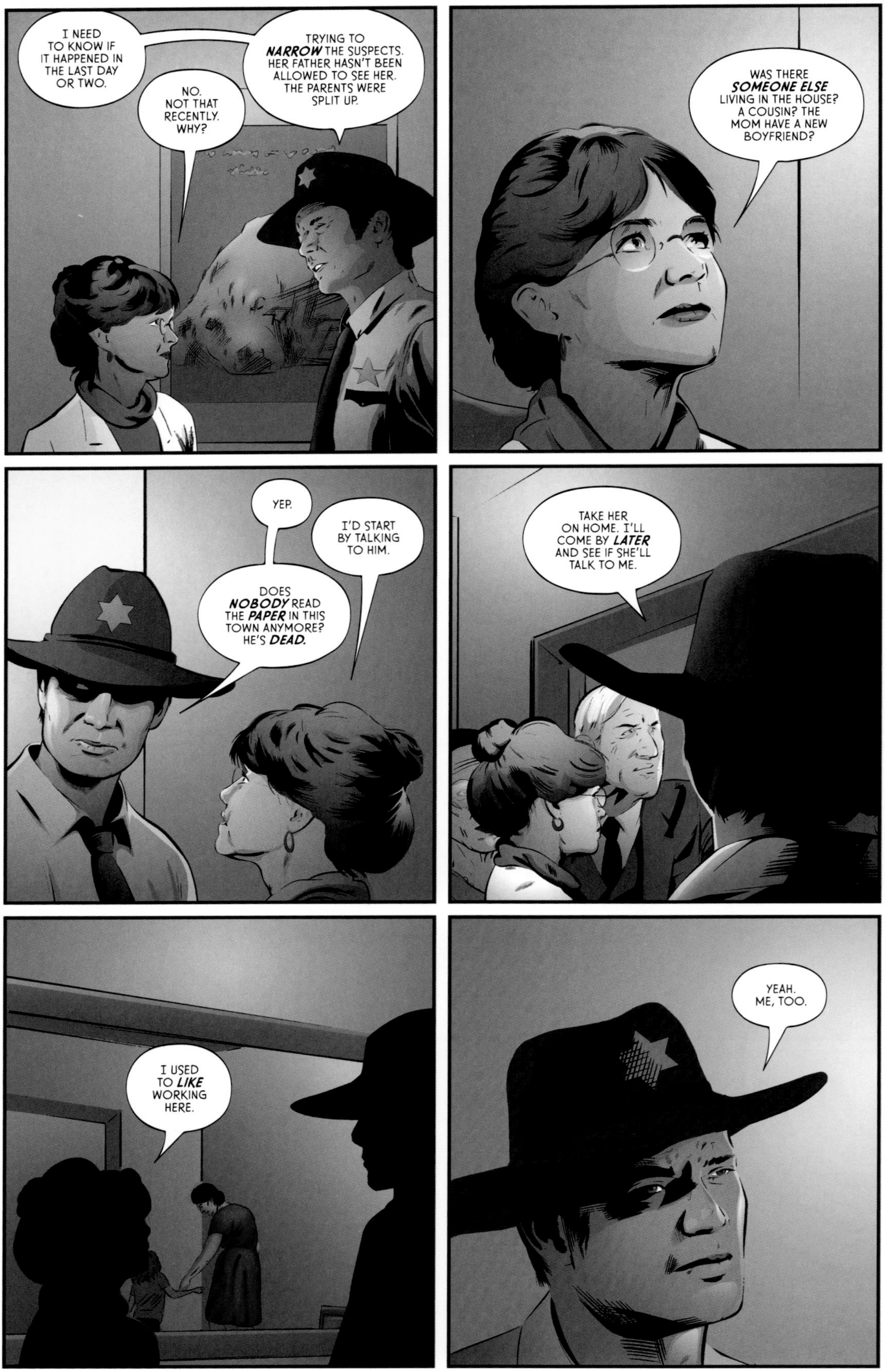
I NEED TO KNOW IF IT HAPPENED IN THE LAST DAY OR TWO.
NO. NOT THAT RECENTLY. WHY?
TRYING TO *NARROW* THE SUSPECTS. HER FATHER HASN'T BEEN ALLOWED TO SEE HER. THE PARENTS WERE SPLIT UP.
WAS THERE *SOMEONE ELSE* LIVING IN THE HOUSE? A COUSIN? THE MOM HAVE A NEW BOYFRIEND?
YEP.
I'D START BY TALKING TO HIM.
DOES *NOBODY* READ THE *PAPER* IN THIS TOWN ANYMORE? HE'S *DEAD.*
TAKE HER ON HOME. I'LL COME BY *LATER* AND SEE IF SHE'LL TALK TO ME.
I USED TO *LIKE* WORKING HERE.
YEAH. ME, TOO.

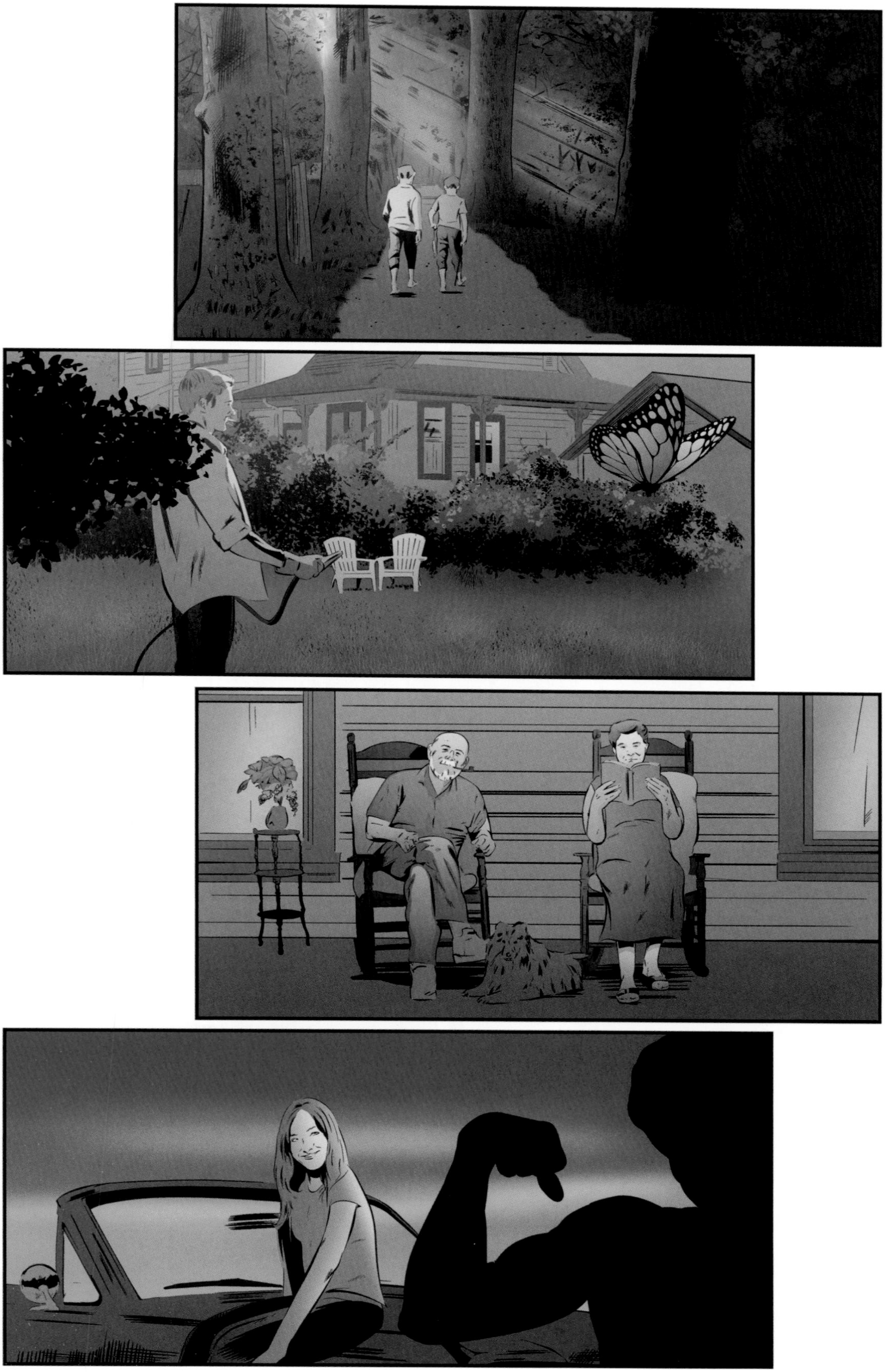

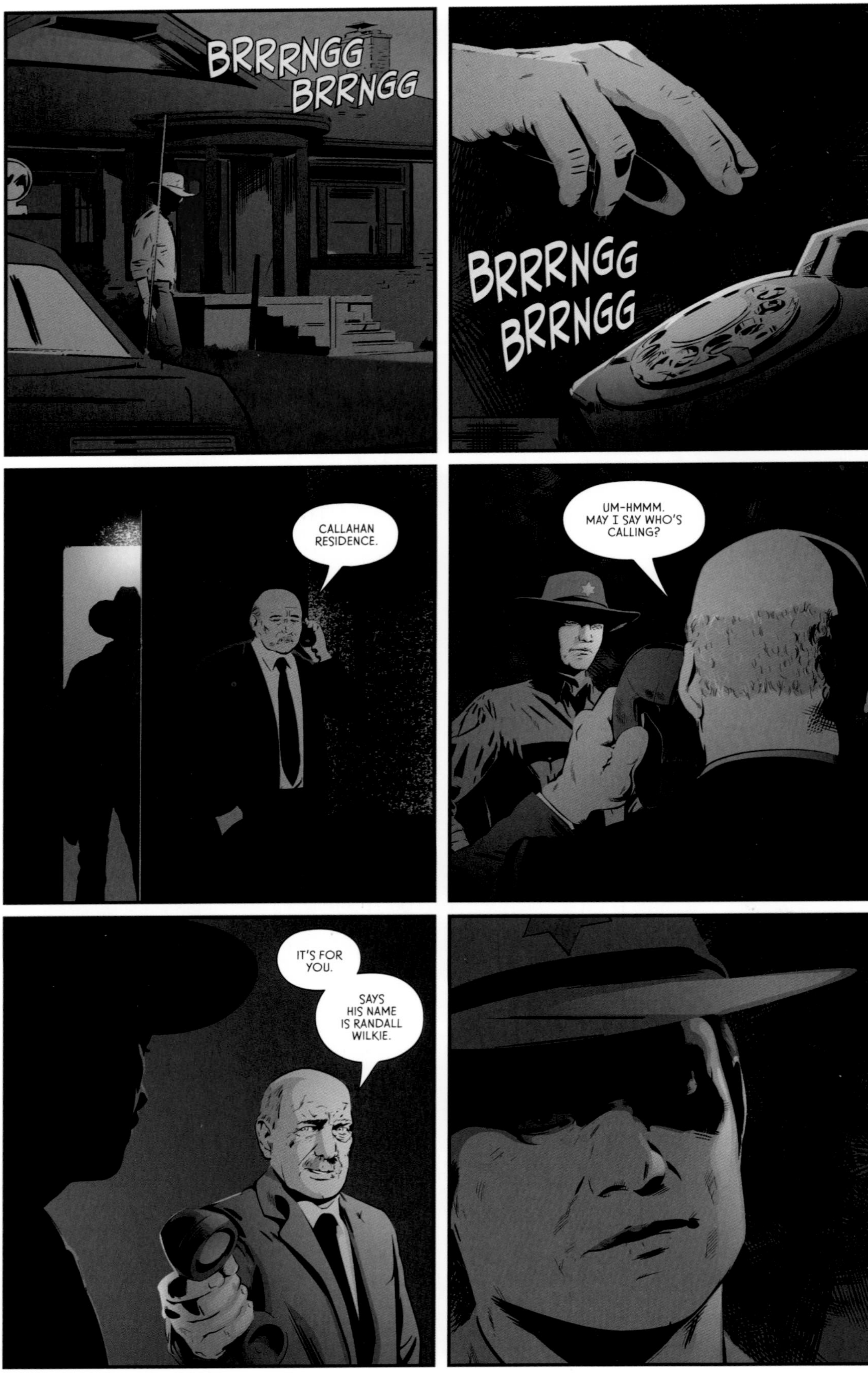
BRRRNGG
BRRNGG
BRRRNGG
BRRNGG
CALLAHAN RESIDENCE.
UM-HMMM. MAY I SAY WHO'S CALLING?
IT'S FOR YOU.
SAYS HIS NAME IS RANDALL WILKIE.

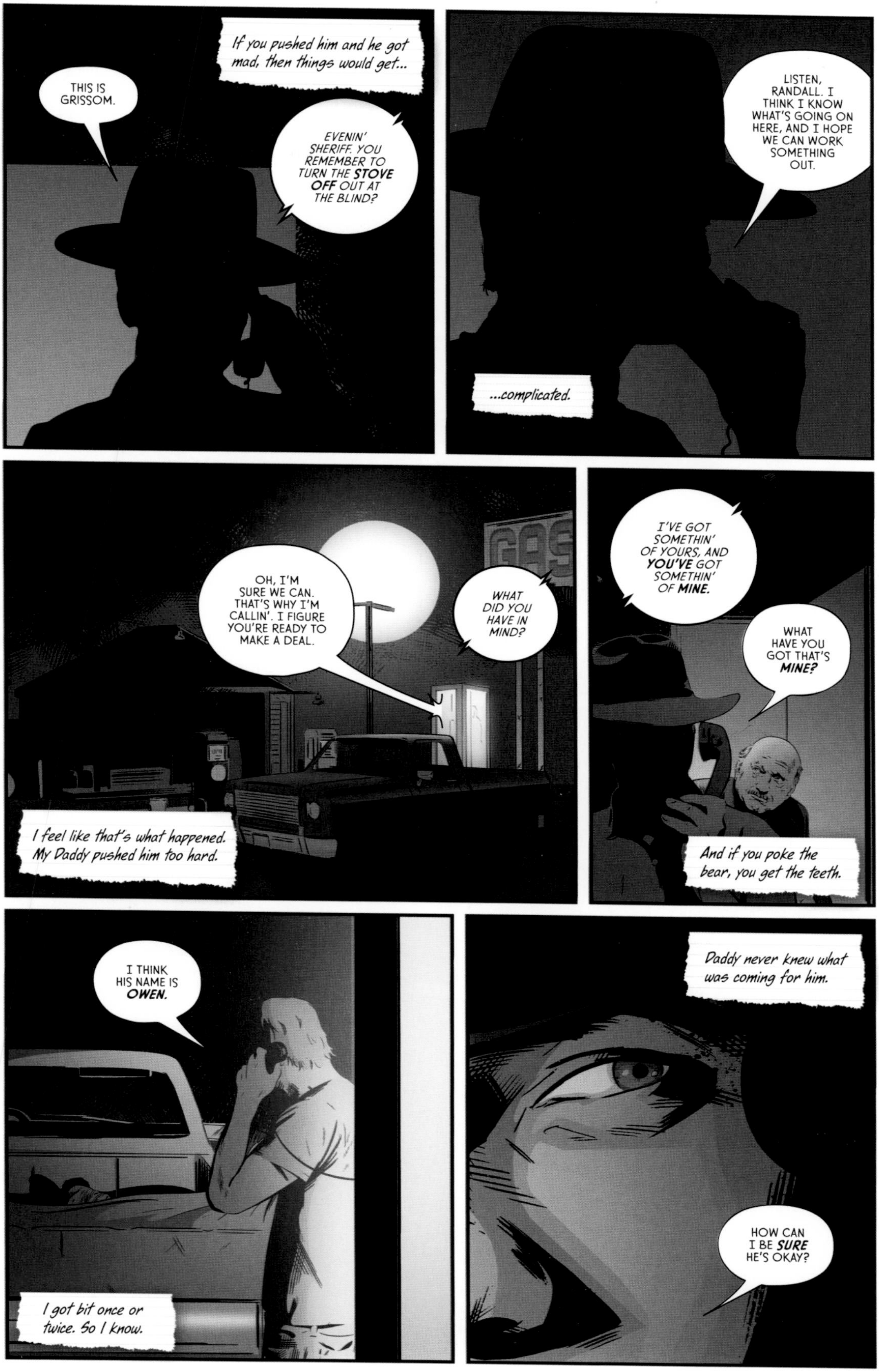
If you pushed him and he got mad, then things would get...
THIS IS GRISSOM.
EVENIN' SHERIFF. YOU REMEMBER TO TURN THE STOVE OFF OUT AT THE BLIND?
LISTEN, RANDALL. I THINK I KNOW WHAT'S GOING ON HERE, AND I HOPE WE CAN WORK SOMETHING OUT.
...complicated.
OH, I'M SURE WE CAN. THAT'S WHY I'M CALLIN'. I FIGURE YOU'RE READY TO MAKE A DEAL.
WHAT DID YOU HAVE IN MIND?
GAS
I feel like that's what happened. My Daddy pushed him too hard.
I'VE GOT SOMETHIN' OF YOURS, AND YOU'VE GOT SOMETHIN' OF MINE.
WHAT HAVE YOU GOT THAT'S MINE?
And if you poke the bear, you get the teeth.
I THINK HIS NAME IS OWEN.
I got bit once or twice. So I know.
Daddy never knew what was coming for him.
HOW CAN I BE SURE HE'S OKAY?

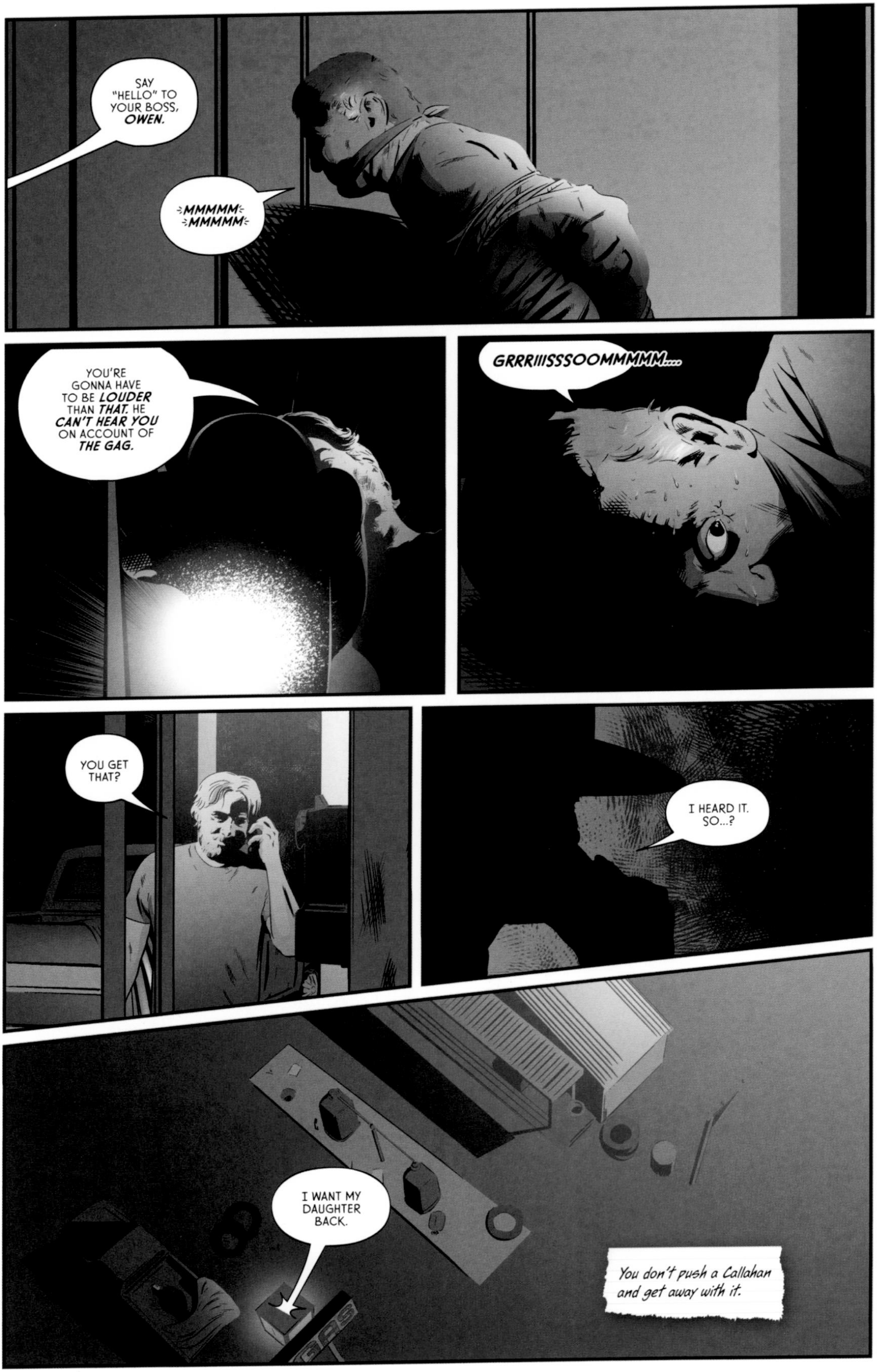
SAY "HELLO" TO YOUR BOSS, OWEN.
MMMMM MMMMM
YOU'RE GONNA HAVE TO BE LOUDER THAN THAT. HE CAN'T HEAR YOU ON ACCOUNT OF THE GAG.
GRRRIIISSSOOMMMMM....
YOU GET THAT?
I HEARD IT. SO...?
I WANT MY DAUGHTER BACK.
You don't push a Callahan and get away with it.

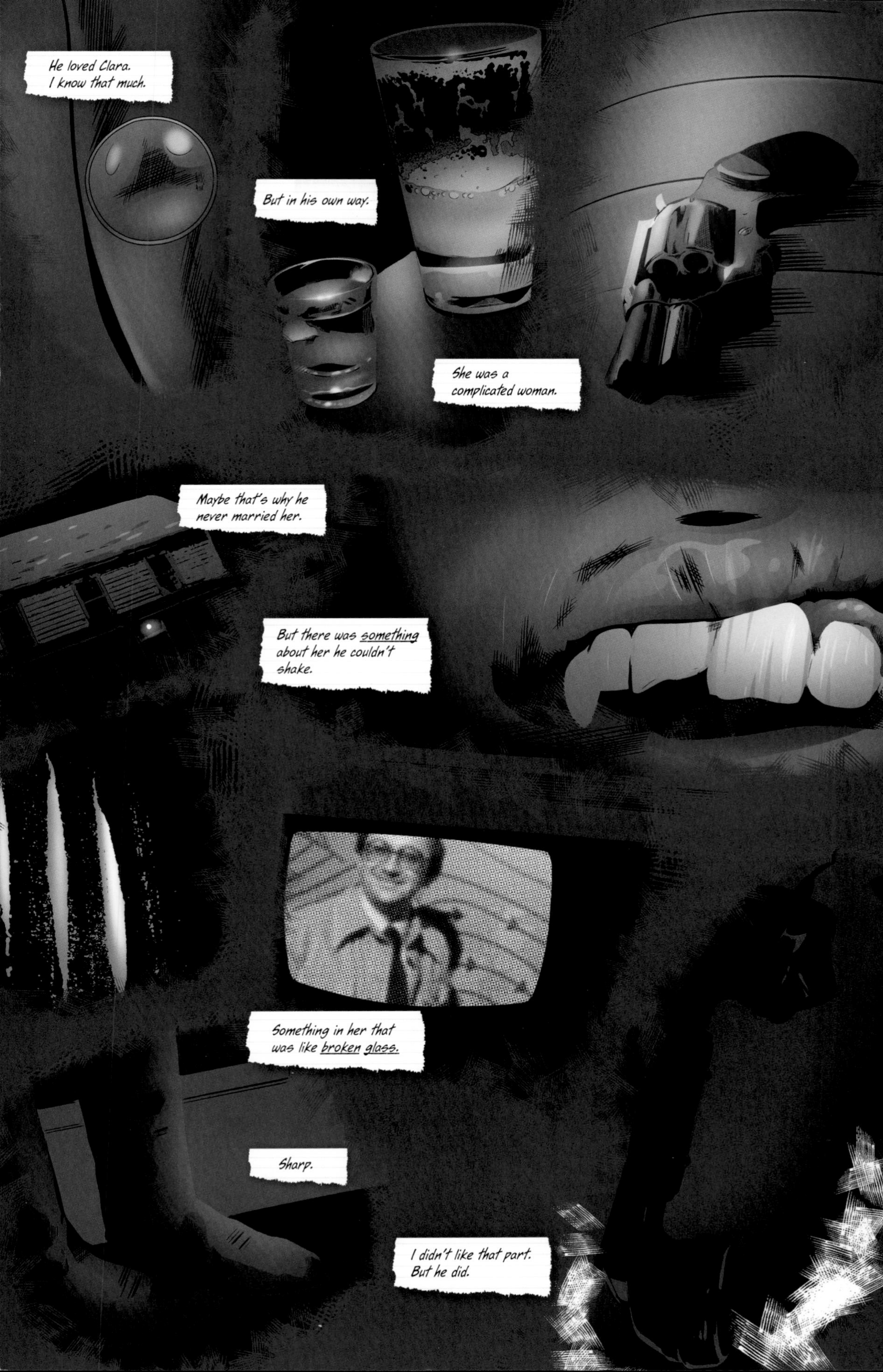
He loved Clara.
I know that much.
But in his own way.
She was a
complicated woman.
Maybe that's why he
never married her.
But there was something
about her he couldn't
shake.
Something in her that
was like broken glass.
Sharp.
I didn't like that part.
But he did.

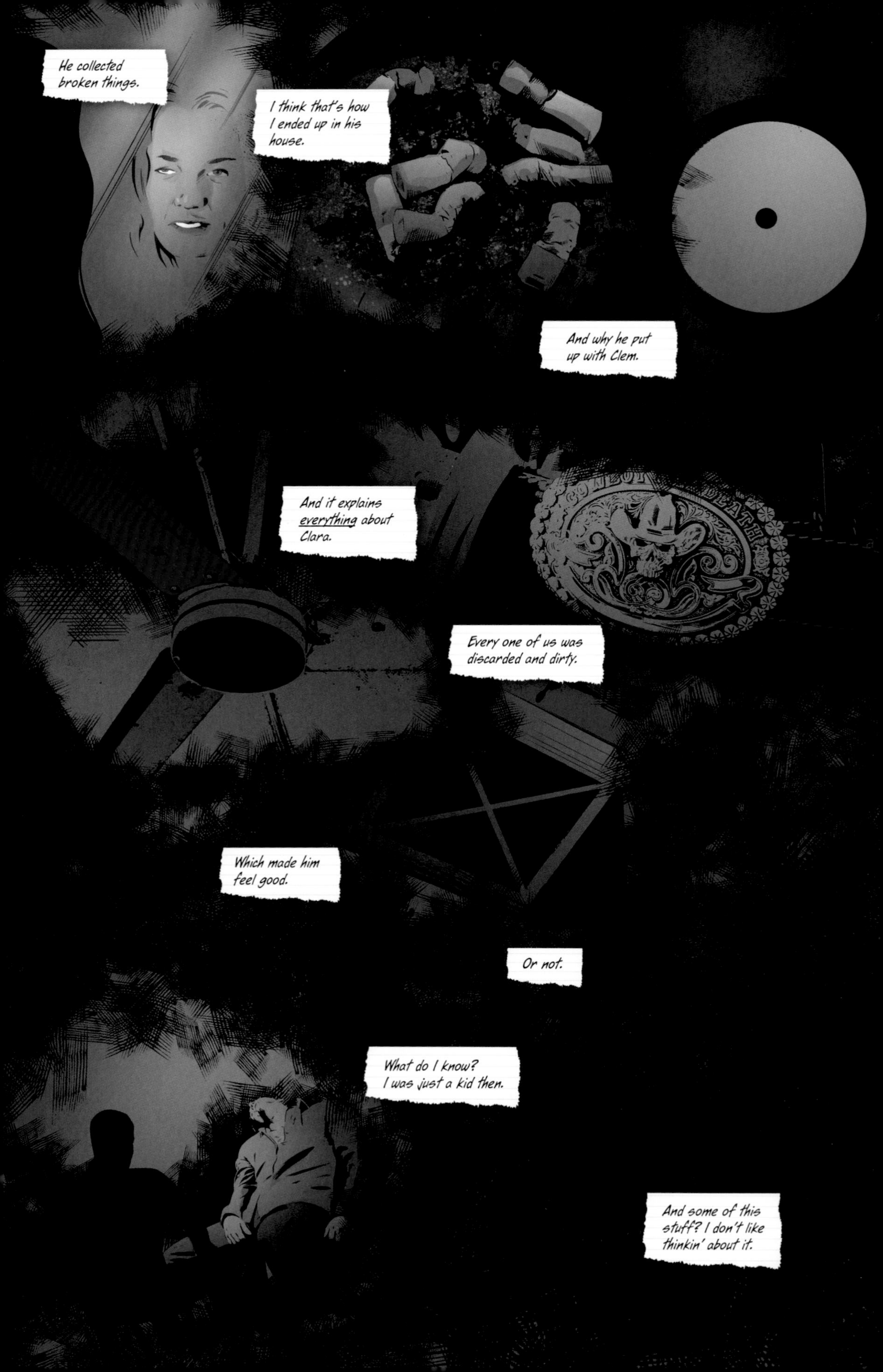
He collected broken things.
I think that's how I ended up in his house.
And why he put up with Clem.
And it explains everything about Clara.
Every one of us was discarded and dirty.
Which made him feel good.
Or not.
What do I know? I was just a kid then.
And some of this stuff? I don't like thinkin' about it.

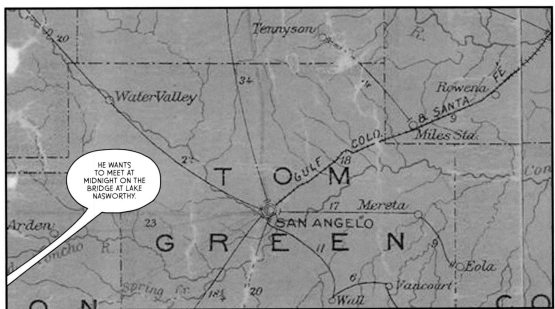

Tennyson
Water Valley
Rowena
SANTA FE
Miles Sta.
GULF COLO.
HE WANTS TO MEET AT MIDNIGHT ON THE BRIDGE AT LAKE NASWORTHY.
TOM GREEN
Mereta
Arden
SAN ANGELO
Eola
Vancourt
Wall
WE MAKE THE SWITCH THERE. IF HE GETS WIND THAT YA'LL ARE ANYWHERE AROUND, HE WON'T SHOW.
I TOOK DOWN A TEN-POINT BUCK LAST YEAR AND I WASN'T EVEN IN A BLIND. I KNOW HOW TO HIDE SO'S NO ONE KNOWS I'M THERE.
YOU'RE A ***LIAR,*** TOO.
AIN'T ***NOBODY*** IN TOM GREEN GOT A ***TEN POINT.*** EVER.
COME ON OVER TO THE HOUSE. HANGIN' ABOVE MY FIREPLACE.
CAN WE FOCUS, PLEASE?
WHY NOT JUST BLOCK THE BRIDGE AFTER YOU MAKE THE SWITCH? WE CAN COVER BOTH ENDS.
AND WHERE WOULD YOU HIDE? IT'S FLAT IN ALL DIRECTIONS. HE'D ***SEE*** YOU. WE CAN'T RISK IT.

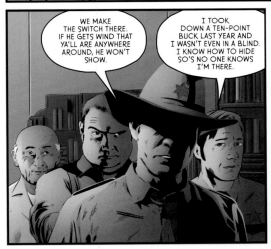

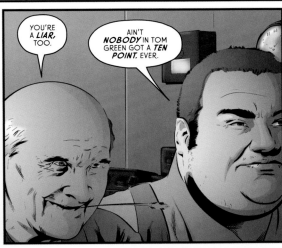

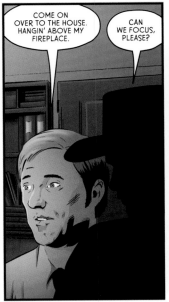

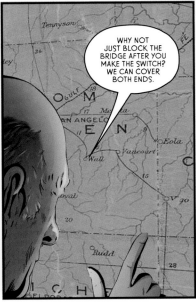

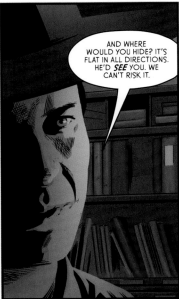

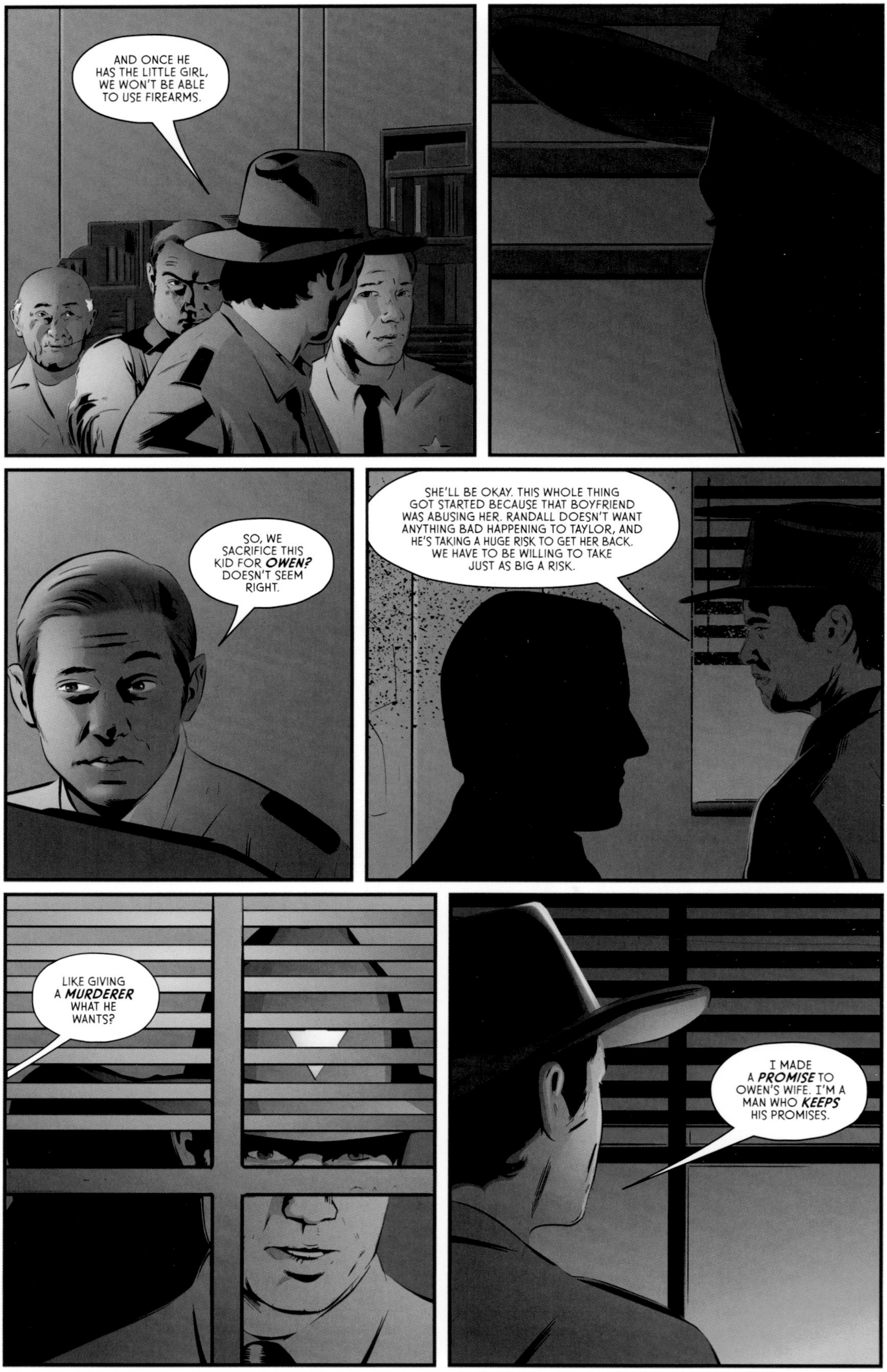
AND ONCE HE HAS THE LITTLE GIRL, WE WON'T BE ABLE TO USE FIREARMS.
SO, WE SACRIFICE THIS KID FOR OWEN? DOESN'T SEEM RIGHT.
SHE'LL BE OKAY. THIS WHOLE THING GOT STARTED BECAUSE THAT BOYFRIEND WAS ABUSING HER. RANDALL DOESN'T WANT ANYTHING BAD HAPPENING TO TAYLOR, AND HE'S TAKING A HUGE RISK TO GET HER BACK. WE HAVE TO BE WILLING TO TAKE JUST AS BIG A RISK.
LIKE GIVING A MURDERER WHAT HE WANTS?
I MADE A PROMISE TO OWEN'S WIFE. I'M A MAN WHO KEEPS HIS PROMISES.

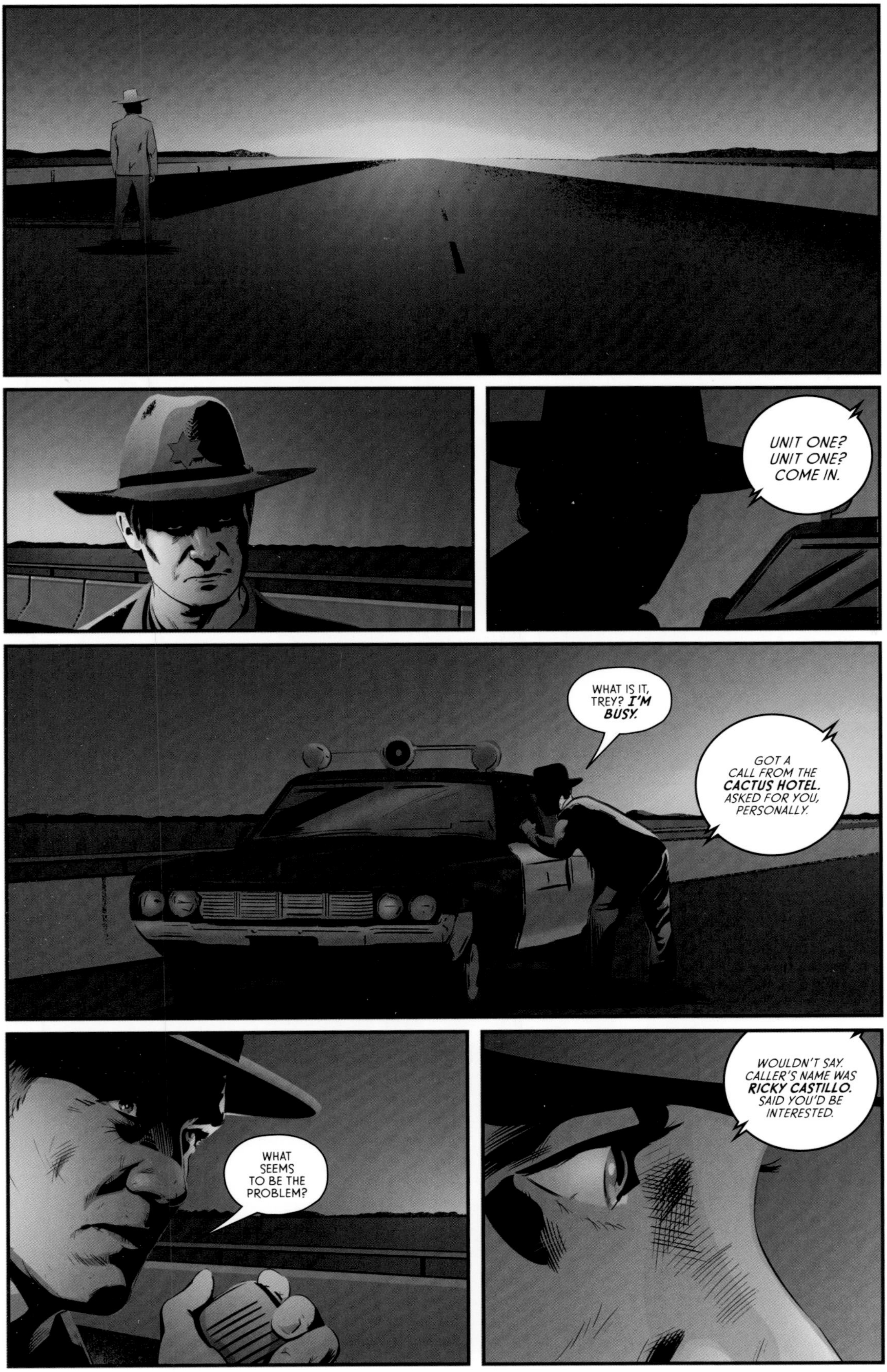
UNIT ONE? UNIT ONE? COME IN.
WHAT IS IT, TREY? I'M BUSY.
GOT A CALL FROM THE CACTUS HOTEL. ASKED FOR YOU, PERSONALLY.
WHAT SEEMS TO BE THE PROBLEM?
WOULDN'T SAY. CALLER'S NAME WAS RICKY CASTILLO. SAID YOU'D BE INTERESTED.

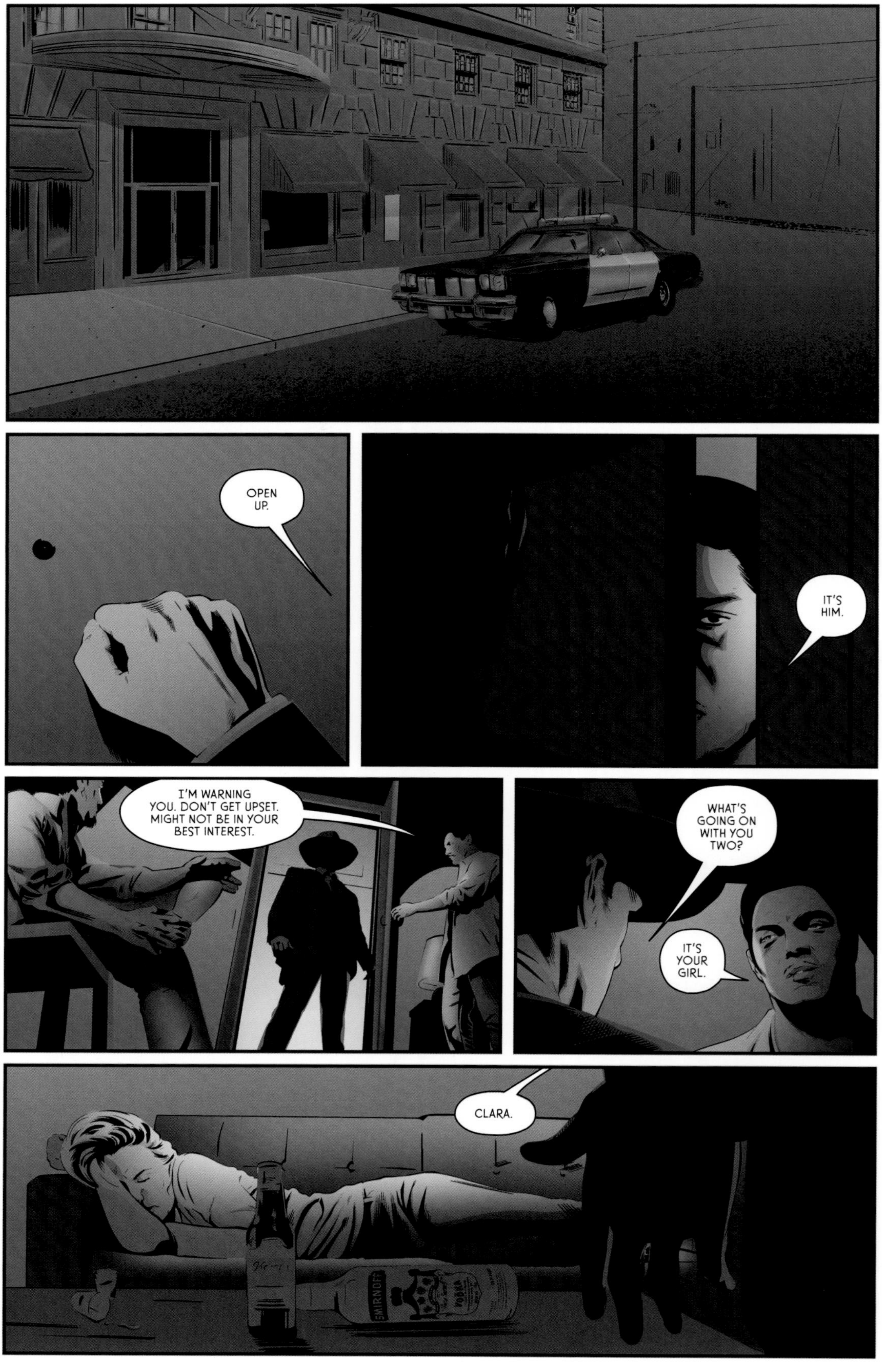
OPEN UP.
IT'S HIM.
I'M WARNING YOU. DON'T GET UPSET. MIGHT NOT BE IN YOUR BEST INTEREST.
WHAT'S GOING ON WITH YOU TWO?
IT'S YOUR GIRL.
CLARA.
SMIRNOFF

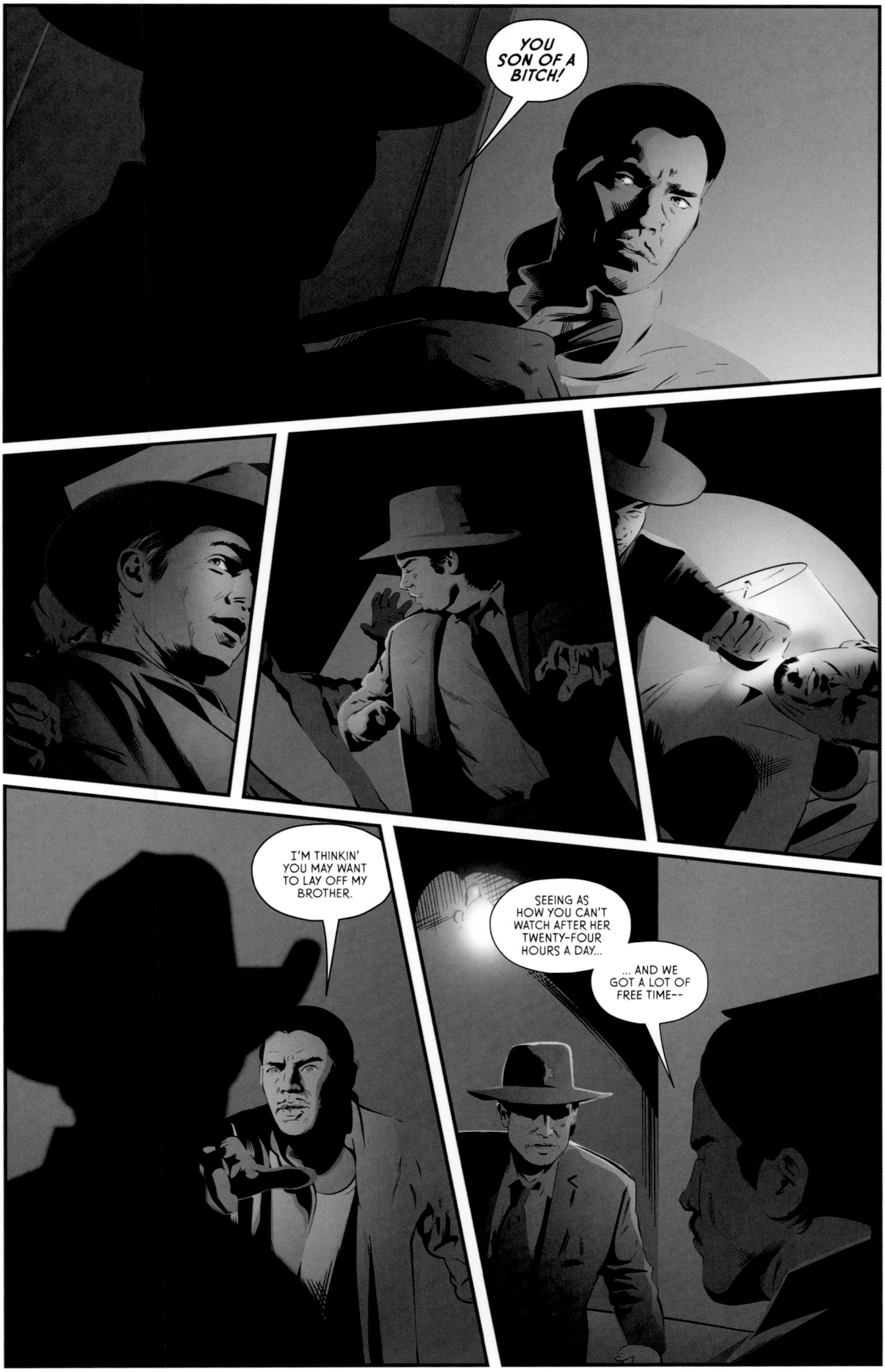
YOU SON OF A BITCH!
I'M THINKIN' YOU MAY WANT TO LAY OFF MY BROTHER.
SEEING AS HOW YOU CAN'T WATCH AFTER HER TWENTY-FOUR HOURS A DAY...
... AND WE GOT A LOT OF FREE TIME--

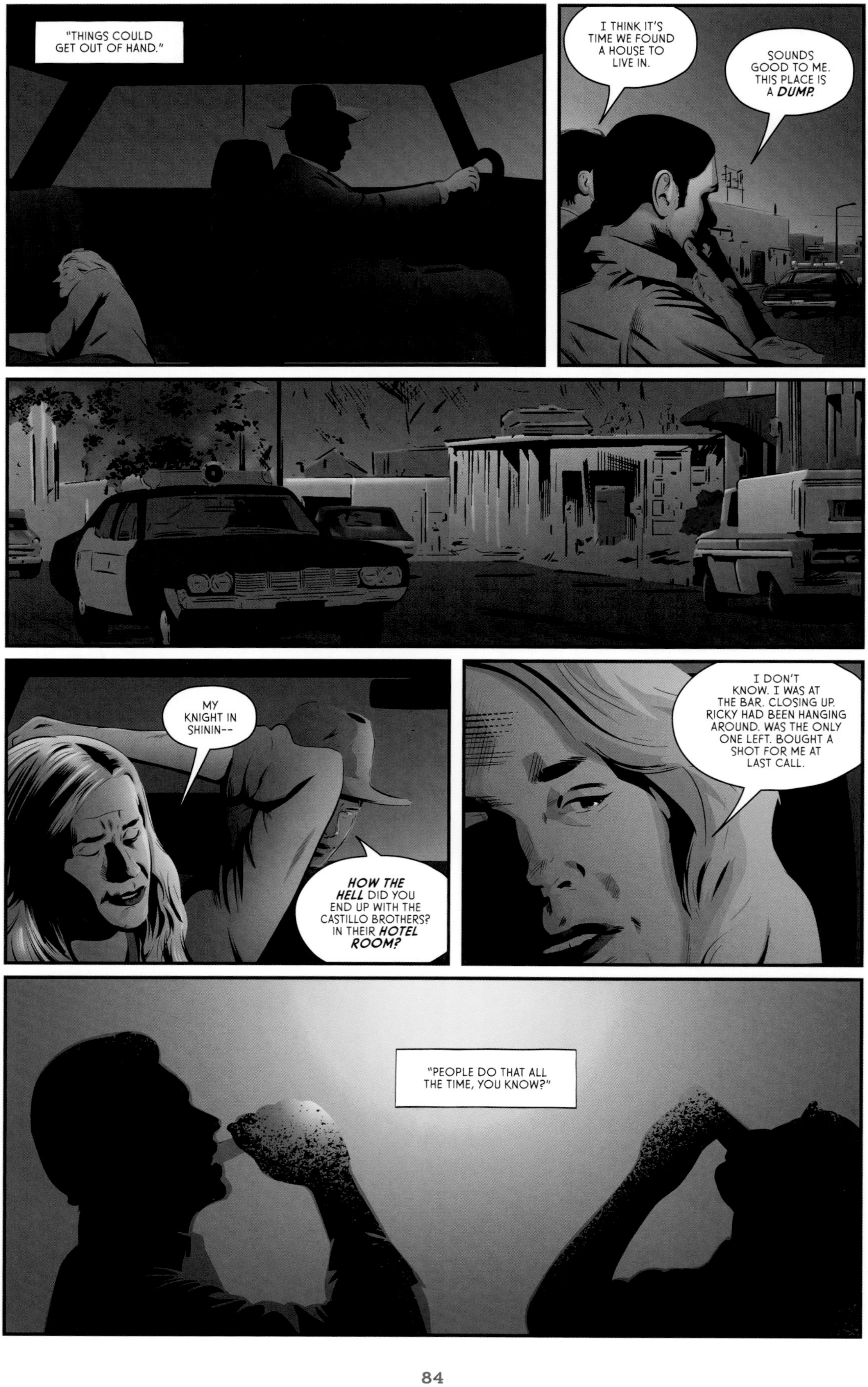
"THINGS COULD GET OUT OF HAND."
I THINK IT'S TIME WE FOUND A HOUSE TO LIVE IN.
SOUNDS GOOD TO ME. THIS PLACE IS A ***DUMP.***
MY KNIGHT IN SHININ--
HOW THE HELL DID YOU END UP WITH THE CASTILLO BROTHERS? IN THEIR ***HOTEL ROOM?***
I DON'T KNOW. I WAS AT THE BAR. CLOSING UP. RICKY HAD BEEN HANGING AROUND. WAS THE ONLY ONE LEFT. BOUGHT A SHOT FOR ME AT LAST CALL.
"PEOPLE DO THAT ALL THE TIME, YOU KNOW?"

THEN I STARTED TO FEEL SICK. WOOZY. LIKE I HADN'T HAD ANYTHING TO EAT ALL DAY.

"RICKY OFFERED TO MAKE SURE I GOT HOME SAFELY. BUT I WASN'T OKAY TO DRIVE.

"I THINK I GAVE HIM MY ADDRESS. I FEEL LIKE HE WAS GONNA TAKE ME HOME."

RED ROOSTER

BUT I GUESS HE DIDN'T. CAN YOU REMEMBER ANYTHING ELSE THAT HAPPENED?

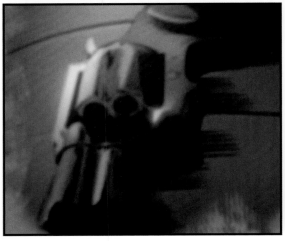

NO.

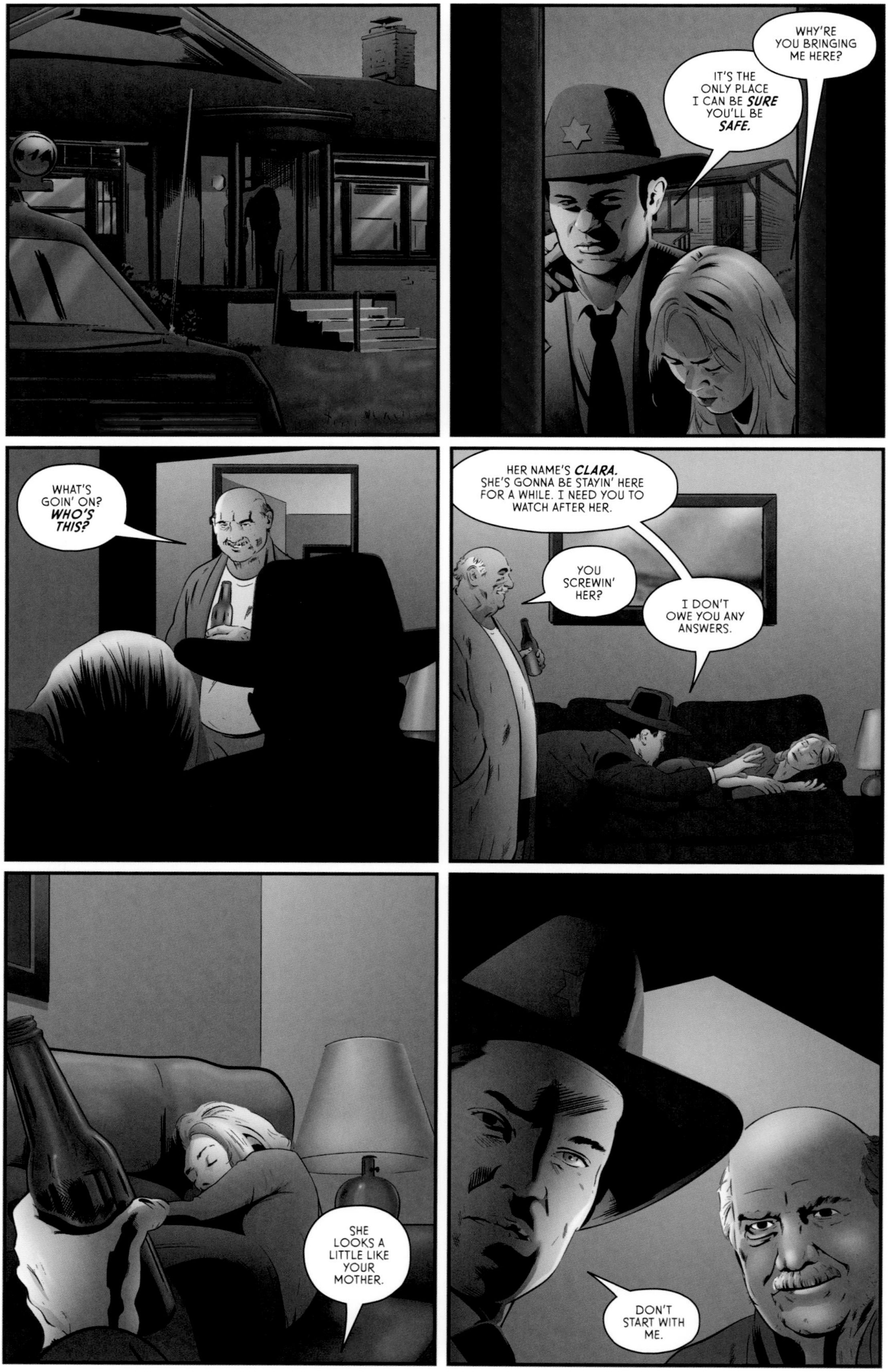
WHY'RE YOU BRINGING ME HERE?
IT'S THE ONLY PLACE I CAN BE SURE YOU'LL BE SAFE.
WHAT'S GOIN' ON? WHO'S THIS?
HER NAME'S CLARA. SHE'S GONNA BE STAYIN' HERE FOR A WHILE. I NEED YOU TO WATCH AFTER HER.
YOU SCREWIN' HER?
I DON'T OWE YOU ANY ANSWERS.
SHE LOOKS A LITTLE LIKE YOUR MOTHER.
DON'T START WITH ME.

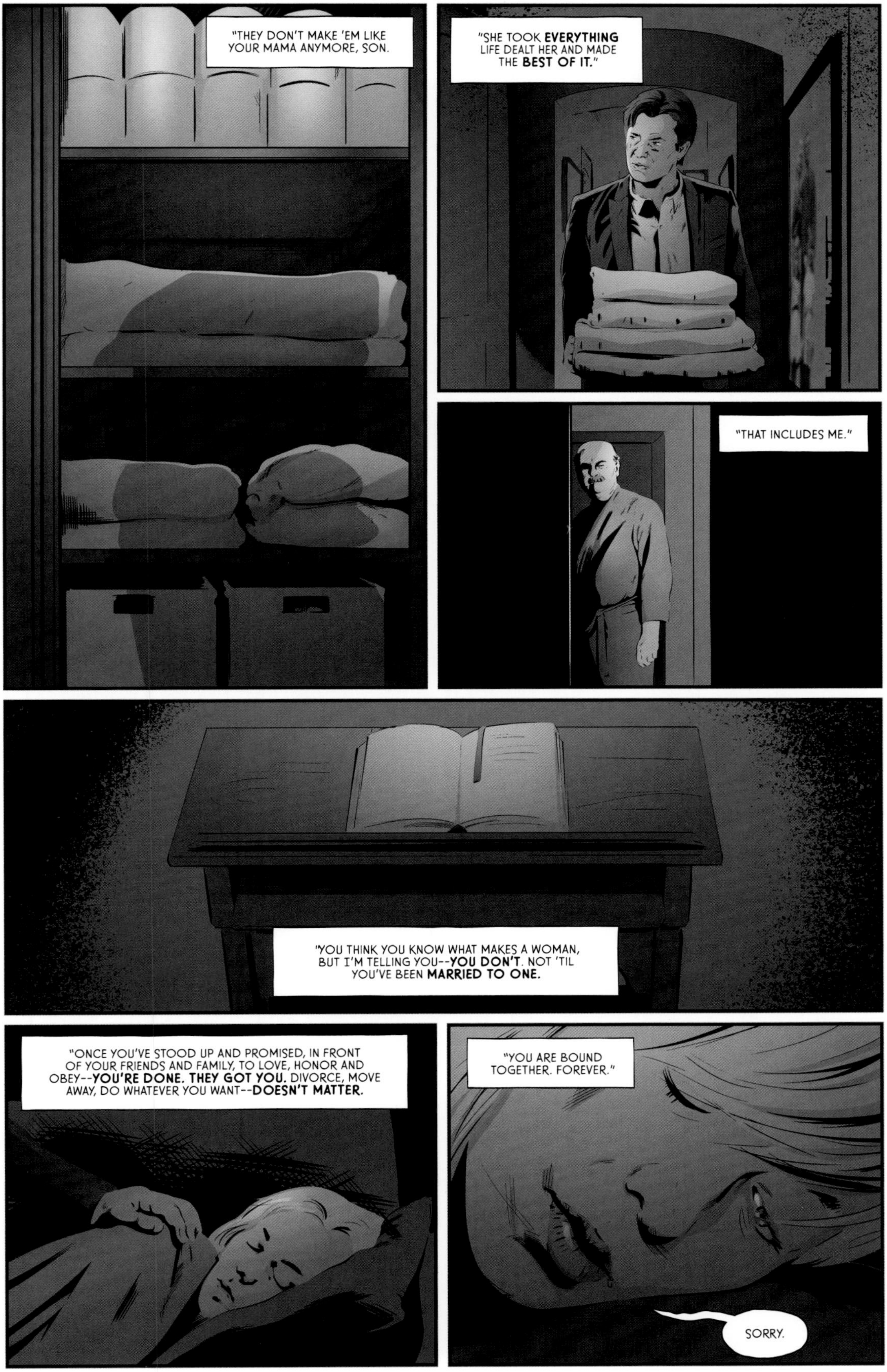
"THEY DON'T MAKE 'EM LIKE YOUR MAMA ANYMORE, SON.
"SHE TOOK **EVERYTHING** LIFE DEALT HER AND MADE THE **BEST OF IT.**"
"THAT INCLUDES ME."
"YOU THINK YOU KNOW WHAT MAKES A WOMAN, BUT I'M TELLING YOU--**YOU DON'T**. NOT 'TIL YOU'VE BEEN **MARRIED TO ONE.**
"ONCE YOU'VE STOOD UP AND PROMISED, IN FRONT OF YOUR FRIENDS AND FAMILY, TO LOVE, HONOR AND OBEY--**YOU'RE DONE. THEY GOT YOU.** DIVORCE, MOVE AWAY, DO WHATEVER YOU WANT--**DOESN'T MATTER.**
"YOU ARE BOUND TOGETHER. FOREVER."
SORRY.

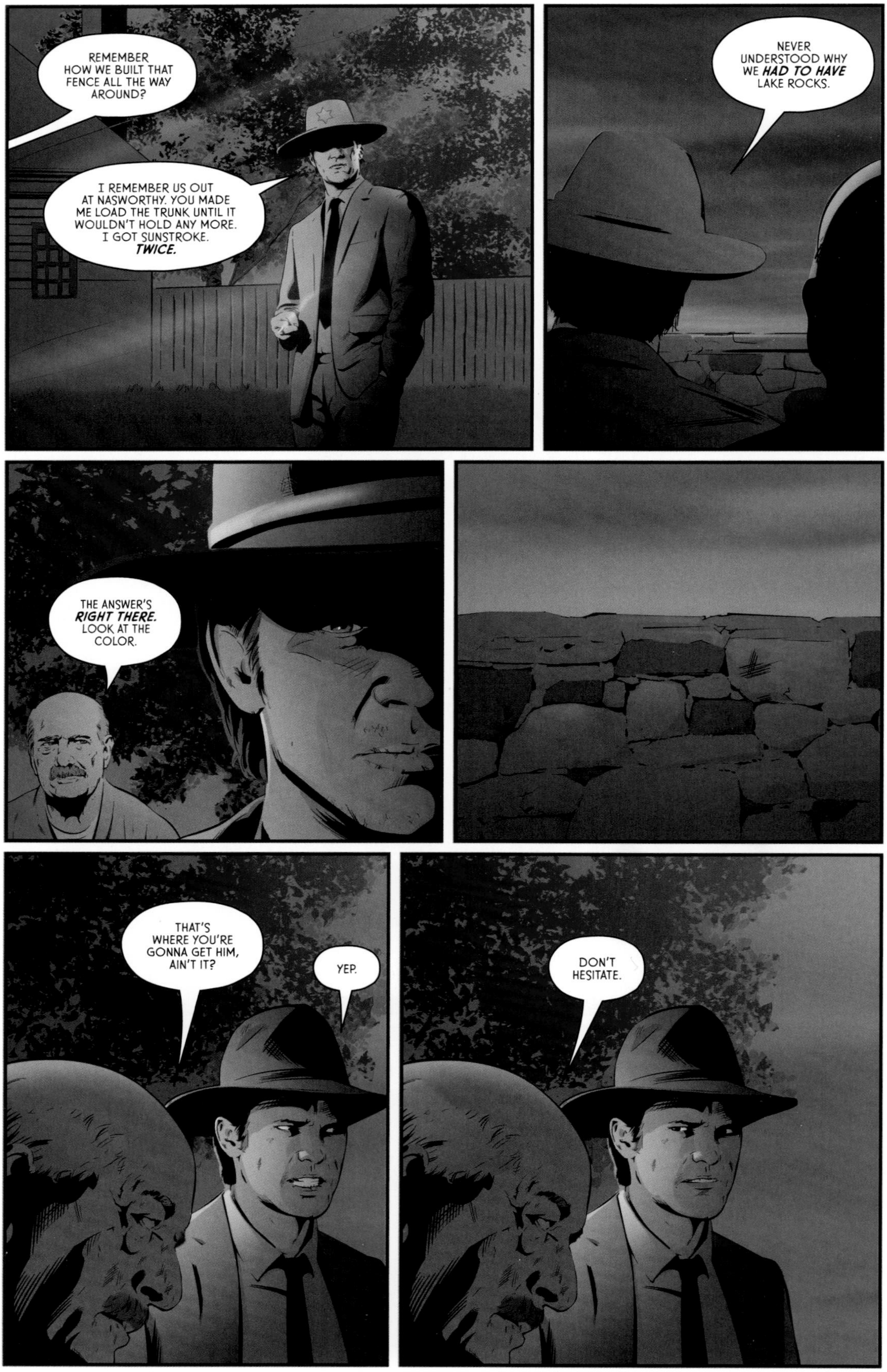
REMEMBER HOW WE BUILT THAT FENCE ALL THE WAY AROUND?
I REMEMBER US OUT AT NASWORTHY. YOU MADE ME LOAD THE TRUNK UNTIL IT WOULDN'T HOLD ANY MORE. I GOT SUNSTROKE. ***TWICE.***
NEVER UNDERSTOOD WHY WE ***HAD TO HAVE*** LAKE ROCKS.
THE ANSWER'S ***RIGHT THERE.*** LOOK AT THE COLOR.
THAT'S WHERE YOU'RE GONNA GET HIM, AIN'T IT?
YEP.
DON'T HESITATE.

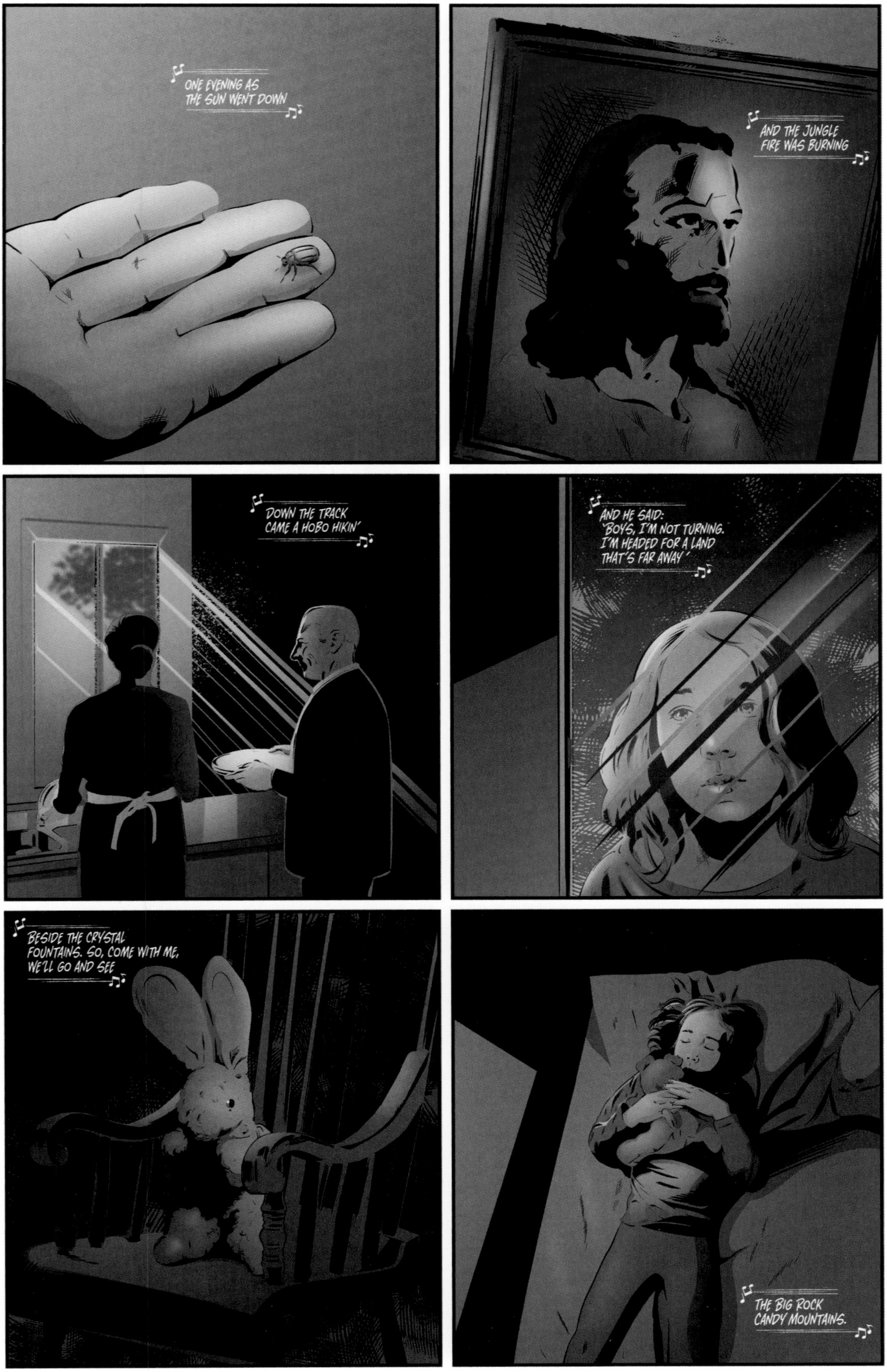
ONE EVENING AS THE SUN WENT DOWN
AND THE JUNGLE FIRE WAS BURNING
DOWN THE TRACK CAME A HOBO HIKIN'
AND HE SAID: 'BOYS, I'M NOT TURNING. I'M HEADED FOR A LAND THAT'S FAR AWAY'
BESIDE THE CRYSTAL FOUNTAINS. SO, COME WITH ME, WE'LL GO AND SEE
THE BIG ROCK CANDY MOUNTAINS.

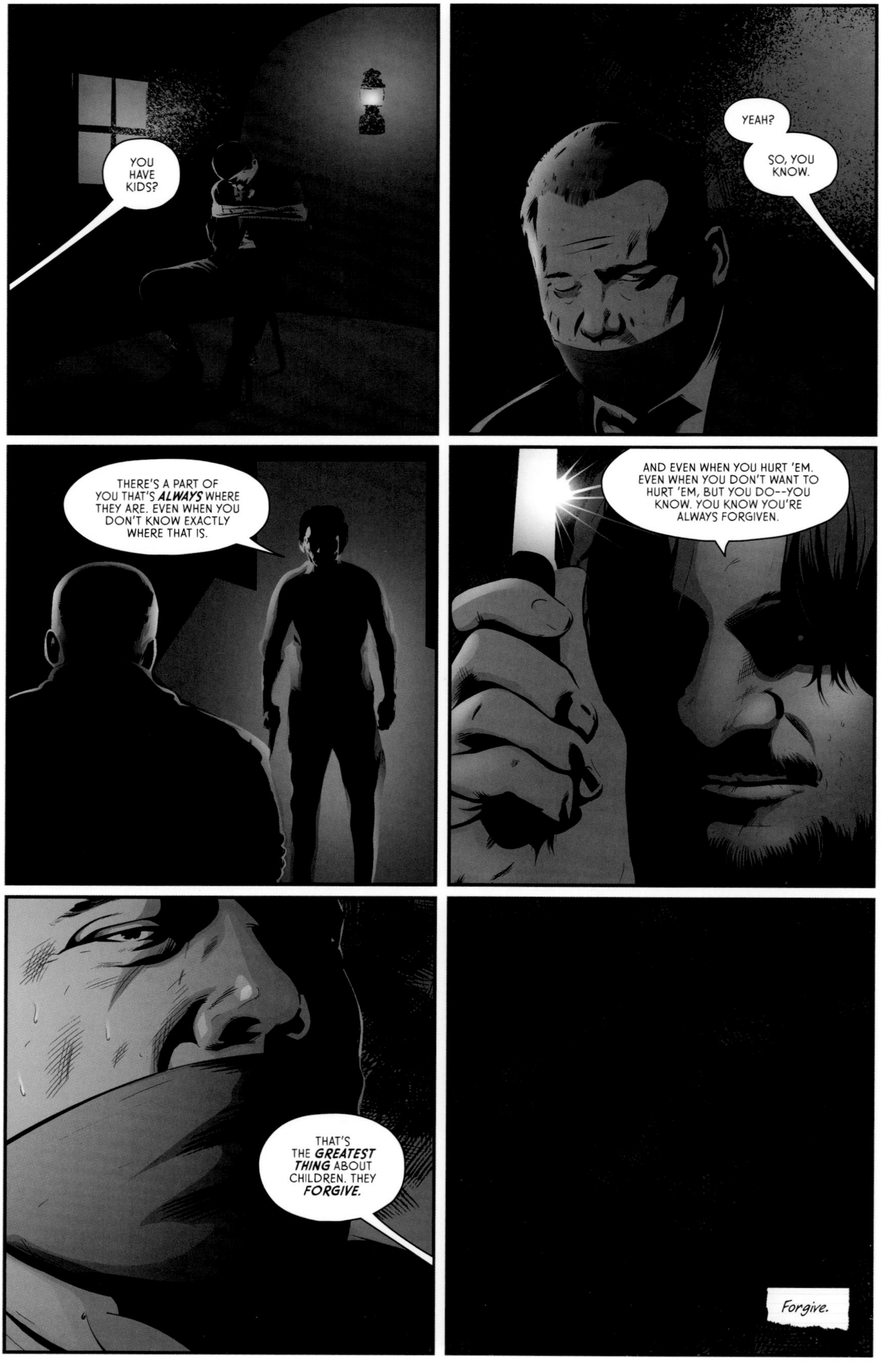
YOU HAVE KIDS?
YEAH?
SO, YOU KNOW.
THERE'S A PART OF YOU THAT'S ***ALWAYS*** WHERE THEY ARE. EVEN WHEN YOU DON'T KNOW EXACTLY WHERE THAT IS.
AND EVEN WHEN YOU HURT 'EM. EVEN WHEN YOU DON'T WANT TO HURT 'EM, BUT YOU DO--YOU KNOW. YOU KNOW YOU'RE ALWAYS FORGIVEN.
THAT'S THE ***GREATEST THING*** ABOUT CHILDREN. THEY ***FORGIVE.***
Forgive.

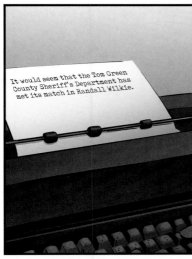

It would seem that the Tom Green County Sheriff's Department has met its match in Randall Wilkie.

With no new leads to follow and the days passing quickly, it would appear that the killer has given the investigators the slip.

Border agents have been alerted.

HEADLINE:
Stockyards Full In Anticipation Of Auction Season.

"BEHOLD, CHILDREN ARE A HERITAGE FROM THE LORD, THE FRUIT OF THE WOMB A REWARD."

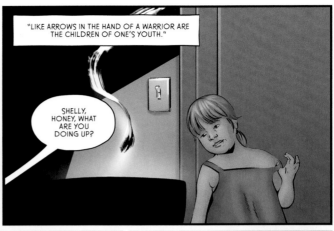

"LIKE ARROWS IN THE HAND OF A WARRIOR ARE THE CHILDREN OF ONE'S YOUTH."

SHELLY, HONEY, WHAT ARE YOU DOING UP?

MY ROLLER-SKATES ARE SINGING.

"BLESSED IS THE MAN WHO FILLS HIS QUIVER WITH THEM!"

OH, BABY. YOU'RE SLEEPWALKING AGAIN. LET'S GO BACK TO BED, OKAY?

"HE SHALL NOT BE PUT TO SHAME WHEN HE SPEAKS WITH HIS ENEMIES AT THE GATE."

DADDY'S DEAD.

PACK YOUR THINGS, TAYLOR. IT'S ALL GOING TO BE OKAY.

HE'S THE SHERIFF, REMEMBER? HE *HELPS* PEOPLE.

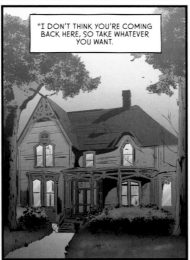

"I DON'T THINK YOU'RE COMING BACK HERE, SO TAKE WHATEVER YOU WANT.

"AND WE HOPE YOU'LL ALWAYS REMEMBER US FONDLY.

"WE'LL KEEP YOU IN OUR PRAYERS.

"ALWAYS."

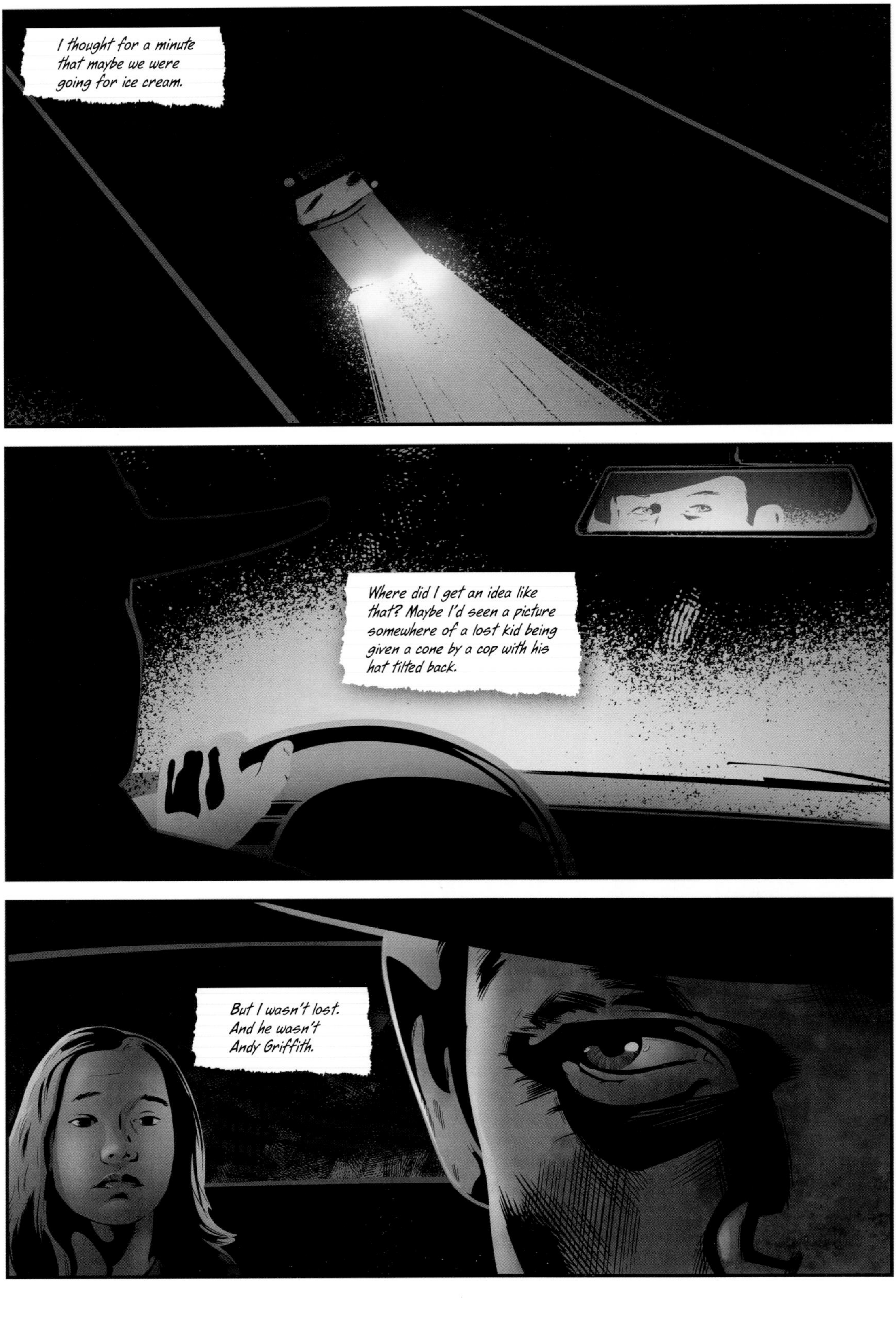
I thought for a minute that maybe we were going for ice cream.
Where did I get an idea like that? Maybe I'd seen a picture somewhere of a lost kid being given a cone by a cop with his hat tilted back.
But I wasn't lost. And he wasn't Andy Griffith.

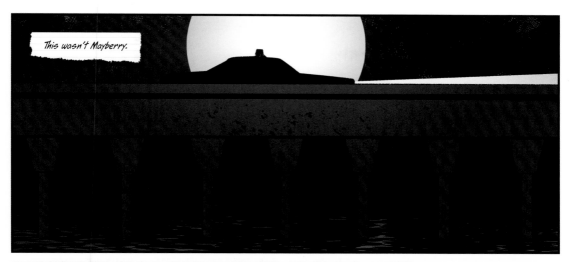

This wasn't Mayberry.

I look back on that night now and remember the smell of moldy green lake water.

I can feel the humidity. And I remember I got two mosquito bites. One on my wrist and one on my ankle.

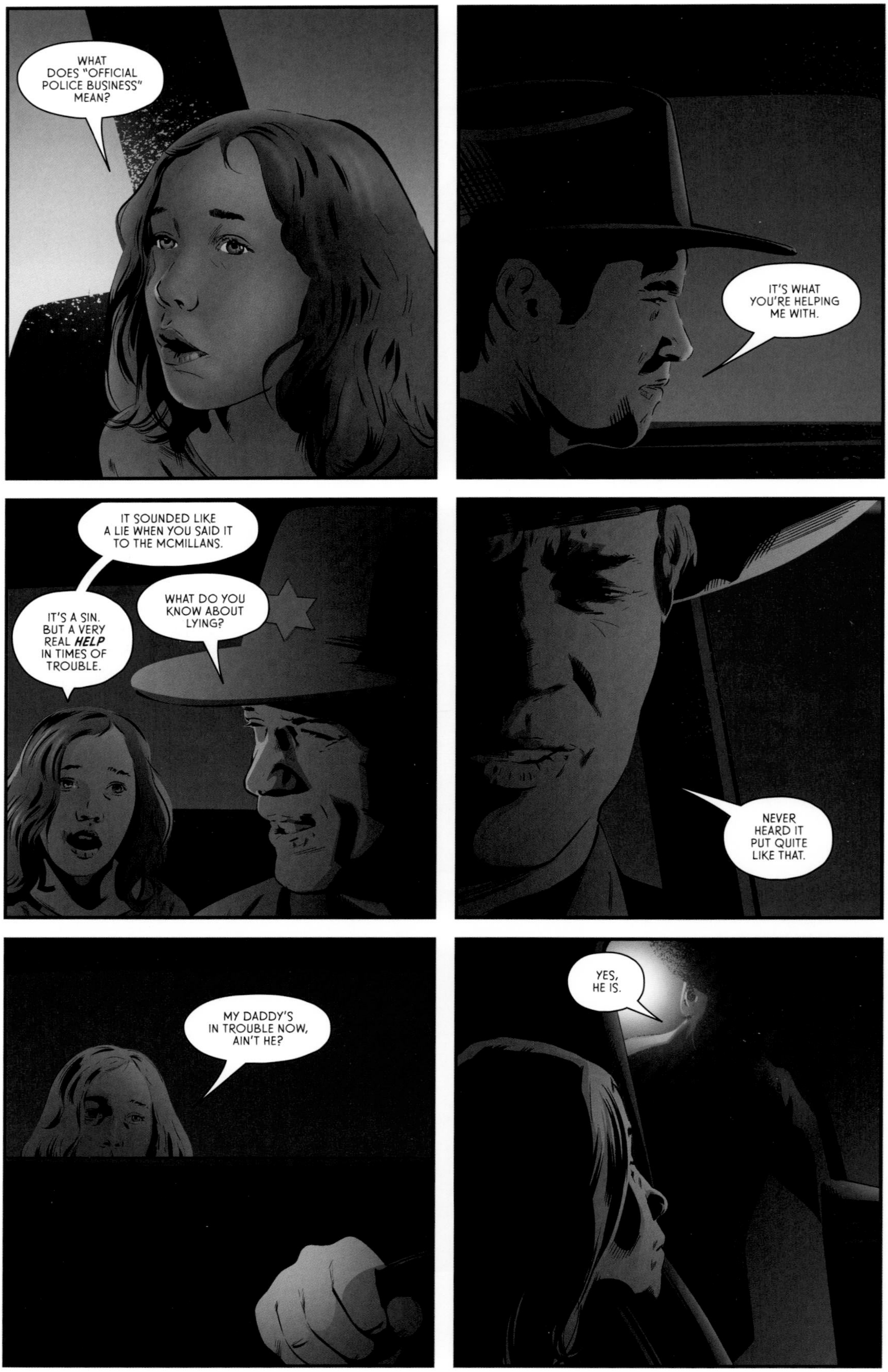
WHAT DOES "OFFICIAL POLICE BUSINESS" MEAN?
IT'S WHAT YOU'RE HELPING ME WITH.
IT SOUNDED LIKE A LIE WHEN YOU SAID IT TO THE MCMILLANS.
WHAT DO YOU KNOW ABOUT LYING?
IT'S A SIN. BUT A VERY REAL **HELP** IN TIMES OF TROUBLE.
NEVER HEARD IT PUT QUITE LIKE THAT.
MY DADDY'S IN TROUBLE NOW, AIN'T HE?
YES, HE IS.

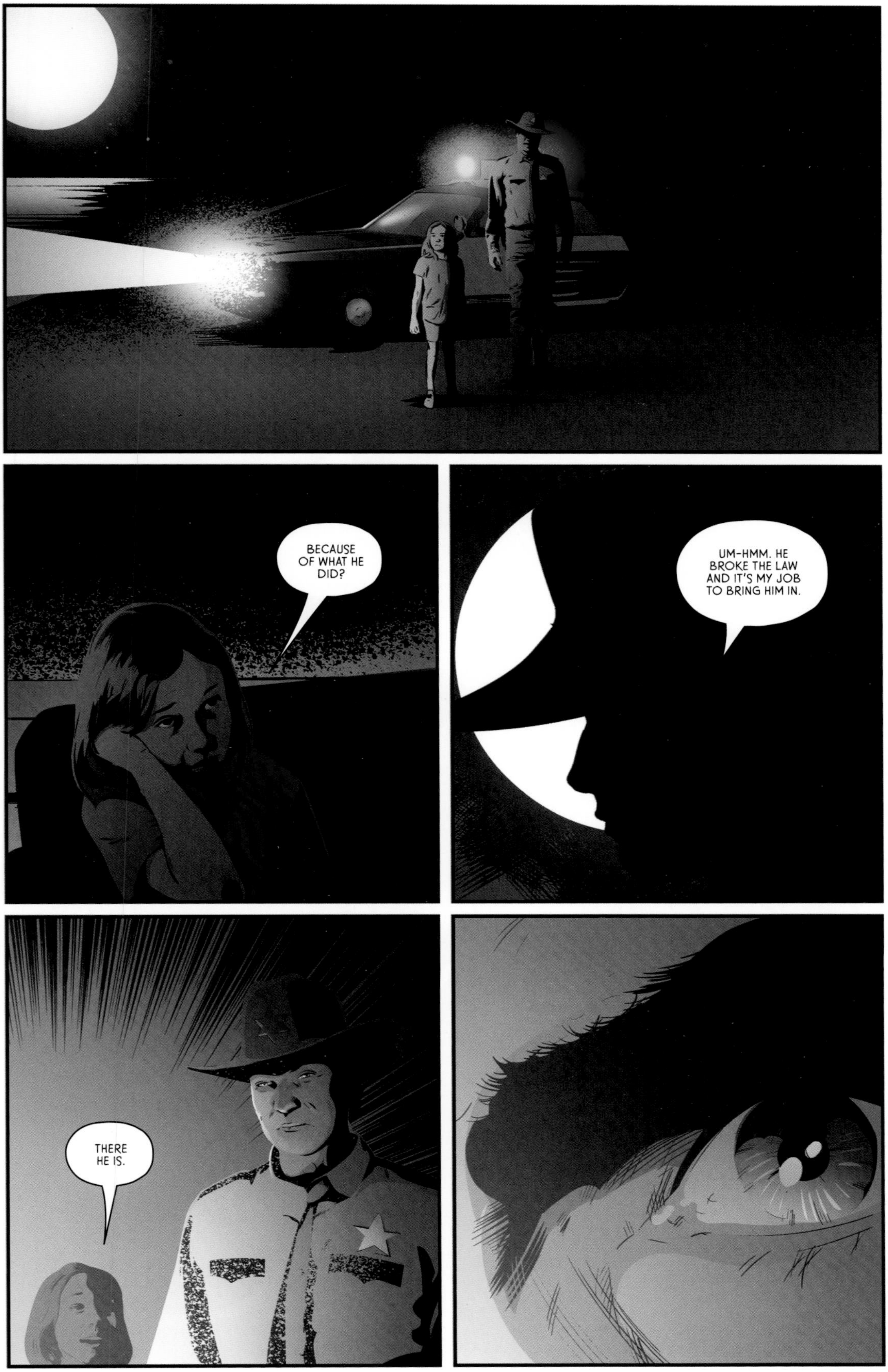
BECAUSE OF WHAT HE DID?
UM-HMM. HE BROKE THE LAW AND IT'S MY JOB TO BRING HIM IN.
THERE HE IS.

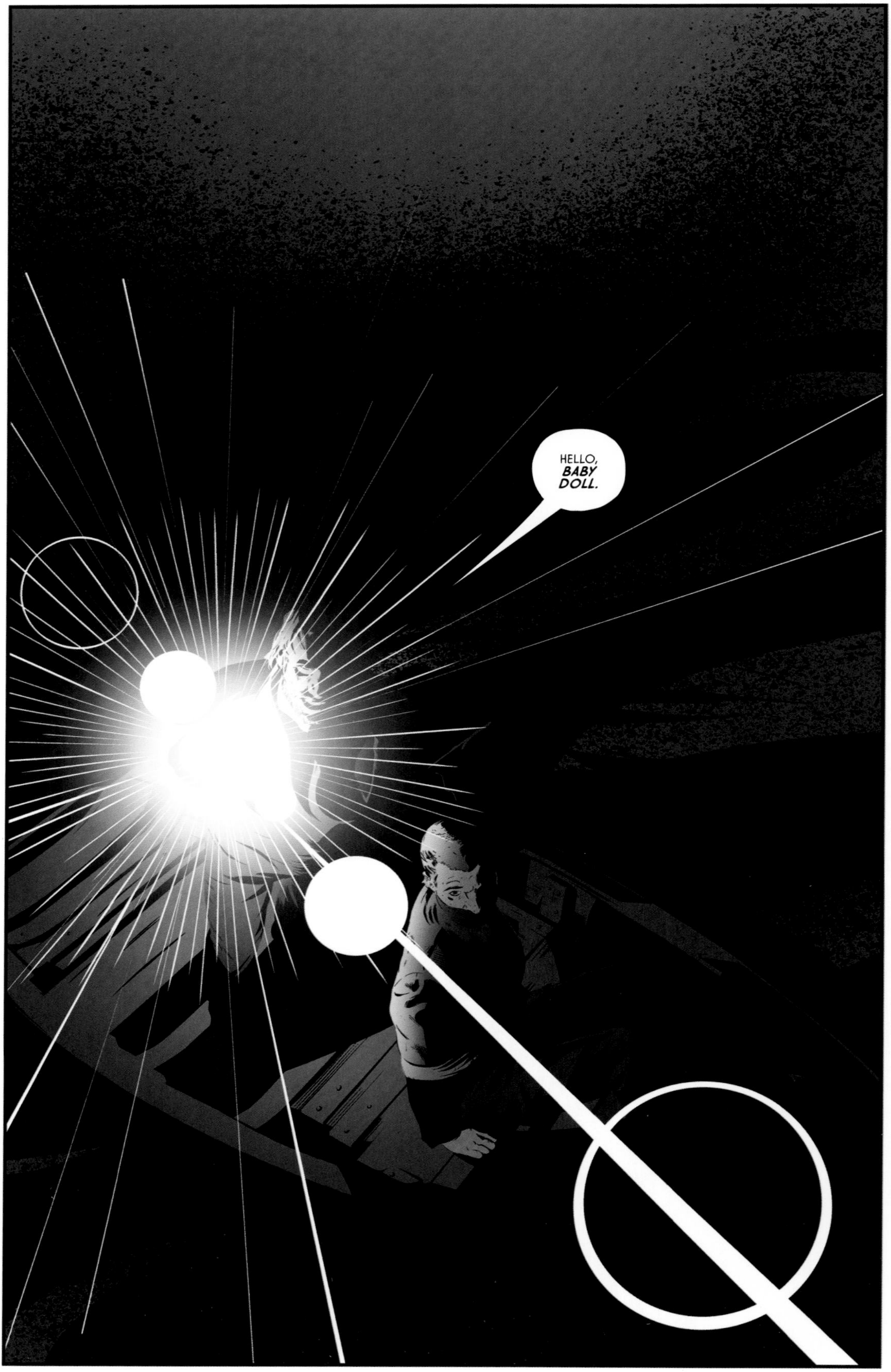
HELLO, *BABY DOLL.*

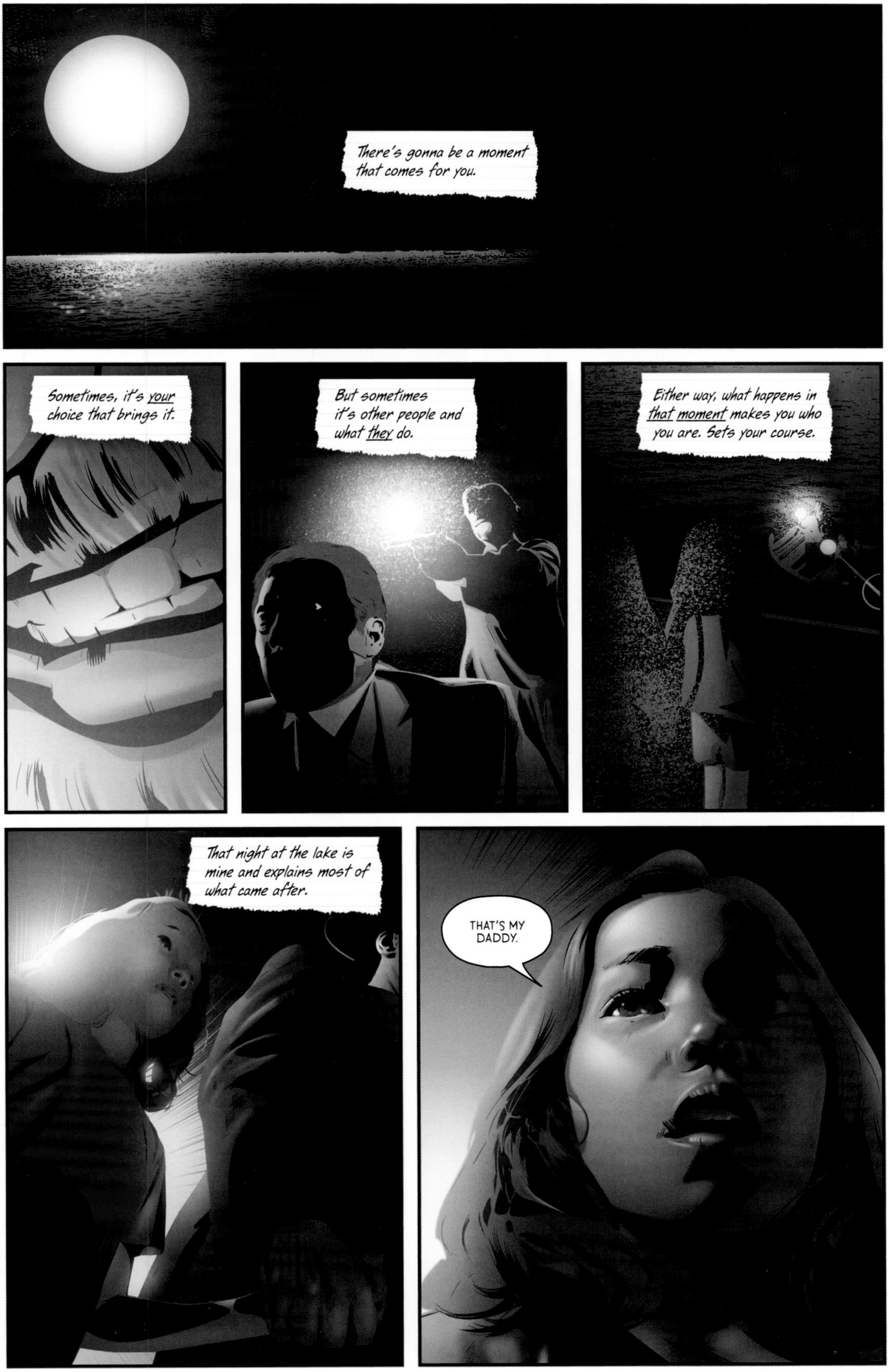
There's gonna be a moment that comes for you.
Sometimes, it's your choice that brings it.
But sometimes it's other people and what they do.
Either way, what happens in that moment makes you who you are. Sets your course.
That night at the lake is mine and explains most of what came after.
THAT'S MY DADDY.

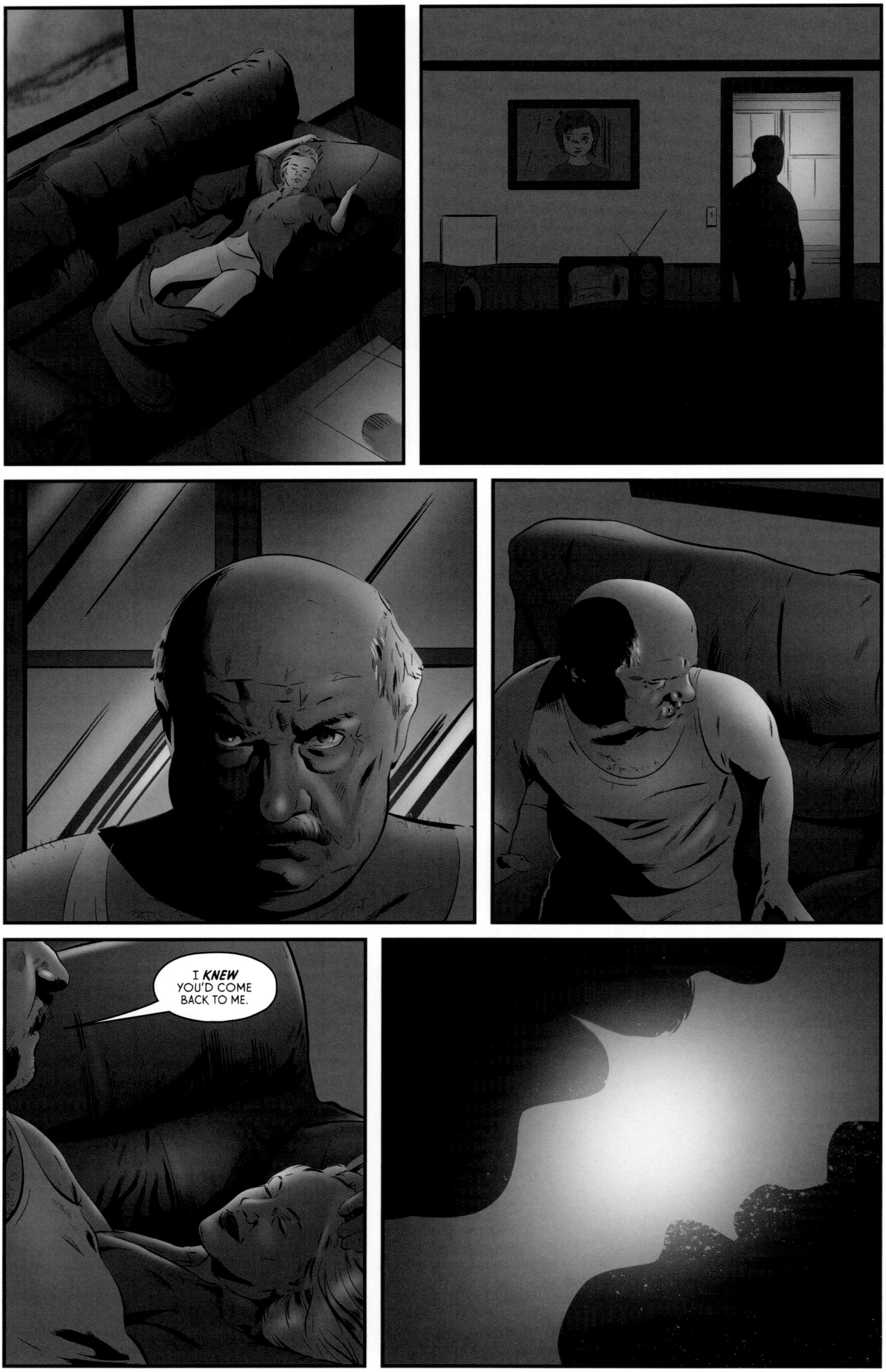
I KNEW YOU'D COME BACK TO ME.

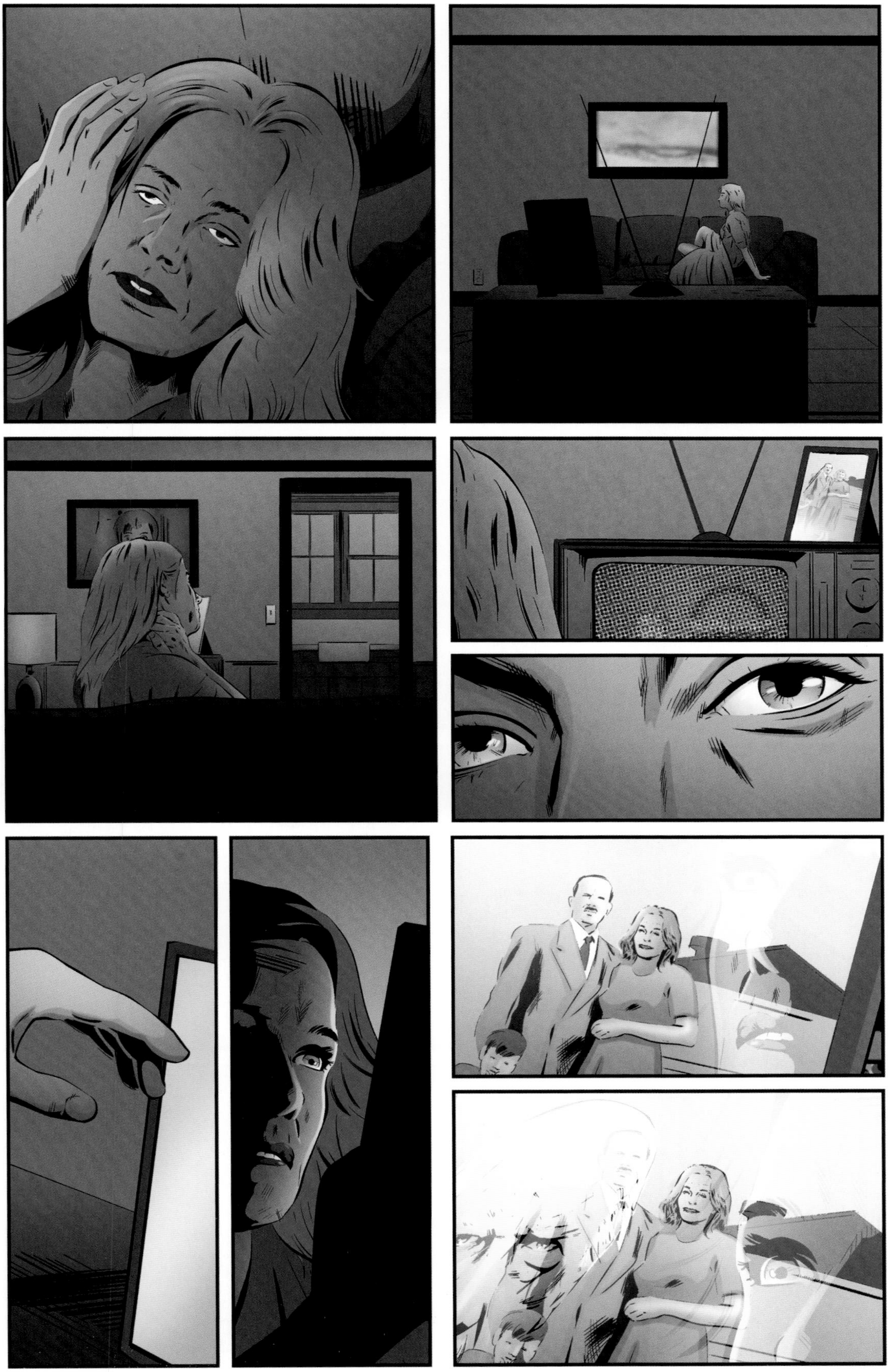

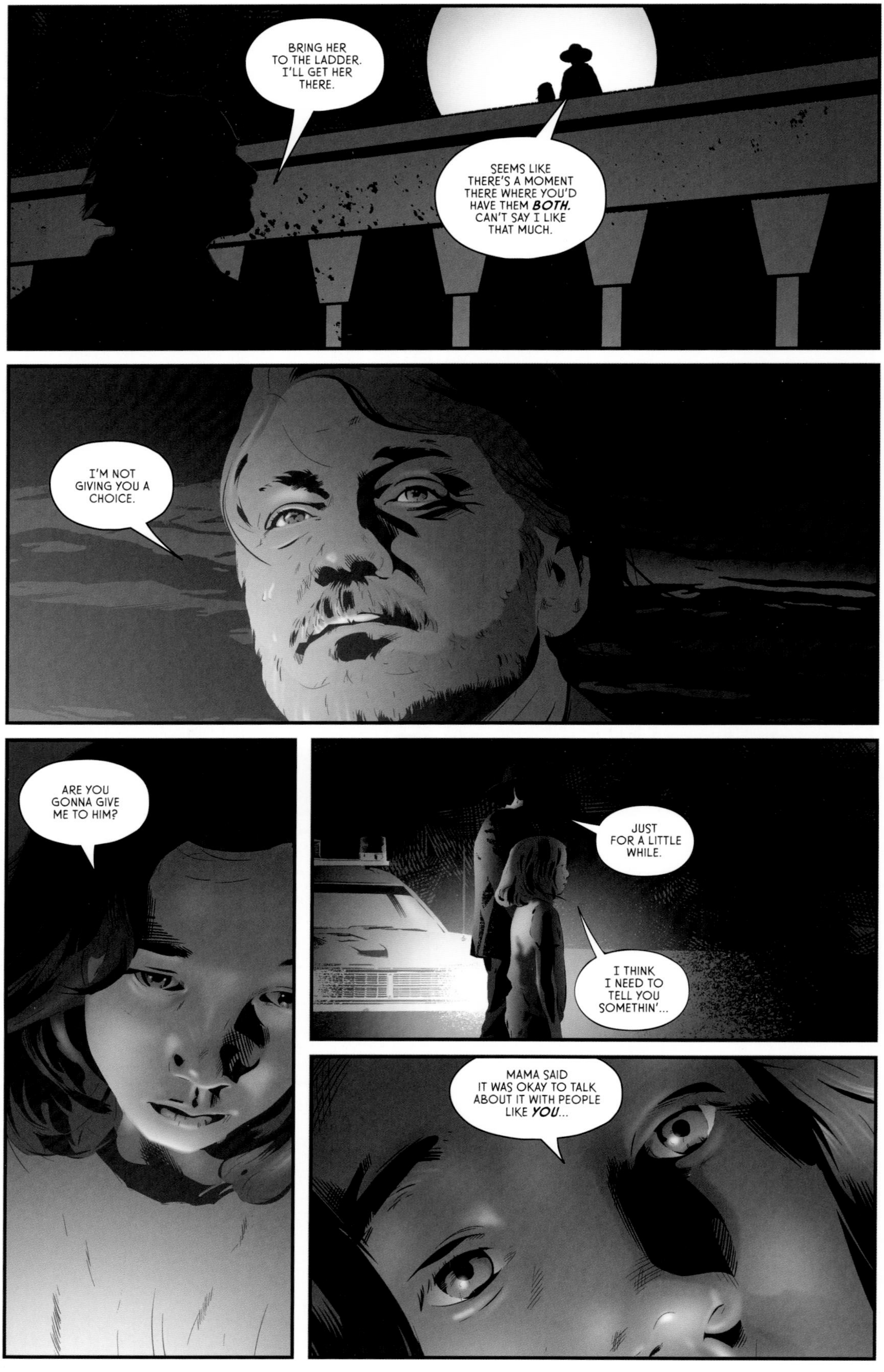
BRING HER TO THE LADDER. I'LL GET HER THERE.
SEEMS LIKE THERE'S A MOMENT THERE WHERE YOU'D HAVE THEM *BOTH.* CAN'T SAY I LIKE THAT MUCH.
I'M NOT GIVING YOU A CHOICE.
ARE YOU GONNA GIVE ME TO HIM?
JUST FOR A LITTLE WHILE.
I THINK I NEED TO TELL YOU SOMETHIN'...
MAMA SAID IT WAS OKAY TO TALK ABOUT IT WITH PEOPLE LIKE *YOU*...

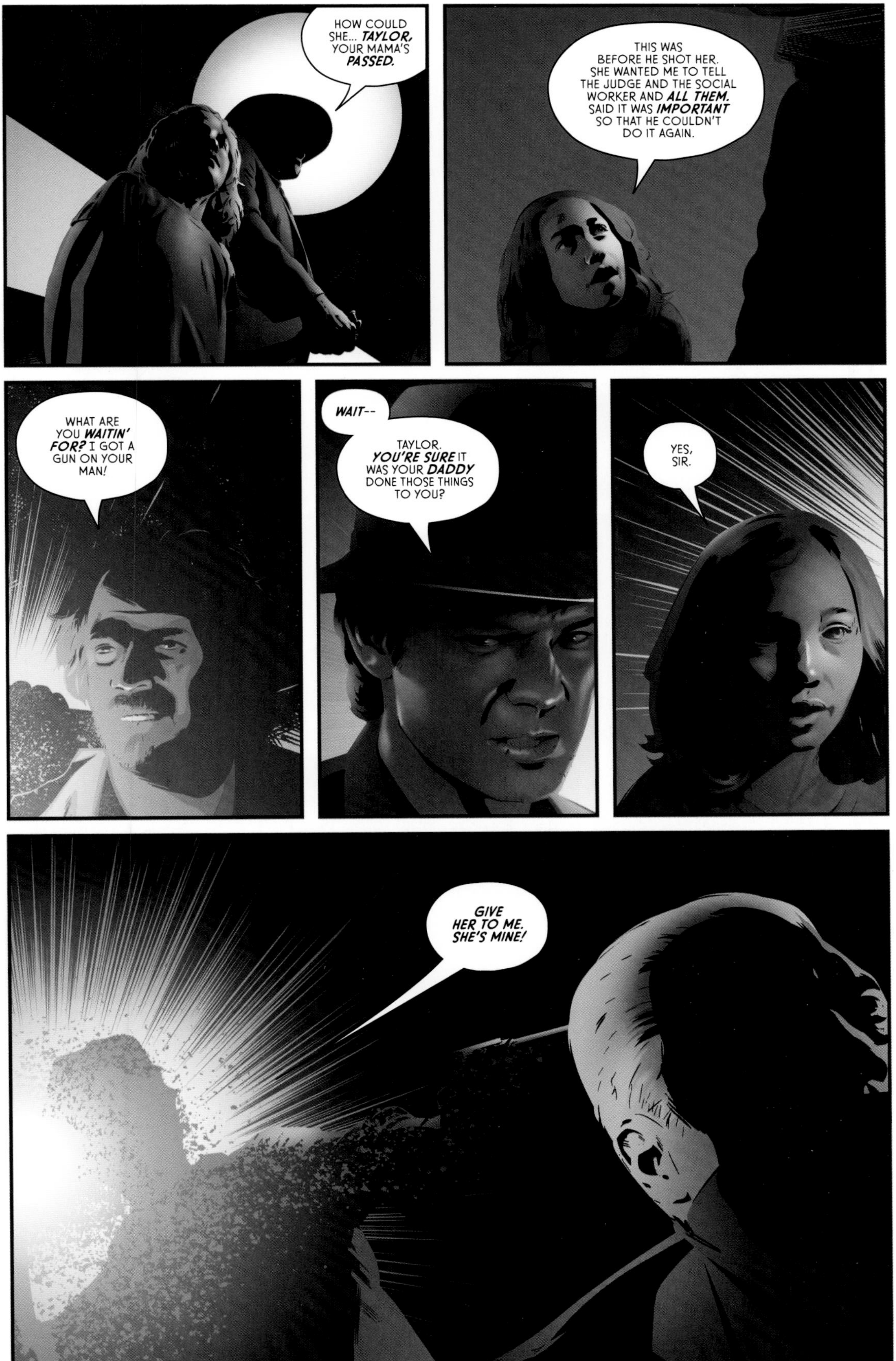
HOW COULD SHE... TAYLOR, YOUR MAMA'S PASSED.
THIS WAS BEFORE HE SHOT HER. SHE WANTED ME TO TELL THE JUDGE AND THE SOCIAL WORKER AND ALL THEM. SAID IT WAS IMPORTANT SO THAT HE COULDN'T DO IT AGAIN.
WHAT ARE YOU WAITIN' FOR? I GOT A GUN ON YOUR MAN!
WAIT--
TAYLOR. YOU'RE SURE IT WAS YOUR DADDY DONE THOSE THINGS TO YOU?
YES, SIR.
GIVE HER TO ME. SHE'S MINE!

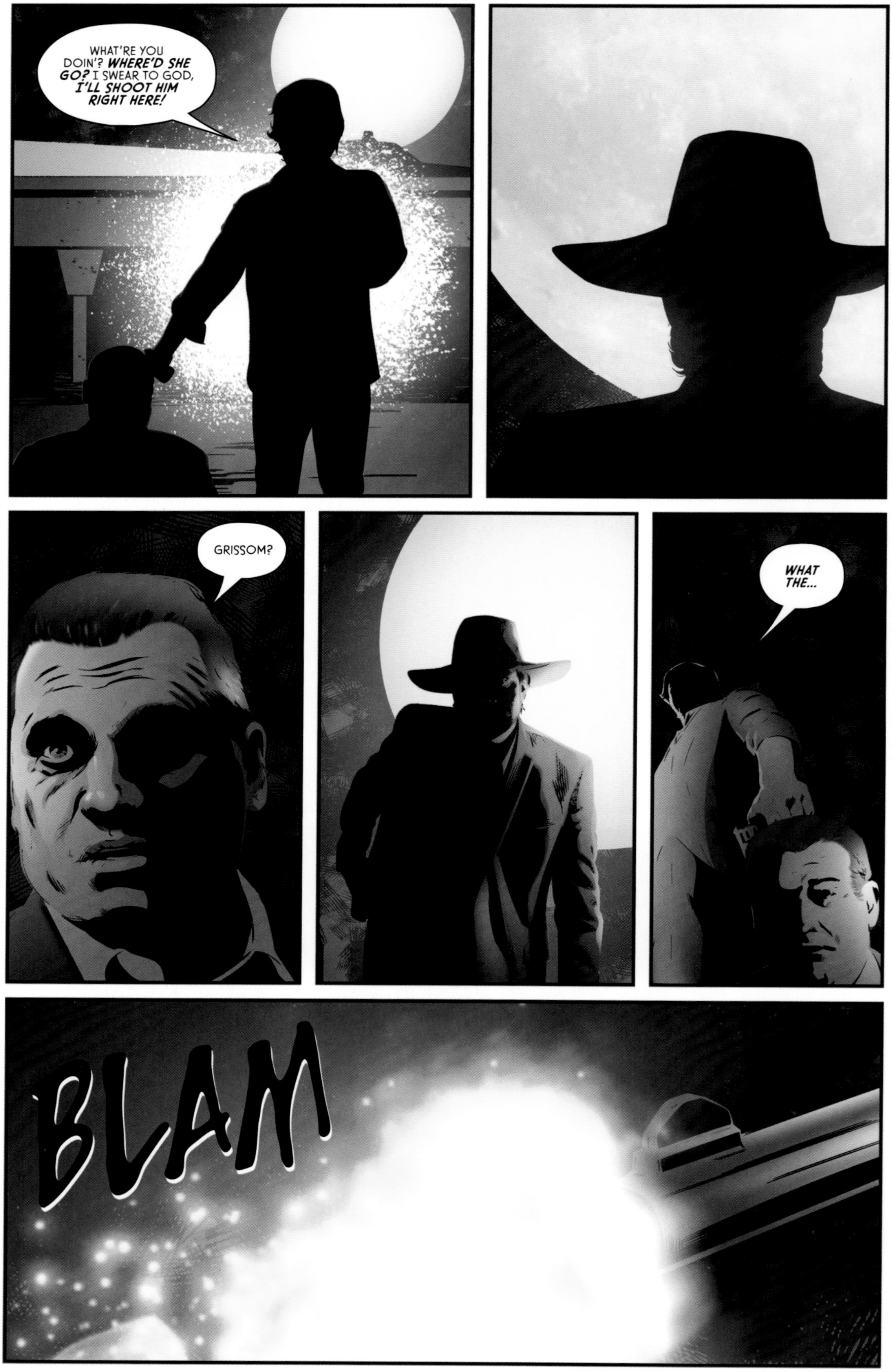
WHAT'RE YOU DOIN'? ***WHERE'D SHE GO?*** I SWEAR TO GOD, ***I'LL SHOOT HIM RIGHT HERE!***
GRISSOM?
WHAT THE...
BLAM

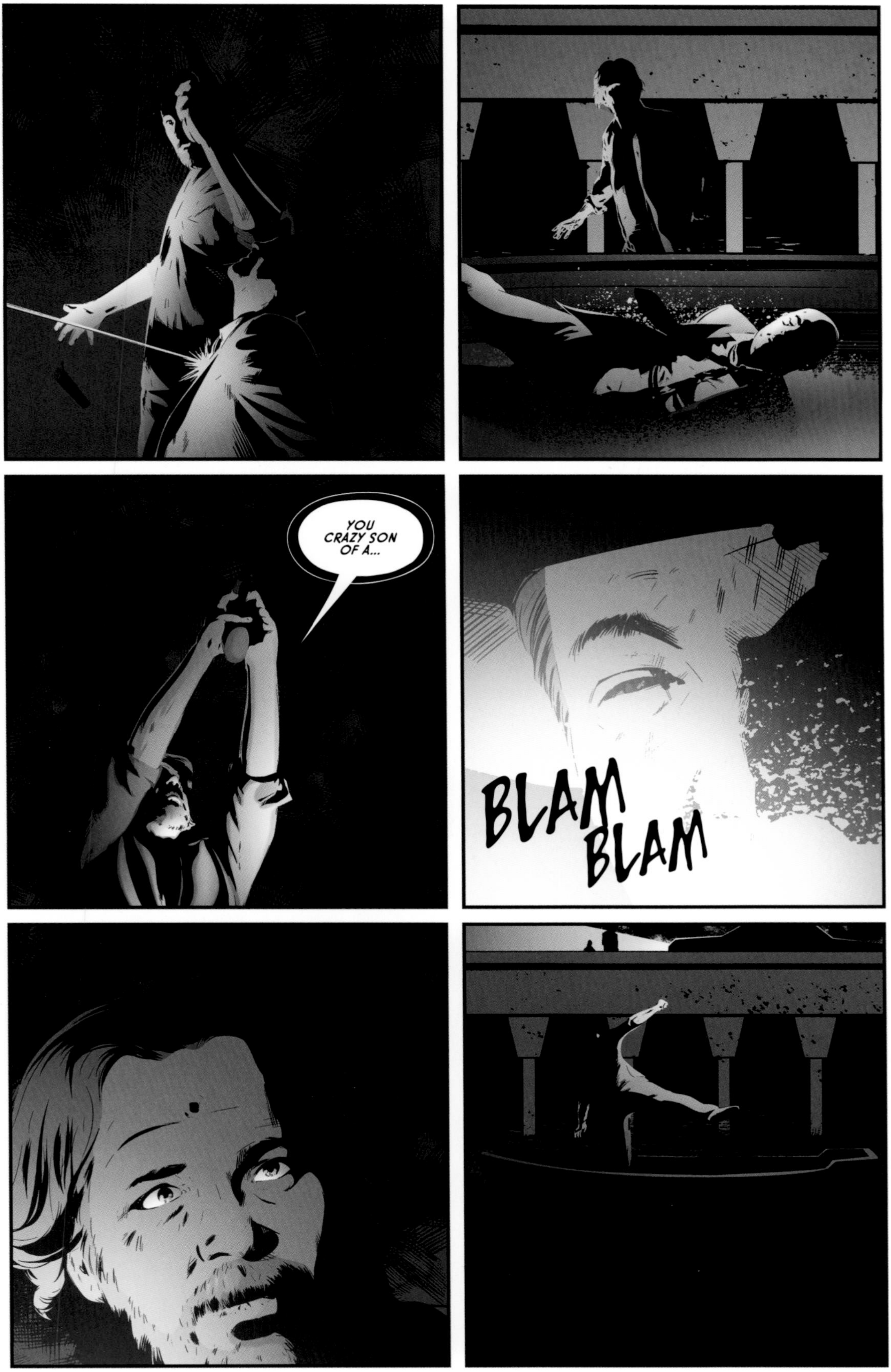
YOU CRAZY SON OF A...
BLAM
BLAM

"IF COULD GO BACK AND CHANGE IT, *I WOULD*.

"IT'S TOO BIG A BURDEN ON HIM. I SHOULDA BEEN MORE CAREFUL.

"A LITTLE BOY SHOULDN'T HAVE TO SEE A THING LIKE THAT. IT *SCARS* A CHILD.

"WHAT I DID TO HIS MAMA I HAD TO DO. BUT HE DIDN'T HAVE TO KNOW. DIDN'T HAVE TO SEE.

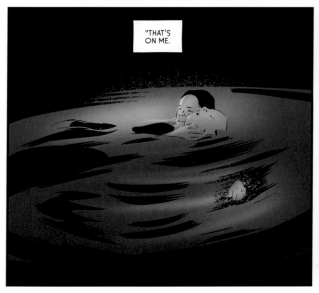

"THAT'S ON ME.

"I DON'T THINK HE'LL *EVER* FORGIVE ME."

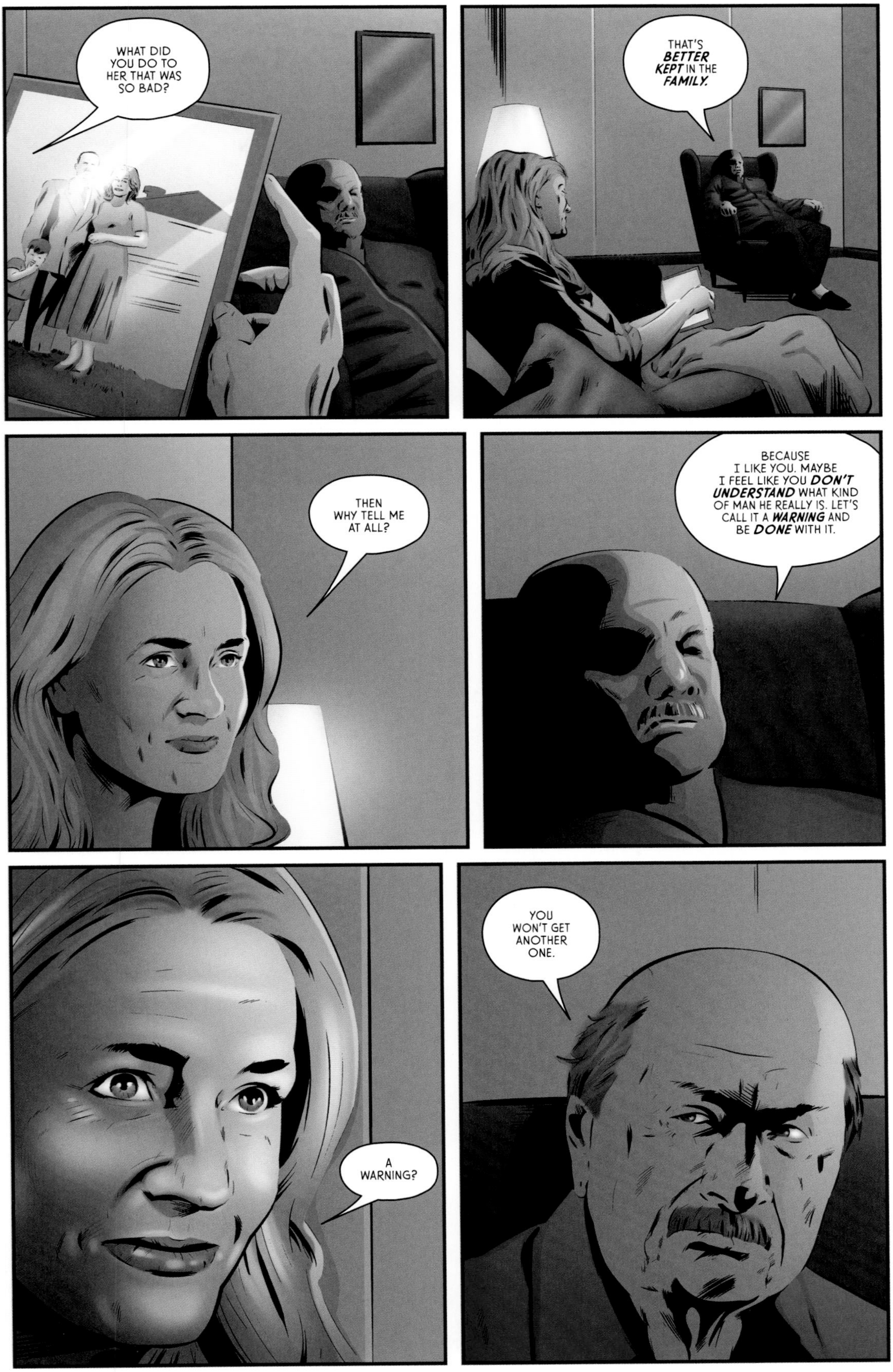
WHAT DID YOU DO TO HER THAT WAS SO BAD?
THAT'S **BETTER KEPT** IN THE **FAMILY.**
THEN WHY TELL ME AT ALL?
BECAUSE I LIKE YOU. MAYBE I FEEL LIKE YOU **DON'T UNDERSTAND** WHAT KIND OF MAN HE REALLY IS. LET'S CALL IT A **WARNING** AND BE **DONE** WITH IT.
A WARNING?
YOU WON'T GET ANOTHER ONE.

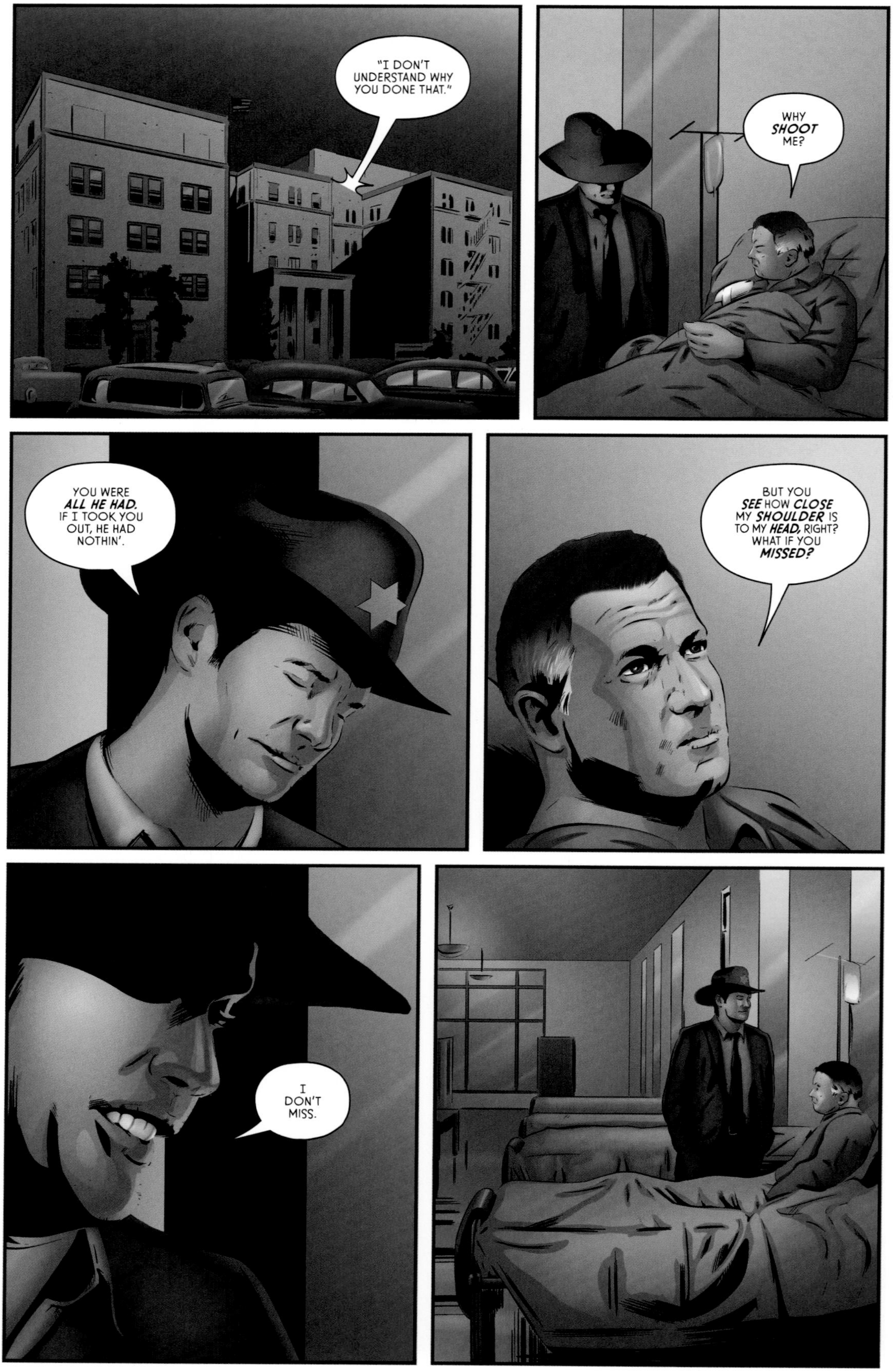
"I DON'T UNDERSTAND WHY YOU DONE THAT."
WHY SHOOT ME?
YOU WERE ALL HE HAD. IF I TOOK YOU OUT, HE HAD NOTHIN'.
BUT YOU SEE HOW CLOSE MY SHOULDER IS TO MY HEAD, RIGHT? WHAT IF YOU MISSED?
I DON'T MISS.

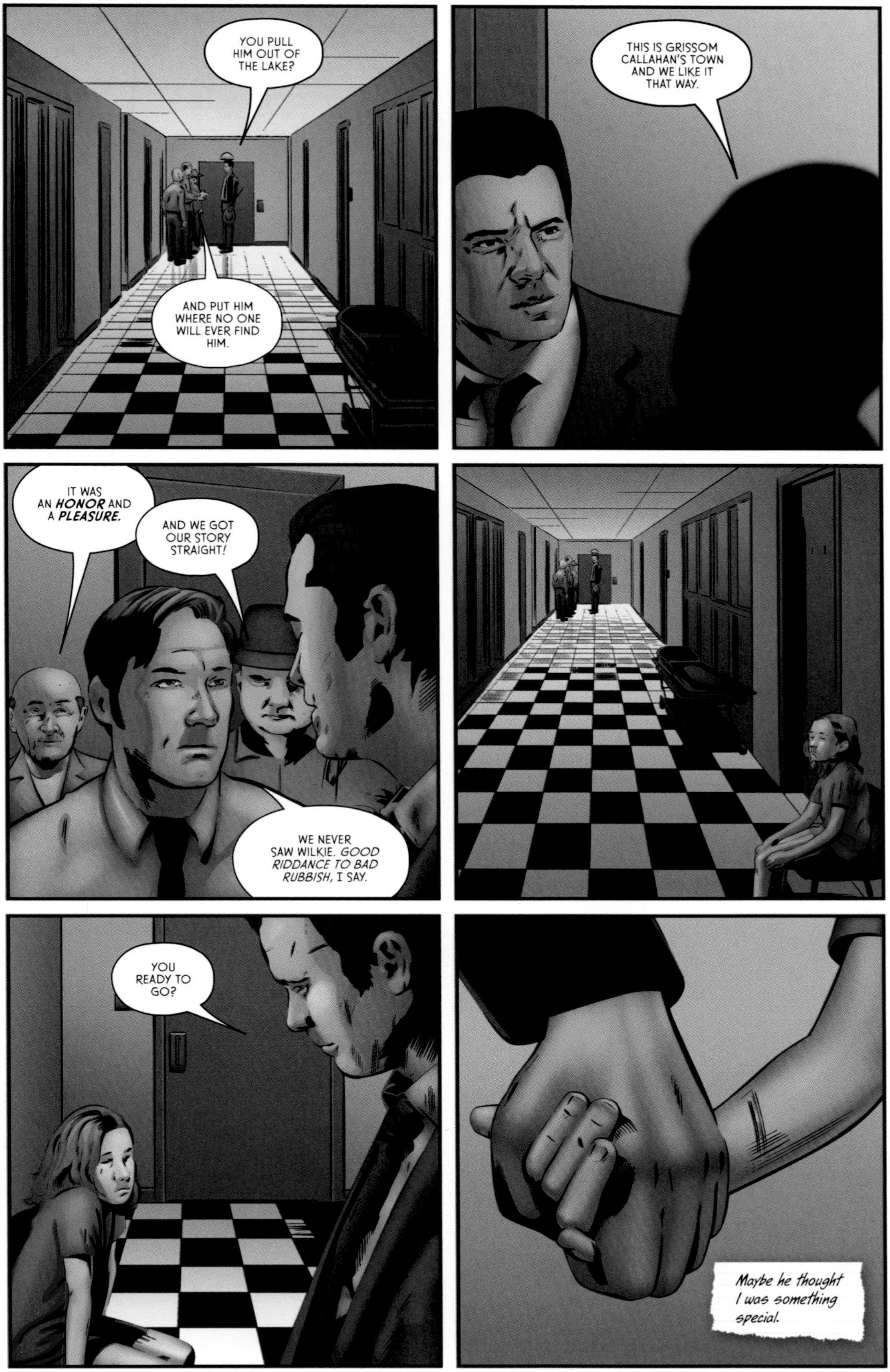
YOU PULL HIM OUT OF THE LAKE?
AND PUT HIM WHERE NO ONE WILL EVER FIND HIM.
THIS IS GRISSOM CALLAHAN'S TOWN AND WE LIKE IT THAT WAY.
IT WAS AN **HONOR** AND A **PLEASURE.**
AND WE GOT OUR STORY STRAIGHT!
WE NEVER SAW WILKIE. *GOOD RIDDANCE TO BAD RUBBISH*, I SAY.
YOU READY TO GO?
Maybe he thought I was something special.

A second chance.

A redemption.

But it doesn't work that way, does it?

Some things can't be bought back.

Or forgotten.

No matter how hard we try.

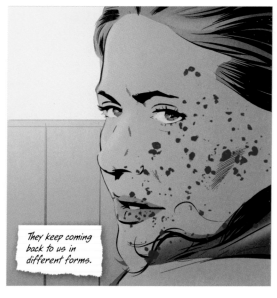

They keep coming back to us in different forms.

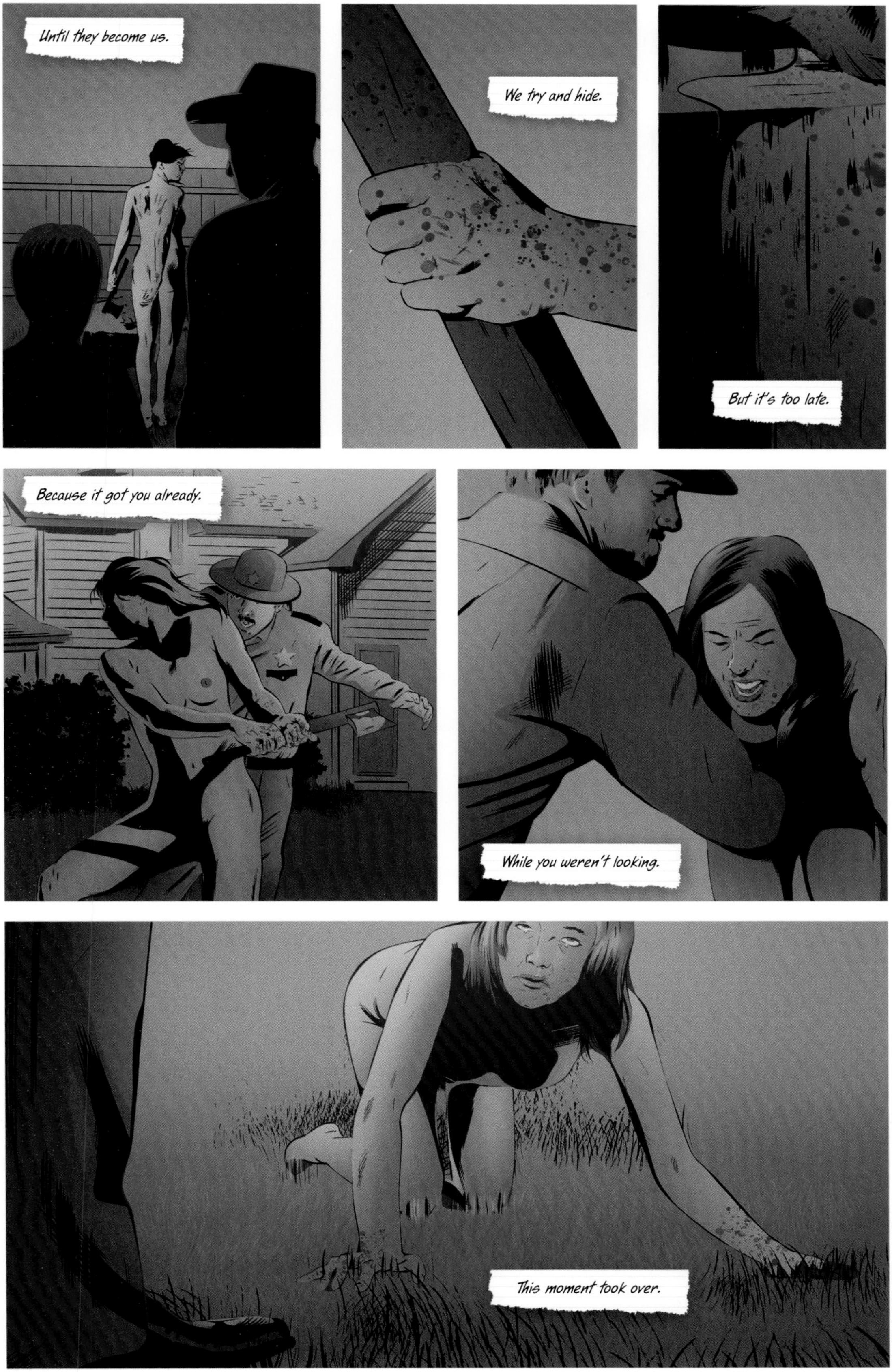
Until they become us.
We try and hide.
But it's too late.
Because it got you already.
While you weren't looking.
This moment took over.

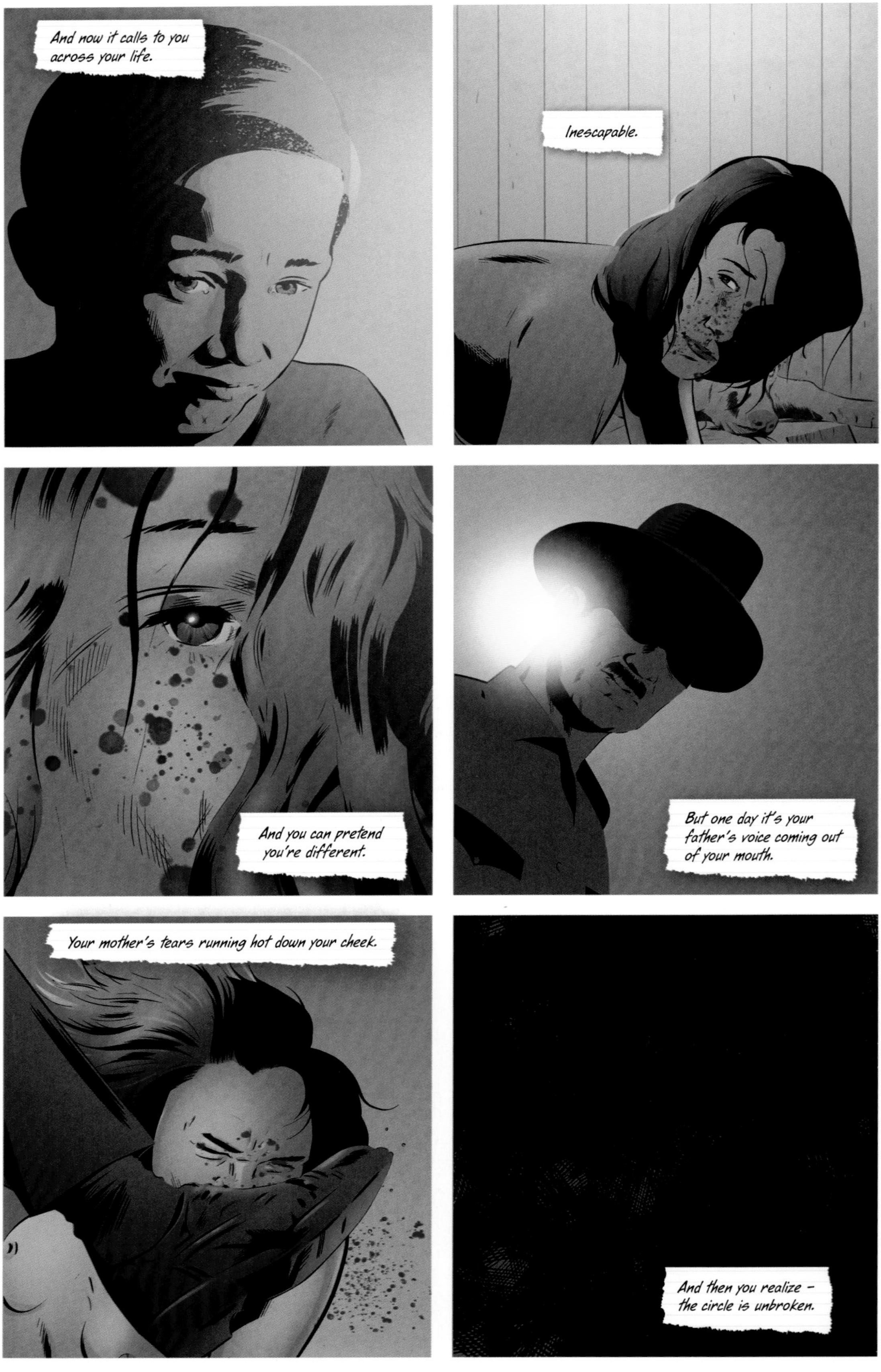
And now it calls to you across your life.
Inescapable.
And you can pretend you're different.
But one day it's your father's voice coming out of your mouth.
Your mother's tears running hot down your cheek.
And then you realize – the circle is unbroken.

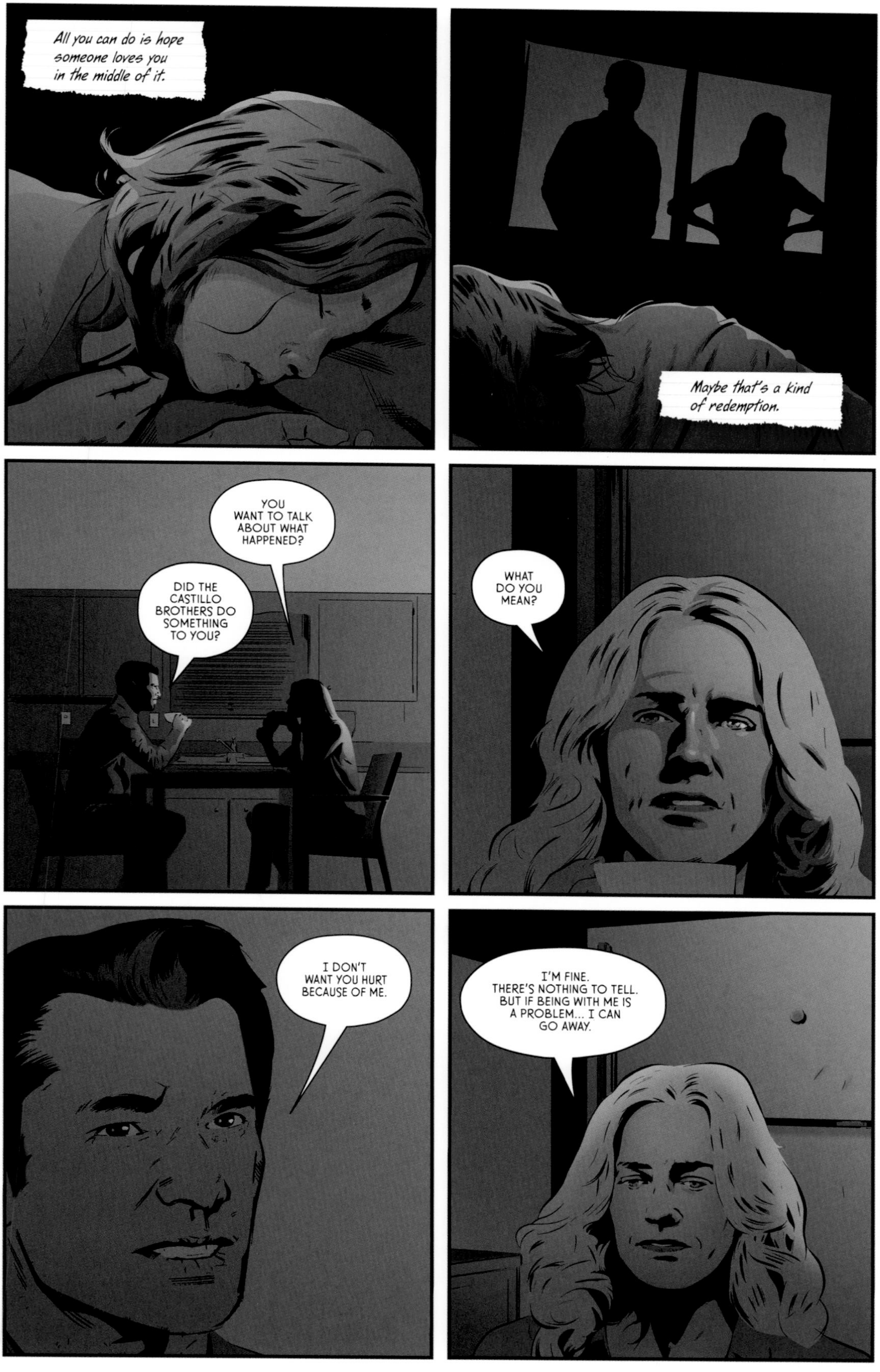
All you can do is hope someone loves you in the middle of it.
Maybe that's a kind of redemption.
YOU WANT TO TALK ABOUT WHAT HAPPENED?
DID THE CASTILLO BROTHERS DO SOMETHING TO YOU?
WHAT DO YOU MEAN?
I DON'T WANT YOU HURT BECAUSE OF ME.
I'M FINE. THERE'S NOTHING TO TELL. BUT IF BEING WITH ME IS A PROBLEM... I CAN GO AWAY.

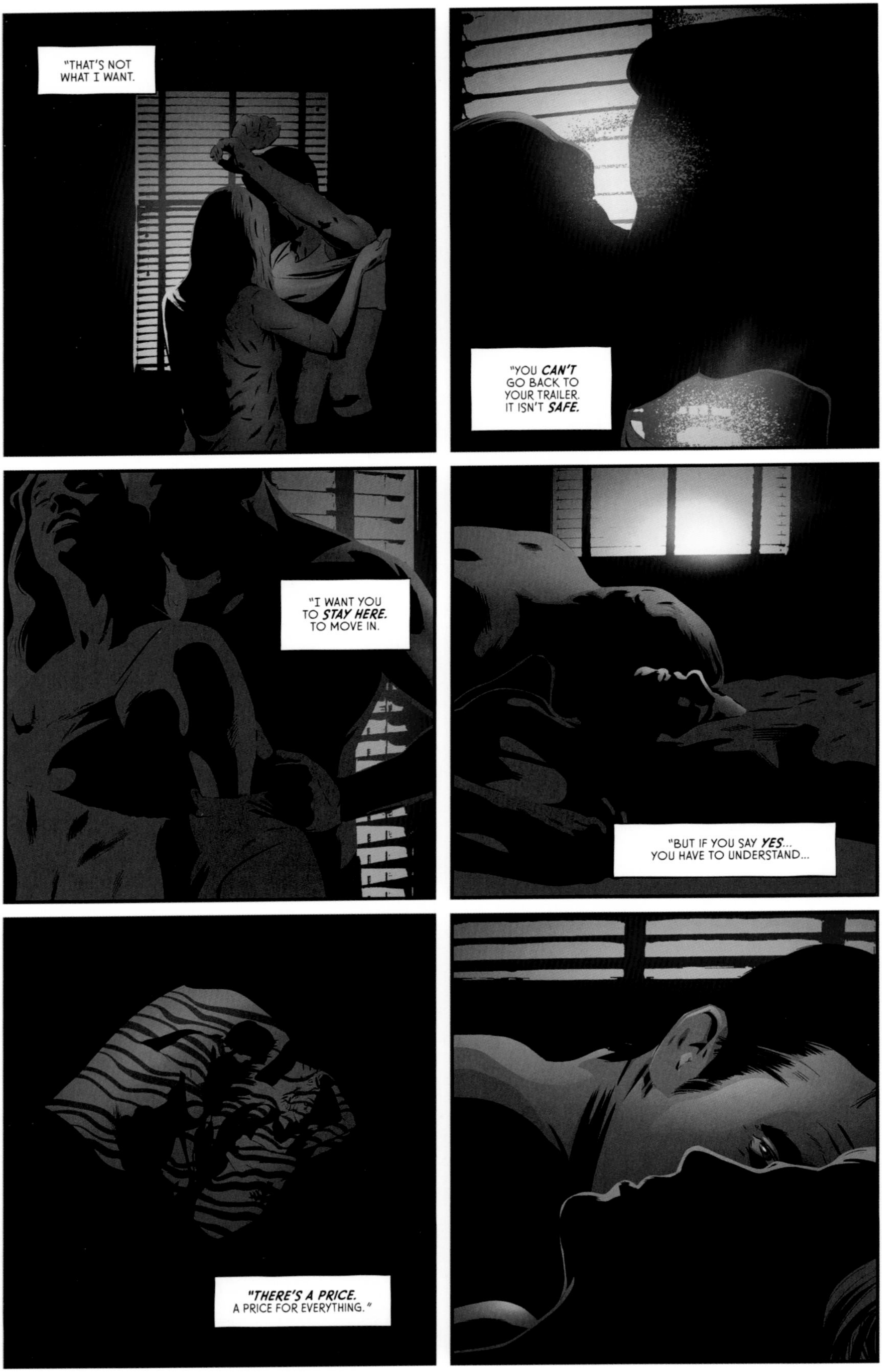
"THAT'S NOT WHAT I WANT.
"YOU CAN'T GO BACK TO YOUR TRAILER. IT ISN'T SAFE.
"I WANT YOU TO STAY HERE. TO MOVE IN.
"BUT IF YOU SAY YES... YOU HAVE TO UNDERSTAND...
"THERE'S A PRICE. A PRICE FOR EVERYTHING."

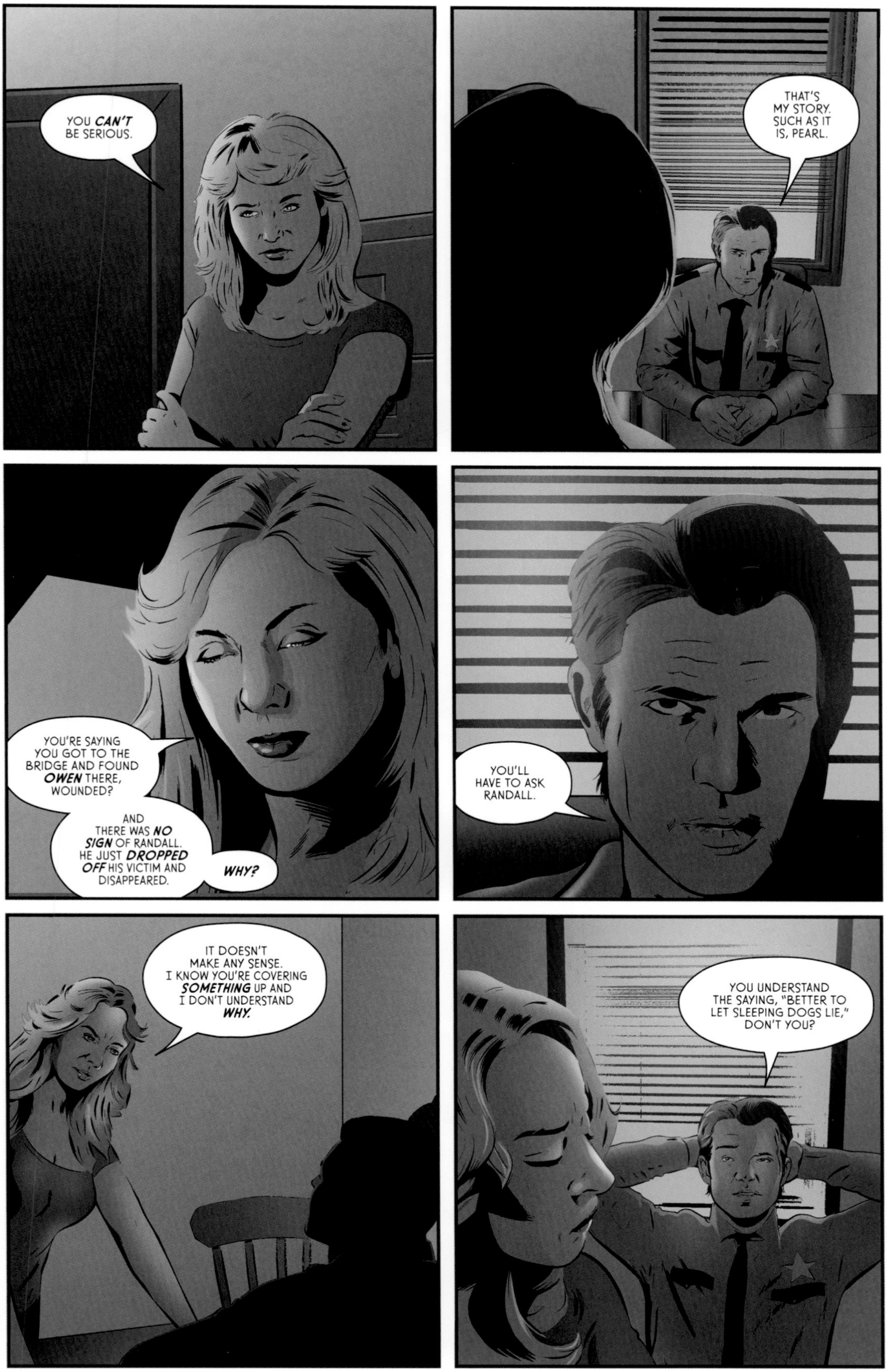

YOU **CAN'T** BE SERIOUS.
THAT'S MY STORY. SUCH AS IT IS, PEARL.
YOU'RE SAYING YOU GOT TO THE BRIDGE AND FOUND **OWEN** THERE, WOUNDED?
AND THERE WAS **NO SIGN** OF RANDALL. HE JUST **DROPPED OFF** HIS VICTIM AND DISAPPEARED.
WHY?
YOU'LL HAVE TO ASK RANDALL.
IT DOESN'T MAKE ANY SENSE. I KNOW YOU'RE COVERING **SOMETHING** UP AND I DON'T UNDERSTAND **WHY.**
YOU UNDERSTAND THE SAYING, "BETTER TO LET SLEEPING DOGS LIE," DON'T YOU?

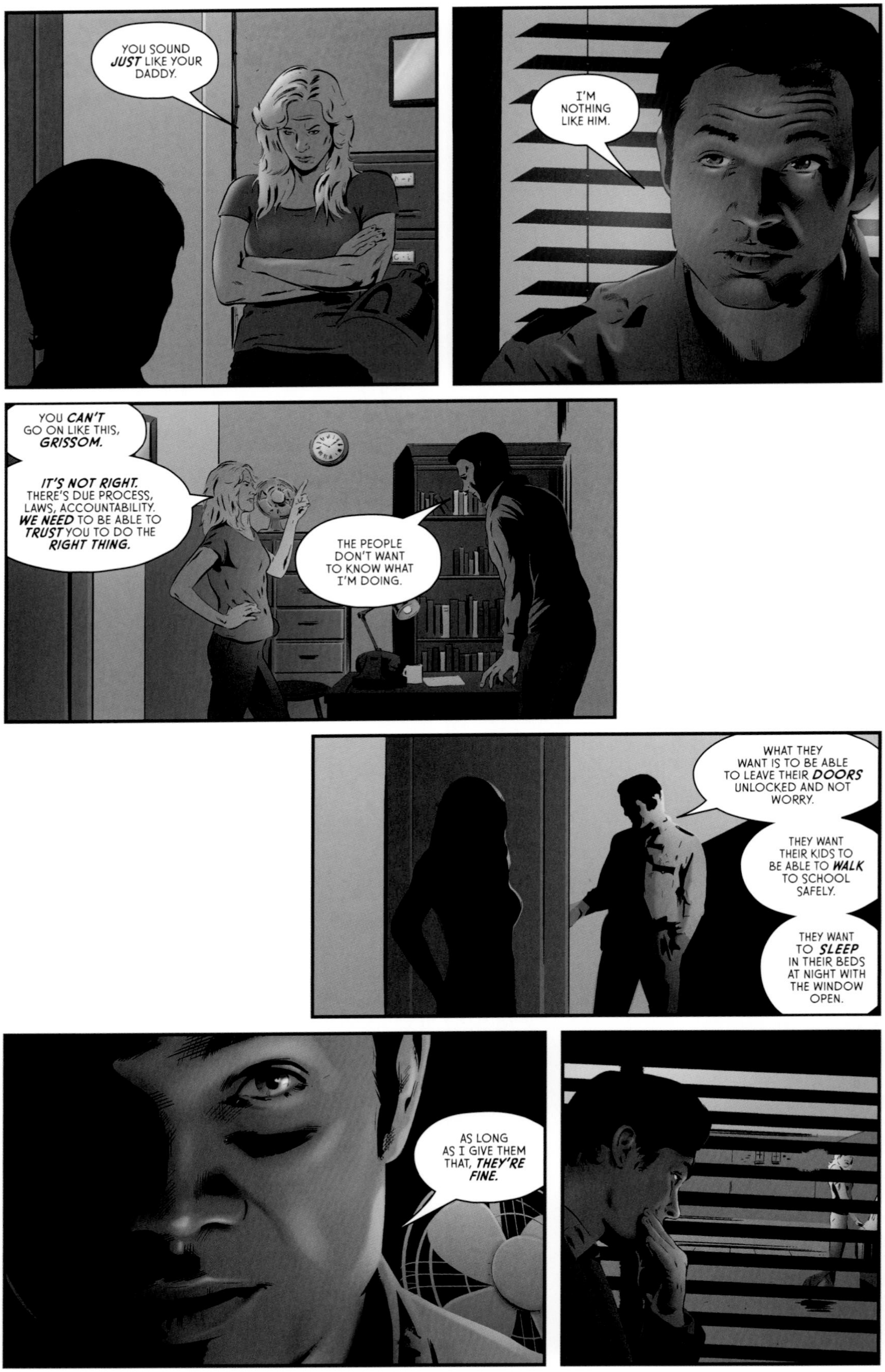
YOU SOUND *JUST* LIKE YOUR DADDY.
I'M NOTHING LIKE HIM.
YOU *CAN'T* GO ON LIKE THIS, *GRISSOM.*
IT'S NOT RIGHT. THERE'S DUE PROCESS, LAWS, ACCOUNTABILITY. *WE NEED* TO BE ABLE TO *TRUST* YOU TO DO THE *RIGHT THING.*
THE PEOPLE DON'T WANT TO KNOW WHAT I'M DOING.
WHAT THEY WANT IS TO BE ABLE TO LEAVE THEIR *DOORS* UNLOCKED AND NOT WORRY.
THEY WANT THEIR KIDS TO BE ABLE TO *WALK* TO SCHOOL SAFELY.
THEY WANT TO *SLEEP* IN THEIR BEDS AT NIGHT WITH THE WINDOW OPEN.
AS LONG AS I GIVE THEM THAT, *THEY'RE FINE.*

"I GOT A JOB FOR YOU, TREY.

"GO ON OVER TO THE BANK. FIND OUT HOW MUCH PEARL OWES ON HER HOUSE, WILL YOU? TELL BERT IT'S OFFICIAL POLICE BUSINESS."

And that's what he did.

He used every trick in the book.

Dear Miss Breckenridge,

Congratulations on paying off your home mortgage with San Angelo National Bank. Enclosed are the documents related to home.

To make people feel safe.

And it worked. For a while.

119

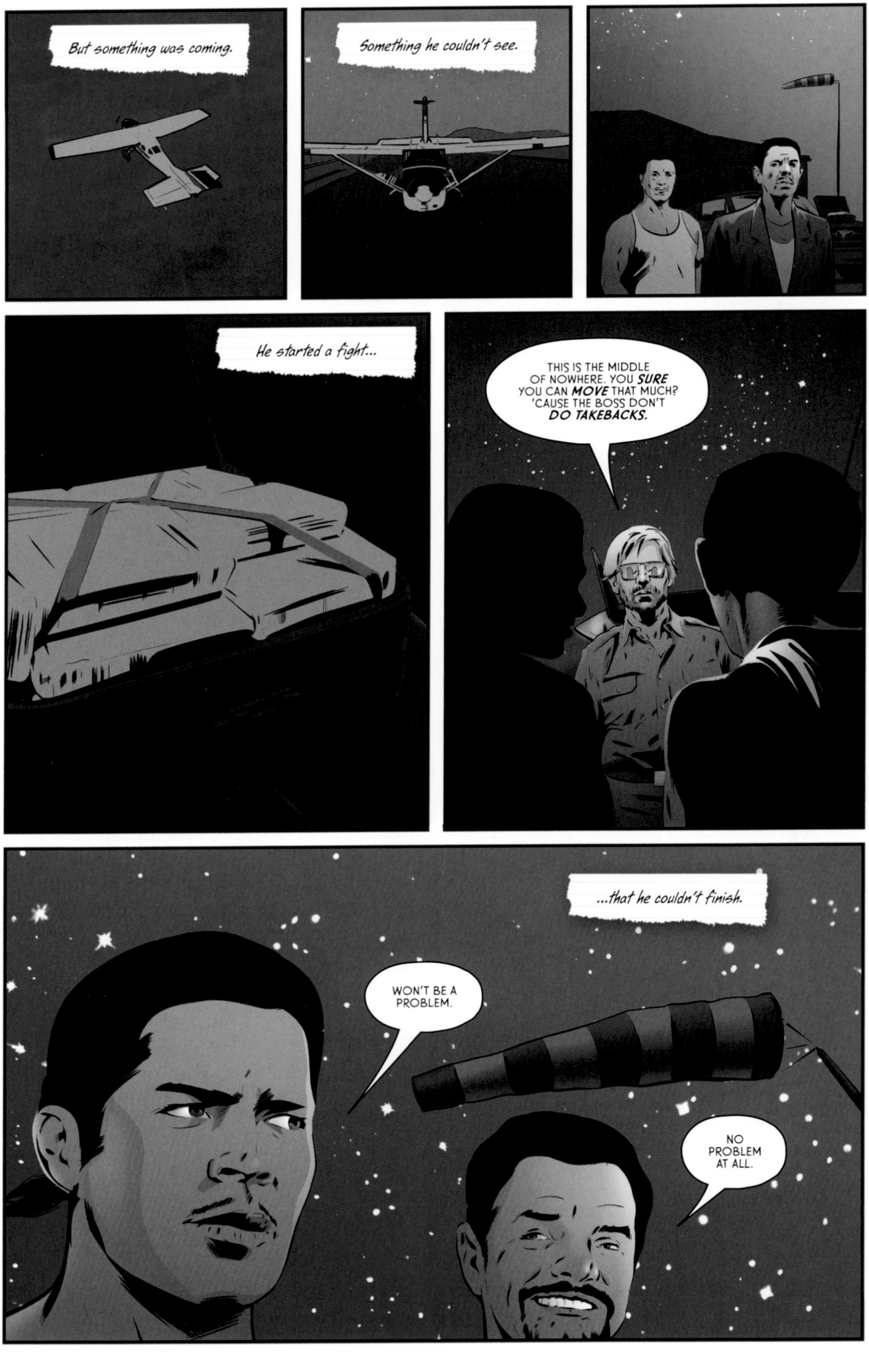

But something was coming.
Something he couldn't see.
He started a fight...
THIS IS THE MIDDLE OF NOWHERE. YOU **SURE** YOU CAN **MOVE** THAT MUCH? 'CAUSE THE BOSS DON'T **DO TAKEBACKS.**
...that he couldn't finish.
WON'T BE A PROBLEM.
NO PROBLEM AT ALL.

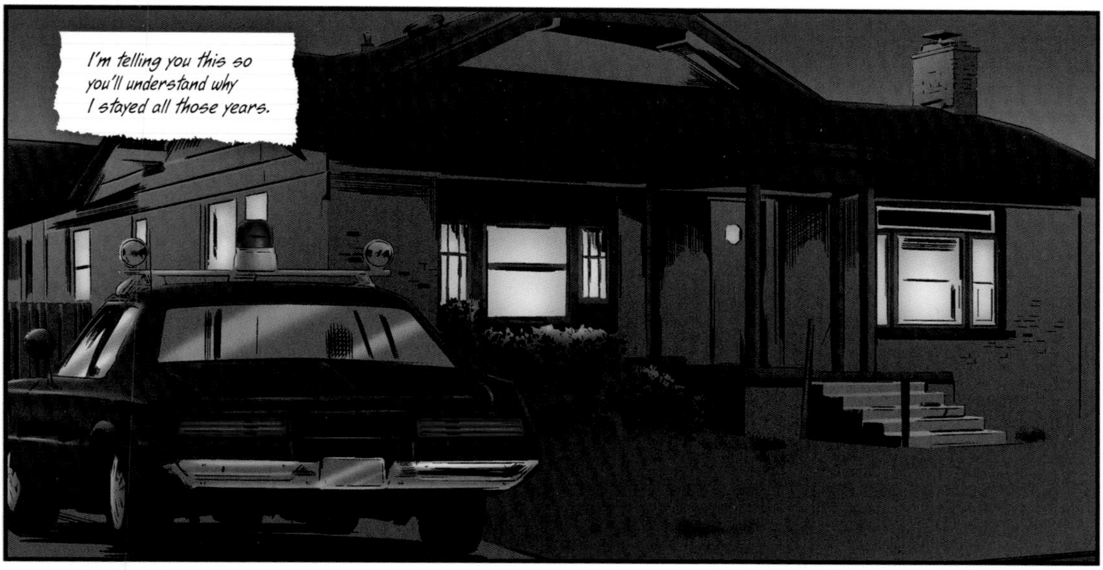
I'm telling you this so you'll understand why I stayed all those years.

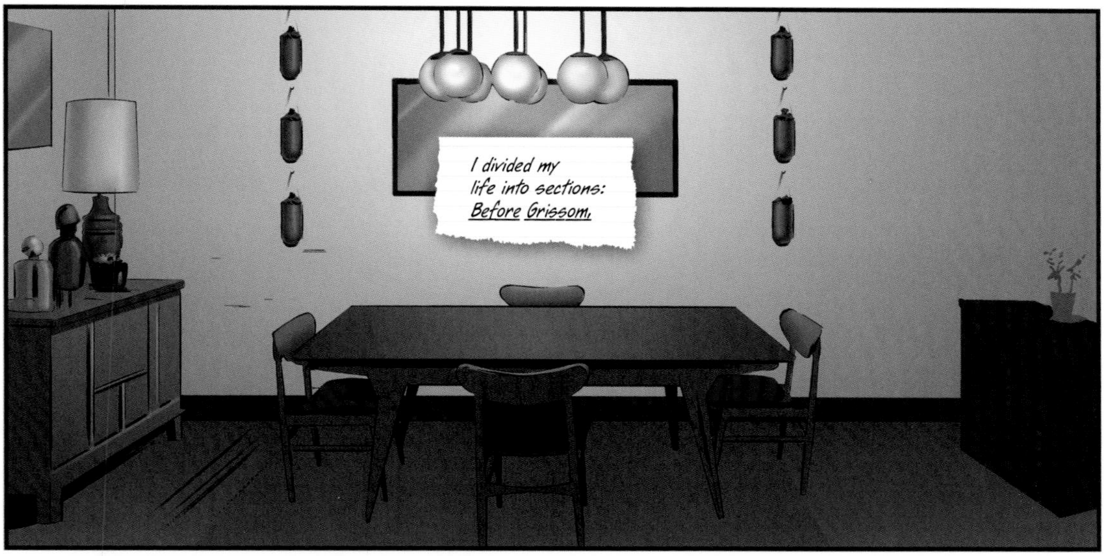
I divided my life into sections: Before Grissom,

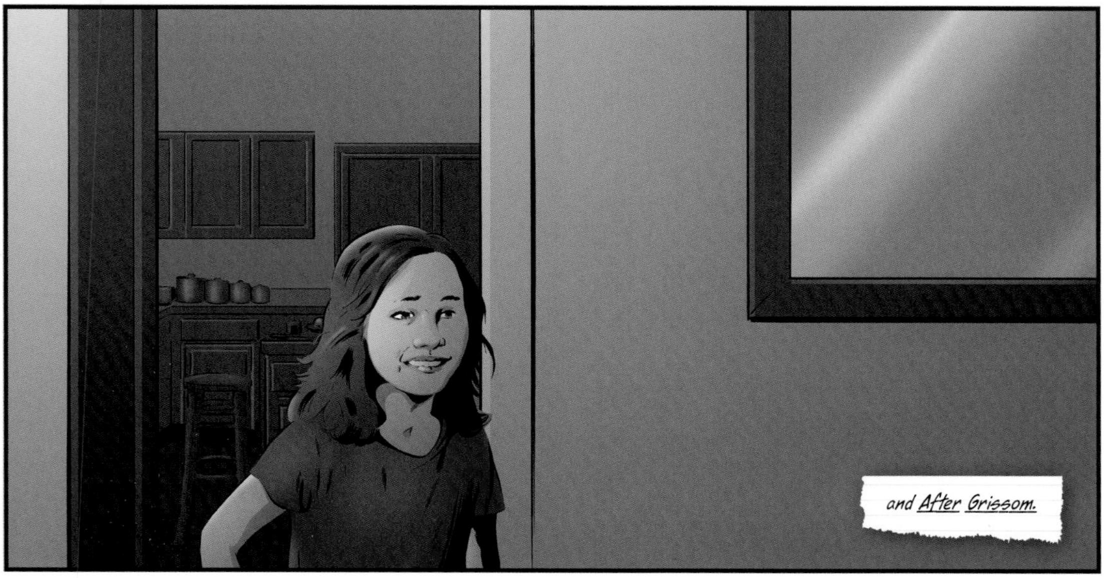
and After Grissom.

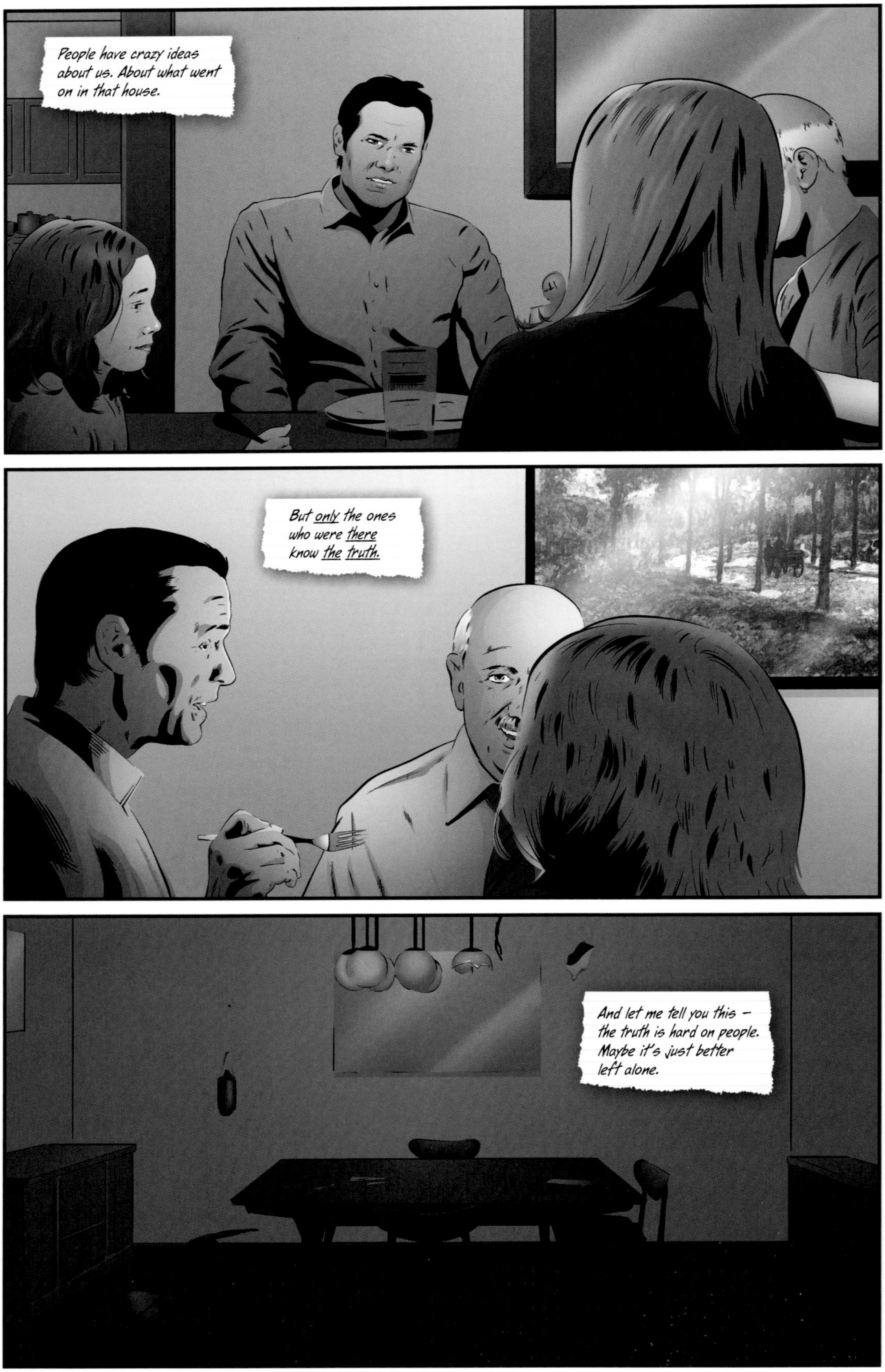
People have crazy ideas about us. About what went on in that house.
But only the ones who were there know the truth.
And let me tell you this – the truth is hard on people. Maybe it's just better left alone.

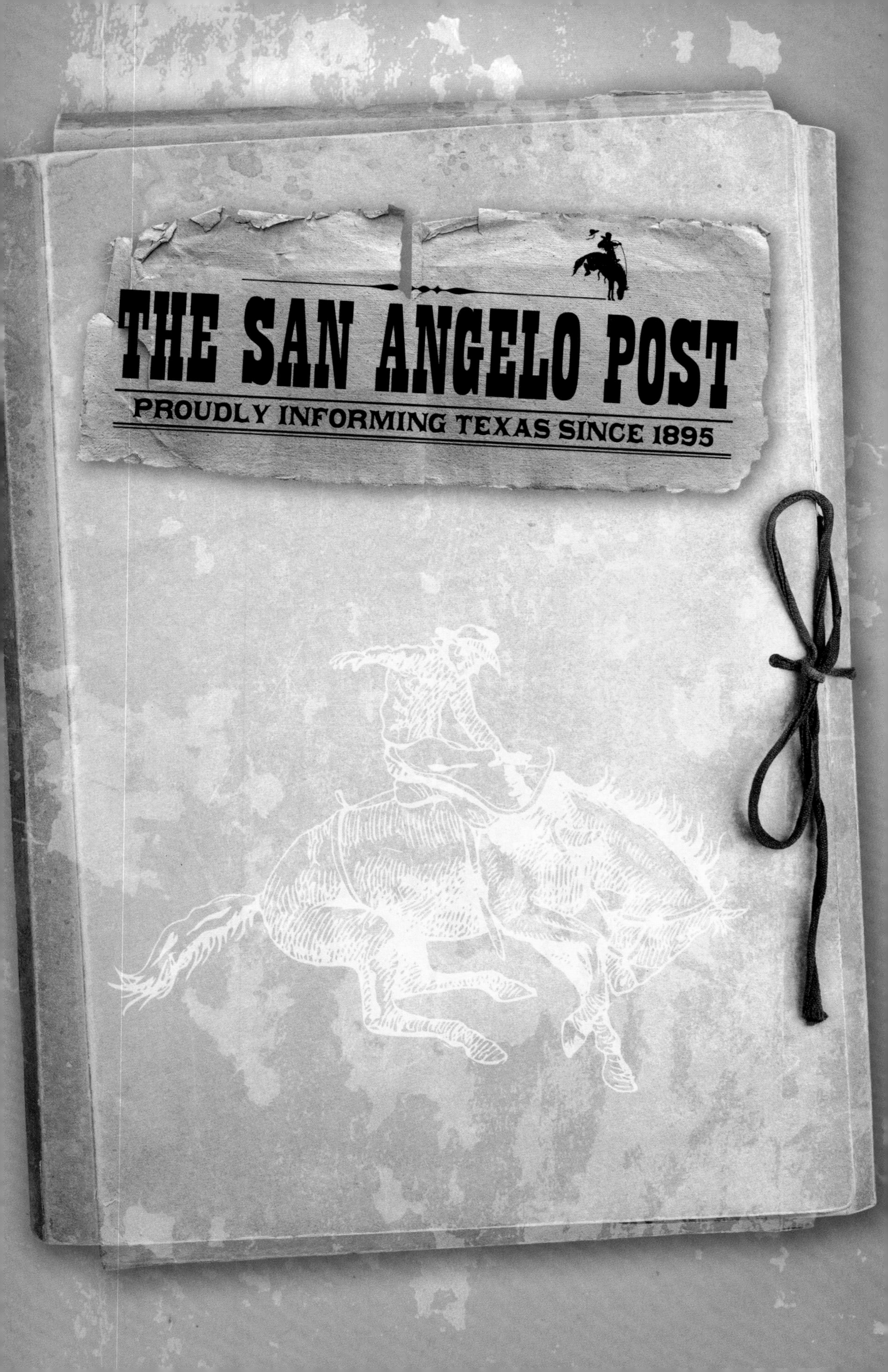
THE SAN ANGELO POST
PROUDLY INFORMING TEXAS SINCE 1895

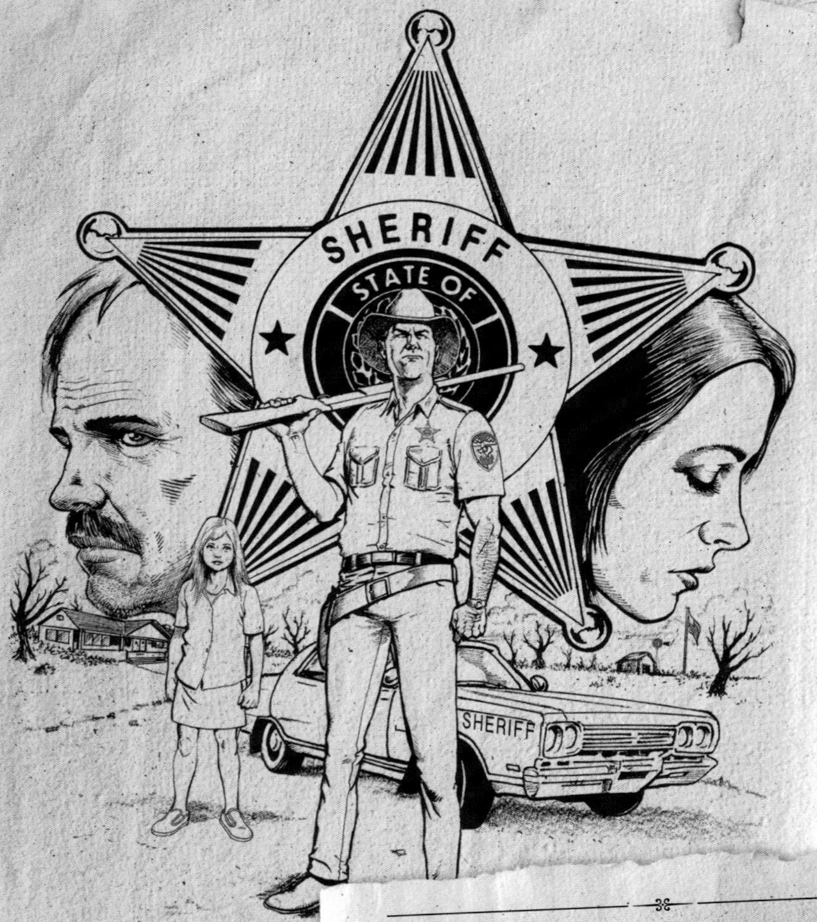
SHERIFF
STATE OF
SHERIFF

MANHUNT CONTINUES FOR KILLER OF TWO

By **Pearl Breckenridge**
San Angelo Post Staff Writer

It seems Randall Wilkie has given San Angelo's finest the slip. Sheriff Grissom Callahan reports that the suspected killer of two and kidnapper of Deputy Owen Wayne has disappeared without a trace. In what Sheriff Callahan characterized as "a confusing set of circumstances," a wounded Deputy Wayne was left tied up and alone on the Lake Nasworthy Bridge last night where he was discovered by the Sheriff and brought to Shannon Hospital for treatment. There was no sign of the suspect and attempts to talk to Deputy Wayne have been denied. "This is an ongoing investigation and we encourage anyone with information to contact the San Angelo Sheriff's Office immediately," said Sheriff Callahan. The suspect is to be considered armed and dangerous.

CALLAHAN FAMILY RECOGNIZED FOR DECADES OF SERVICE

By **Jim Henderson**
San Angelo Post Staff Writer

Former Sheriff Clem Callahan wasn't going to let a little thing like a wheelchair hold him back. At the annual Rotary Club Recognition Award Ceremony on Saturday night, the man most San Angelo residents still refer to as "The Sheriff" rose from said wheelchair and strode across the stage with the same swagger he had thirty years ago in his prime. Taking the award in hand and flanked by his son and current Sheriff, Grissom, Clem told the crowd in a loud and confident manner that he was prepared to return to the force if anyone was willing to nominate him. A rousing round of applause followed.

The Callahan family has served the citizens of San Angelo in some form of law enforcement for over fifty years. Clem's father Otto first moved to Tom Green County at about the same time this very newspaper was established. He quickly positioned himself as a peace officer before fulfilling the requirements to join the bench where he became the only local judge. One of five boys, Clem followed in his father's footsteps to become Sheriff in 1948 after returning from WWII.

DECONSTRUCTING TEXAS

Cover artist Darick Robertson created this illustration based on the scene where Grissom Callahan goes after Randall Wilkie in Christoval. It was drawn before interior artist Dennis Calero started working on said pages. As a result, there are differences: Grissom is in full Police uniform in this piece, and Wilkie holds a rifle instead of a pistol.

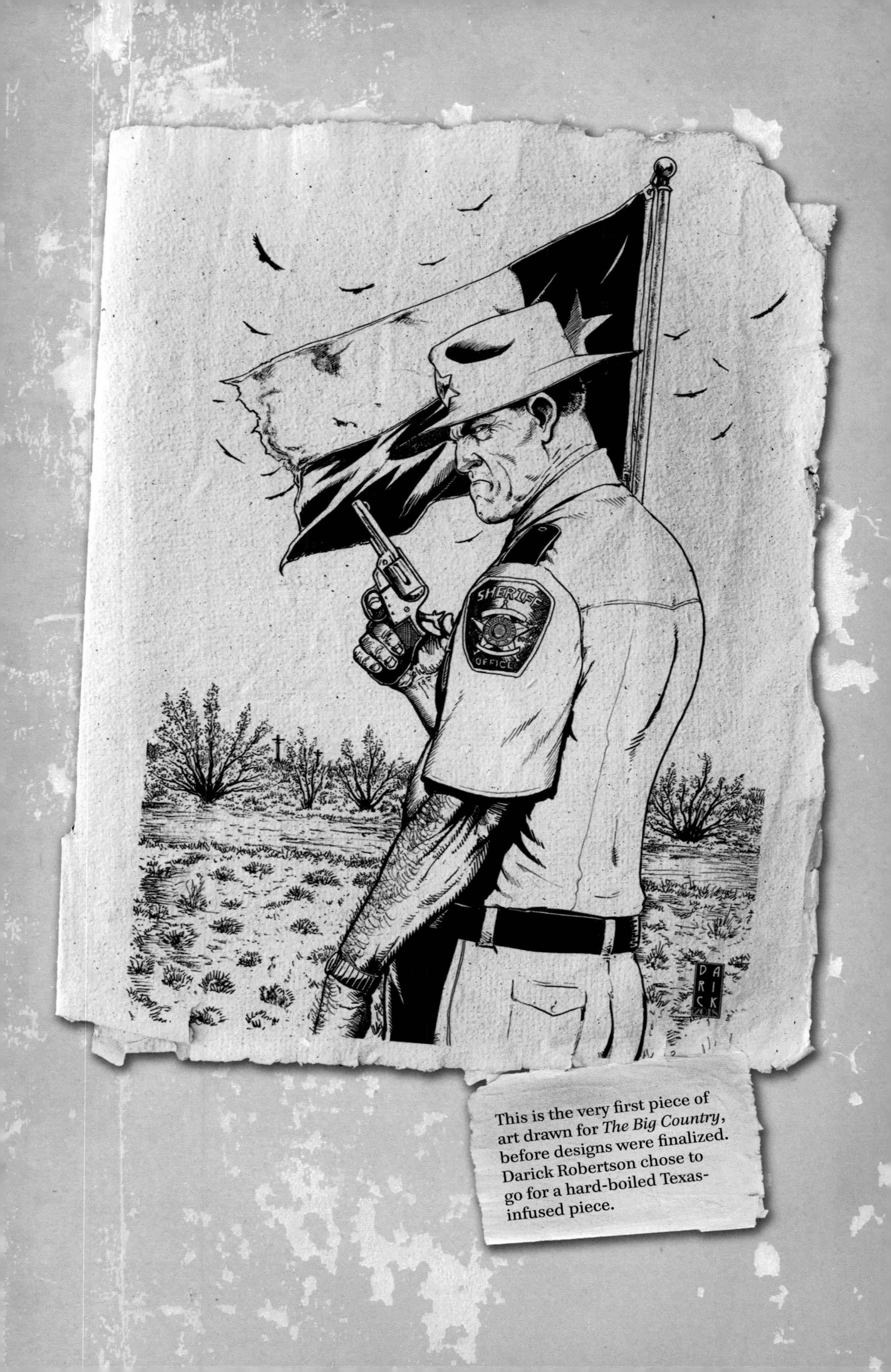
SHERIFF
OFFICE

This is the very first piece of art drawn for *The Big Country*, before designs were finalized. Darick Robertson chose to go for a hard-boiled Texas-infused piece.

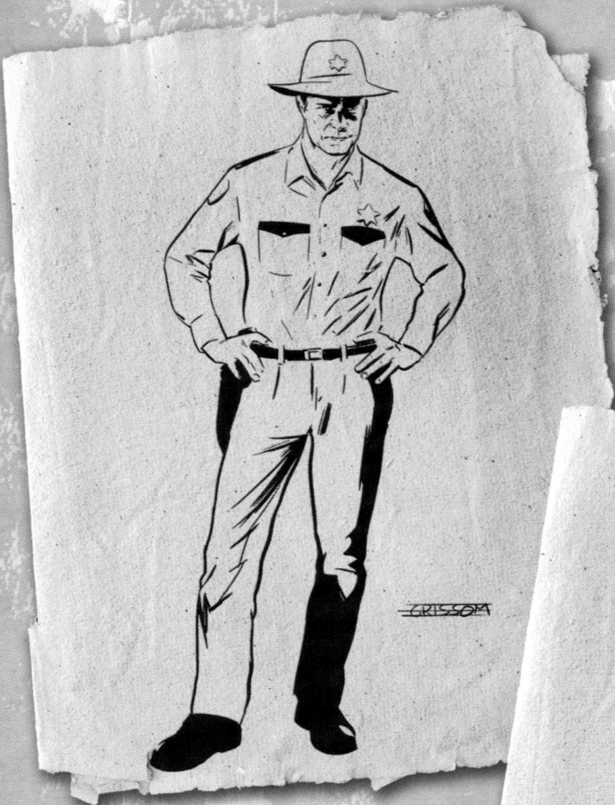
GRISSOM

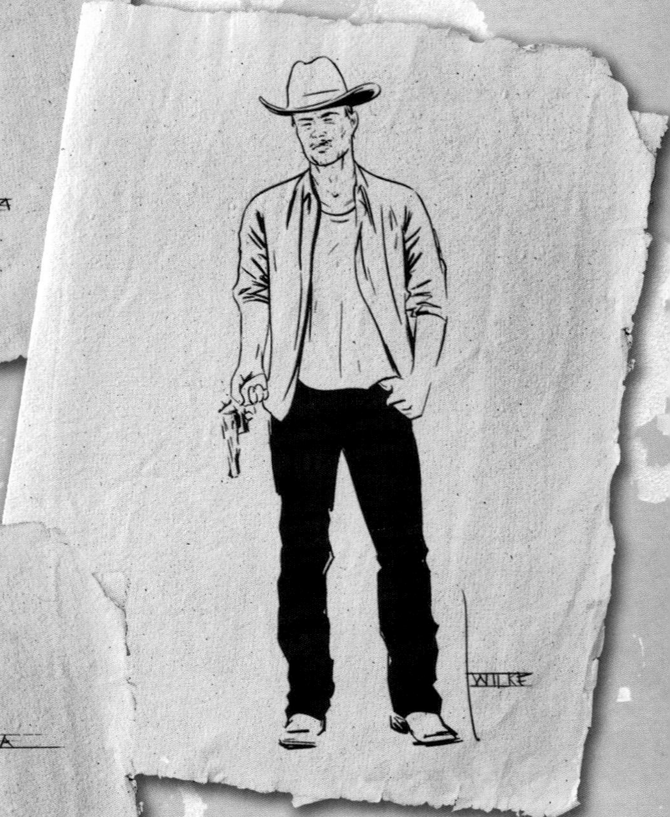
WILKE

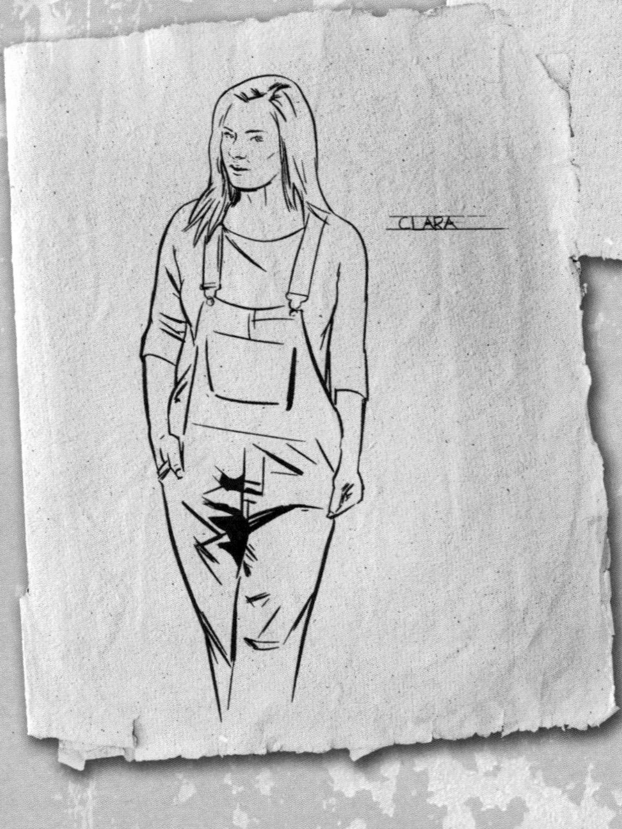
CLARA

Character designs evolved greatly as this book was put together. These were the original designs proposed by Dennis Calero.